Se̶ ̶̶̶̶es

Strike A Match Book 1

Frank Tayell

Dedicated to my family

Published by Frank Tayell
Copyright 2015

ISBN-13: 978-1519157577
ISBN-10: 1519157576

All people, places, and (especially) events are fictional.

Other titles:
Strike A Match
1. Serious Crimes

Work. Rest. Repeat.
A Post-Apocalyptic Detective Novel

Surviving The Evacuation
Book 0.5: Zombies vs The Living Dead
Book 1: London
Book 2: Wasteland
Book 3: Family
Book 4: Unsafe Haven
Book 5: Reunion
Book 6: Harvest
Book 7: Home

For more information visit:
http://blog.franktayell.com
http://twitter.com/FrankTayell
http://www.facebook.com/FrankTayell

Prologue: Progress
16th September 2039

"Roll on winter," Detective Sergeant Henry Mitchell grumbled as he ran a finger around his sweat-drenched collar. He hated being back in uniform, and not just because the woollen coat was completely impractical in the unseasonably blazing heat. When he'd left the police, his uniform had been whatever blue clothes he could find. All that had mattered was the badge. He'd come back to find it wasn't only the clothing that had changed. Everything had become rigid, from the rules to the ranks.

"Just like the old world. Progress, ha!" he muttered. He'd returned to Twynham intending to stay in the force long enough to see if the legendary beast they called a pension was real or a myth. Now he was almost certain he would resign in three months.

"Three months, assuming she passes." But of course she would pass. As her new commanding officer, Mitchell could be certain of that. She wasn't the reason he'd returned. Not entirely. It was duty that had drawn him back to southern England. And it was duty that had caused him to say the right thing at the wrong time, and so get demoted to sergeant.

He shrugged his shoulders and plucked at cloth, trying to dislodge the pool of sweat slowly turning into a reservoir beneath the straps of his bulletproof vest. That wasn't part of the uniform but, after what he'd been through in the last twenty years, he knew that particular discomfort was better than the alternative.

A mocking giggle came from behind him. He turned around and saw two children pointing and laughing at the muttering, squirming policeman. He threw them a glare. It had no effect, so he turned it into a pointed stare at the small cart the children had been pulling through the street. They followed his gaze until all three were staring at the small cargo of coal half filling the cart. Suddenly, the older child's eyes opened wide in understanding. With one hand the boy grabbed the cart, with the other he grabbed the girl's arm. They took off, the cart rattling behind them.

A lump of coal bounced out to land in the street. The girl darted back and half bent to pick it up. She looked at Mitchell, changed her mind, and ran.

For the first time that week, Mitchell found a smile sneaking across his lips. Technically, coal that fell from a steam engine's tender still belonged to the Railway Company so collecting it from the side of the tracks was theft. Technically. No one from his generation cared. They remembered the freezing winters after The Blackout too well to begrudge the meagre warmth a few lumps of coal would bring. And, the current heat notwithstanding, if the newspaper was to be believed, this winter was going to be one of the coldest in a decade.

The smile stayed on Mitchell's lips as he remembered his own, so very different, childhood in Montana. It truly was a lifetime ago. Then he looked up and saw the nearly complete radio antenna towering above the rooftops to the south. The smile vanished. There were some technophobes who claimed it was the harbinger of a second, final apocalypse. Most people saw it as a promise that things were returning to 'normal', whatever that was. That morning, the newspaper's front page had led with an artist's sketch of the antenna underneath the single word 'Progress!' Mitchell bit down on another scoffing retort. As he got closer to where they were building the outdoor stage, the roads were getting busier. Being thought an eccentric, muttering policeman by children was one thing. Amongst the adults tending their vegetable patches, heading out to the pub, or home for dinner, it was something else entirely.

The metropolis of Twynham was nothing like the cities that Mitchell remembered from his American youth. It was a sprawling suburb of towns and villages, hamlets and homes, factories and farms, created out of the buildings and land that hadn't been destroyed during The Blackout. Excluding the cratered remains of Bournemouth, it stretched from the New Forest in the east to Poole in the west, and for a dozen miles in land.

Close to a quarter of a million people now lived along the southern English coast. A million more worked the farms in Devon, Dorset, and Hampshire, and in the great orchards of Kent. Middle England was a wasteland. Its only inhabitants were loners and solitary kings who ruled over insects and birds from tower blocks they called their castles. Beyond that devastated expanse were the mobile mining cities of Wales and the factory towns of northern Scotland. They said farmers had to sleep with one eye open to watch for bandits raiding from the wasteland. Each year there were fewer raids, and fewer bandits to commit them. Each summer, more train tracks were laid, and more land was returned to the plough. It was piracy that was getting worse, particularly off the coast of Kent. But that was a matter for the Navy, not the police, and certainly not for Henry Mitchell.

He was close enough to the stage to make out the stick-like figures moving up and down the scaffolding. They were taking full advantage of the last hour of daylight in their scramble to get the antenna finished before the broadcast. Was it really progress? If you were to believe the newspaper it was one of humanity's greatest achievements. Mitchell rarely believed anything he read in that rag. Not even the weather report. He gave a surreptitious shrug, trying to dislodge the sweat-drenched shirt from where it had stuck to his shoulders. The jacket was part of the uniform, and he couldn't take that off, not yet. Three months, and then he'd take it off for good.

To the north, the smog bank over the power station slowly crept towards the coast. *That* was progress. He'd helped build the coal-fired plant on the site of the old airport. Everyone had helped during those chaotic years when anarchy and lawlessness were as ever-present a threat as starvation. All because of The Blackout, a brief seventy-two hours when the world had changed.

Everyone knew the story. Mankind had created the artificial intelligences. That's what they called them now, but they'd acted more like viruses, spreading throughout the connected world. When almost every machine and circuit was under the control of one AI or another, they'd gone to war. Cars, trucks, planes, power stations, dams, refineries, even phones and homes, they'd all become weapons in the AIs attempts to destroy one another. In the end, they'd succeeded. The blasts from nuclear warheads wiped out every power station on the planet. The electromagnetic pulse destroyed every infected circuit. That was the story everyone knew. Mitchell knew it was almost completely wrong.

Humanity had been a bystander, the very definition of collateral damage in that brief war. When the survivors had crept out of their underground holes, the world they'd known was gone. Some, like Mitchell, had known to go south. Others followed, not knowing what they might find except that it had to be better than the devastation that surrounded them. Dehydrated, starving, desperate, they'd reached the sea and discovered hundreds of ships had run aground; bulk carriers packed with grain, cargo ships filled with canned food, and cruise ships carrying mostly American tourists. Some called it a miracle. Others dismissed it as luck. A few said it was an ill omen. Again, Mitchell knew they were wrong.

He'd been there when the laws were written, and he'd been there during the dark days when they'd barely kept anarchy and chaos at bay. He'd stood with his back literally to the wall as they'd faced off pirates, bandits, marauders, and worse. His hand went to the decades old scar on his arm, but brushed against the three stripes sewn on the too-thick woollen coat. Self-consciously, his hand fell back to his side. And this was how he was rewarded, demoted to sergeant and assigned to a unit with no duties and fewer responsibilities.

A stray gust carried the sound of sawing and hammering from the coast. It was an ever-present noise, as ubiquitous as that of a train's whistle or a bicycle's bell. It wasn't possible to walk down more than three streets in a row without coming across a neglected house being torn down, or a new workshop being put up. This was different. His feet moving of their own volition, Mitchell set off once more, towards the sound of progress.

As he got closer he saw that there were two distinct groups; the engineers constructing the antenna on the roof of a cliff-top apartment building, and the carpenters building a stage on the grassy common next to it.

"We'll be testing it tomorrow, I hope," an engineer said, coming over to speak to Mitchell.

The woman's face was familiar, but it took a moment for the sergeant to place her. "Joyce Hynes. How are you?" Mitchell asked. Four years before, the woman's fifteen-year-old son had disappeared. Mitchell had assumed the lad had been murdered until he was found using an obviously fake ration book at a boarding house near Caerphilly. The boy had been lured away by the prospect of the high wages offered in a nearby coalmine.

"Busy," Hynes said.

"And your son?"

"Still in mining, though he's moved to Scotland. He's at a deep pit now, working as a loader. He's got the record for the most coal mined in a day," the engineer said with more than a touch of pride in her voice.

"Good for him. You say you're testing the antenna tomorrow?" Mitchell asked. "I thought the ceremony was being advertised as the first transatlantic radio broadcast for two decades."

"Oh, it's hardly that," Hynes said. "We had to make sure the relay stations were operational. It wouldn't do for the broadcast to cut out halfway through the Prime Minister's speech. Valentia Island has been receiving signals from Heart's Content in Newfoundland for over a year now. And we've spent the last month making sure that the floating relay stations are all in place. It would have been so much easier if we could have broadcast the ceremony at night, but they wanted people to listen. It's infuriating," she added, "but I do often find people get in the way of technology."

"Careful," Mitchell said. "If a technophobe were to hear you say that, they'd accuse you of wanting to bring back the AIs."

"Oh, there aren't any of those people working on this project," Hynes said. "No, and we're almost ready. Pinebreak Ferry in Maine and Southbourne here in Twynham are the last two pieces to the puzzle. It helps that the survey ships were in contact by radio over the last decade, but the signing ceremony will be the first *official* broadcast. It's the one that counts, the one that will be recorded as the symbol that we've recovered."

"Recovered?" Mitchell scoffed. "It's taken us twenty years to get back to the stage of what, an eight-minute broadcast?"

"Thirty-two minutes and forty seconds. That's counting the introduction, the musical interlude, and the speeches from two of their Presidents that they're broadcasting from their side of the Atlantic. But," she added, lowering her voice to a conspiratorial whisper, "those have been recorded in case there's a problem with the weather. Still, this is something that could be heard by two million people in Britain, and nearly fifteen million in North America."

"That might be the total population alive," Mitchell said, "but you can't expect every babe in arms to listen."

"Well, no, and I suppose there are places outside of the broadcast's range," she grudgingly admitted. She lowered her voice. "And even if they work night and day they'll almost certainly have to use the recordings to broadcast the address in Juneau. But that, at least, is not my problem. Yes," she added, speaking more normally again, "I do think most people will try to tune in."

"Assuming they can get a radio to work," Mitchell retorted, but he was arguing for the sake of it. There was a roaring clandestine trade among engineers from the Electric Company to which Mitchell and the rest of the police had been told to turn a blind eye. They were making a fortune selling adaptors so old-world radios could be plugged straight into the light socket that was the only working electrical fixture most houses had. The landlord of the pub in which Mitchell rented a room had gone one stage further. He'd hired a scavenger to find a set of working speakers and rigged up the pub as a 'listening room'. An entire evening of entertainment was planned and the tickets had already sold out. His landlord had even given Mitchell a free ticket along with two new candles. The unexpected gift had come with the warning that there would be no electric lighting in his room that night so as the pub didn't exceed its carefully metered allowance of electricity.

"However many tune in," Mitchell said, "they won't be listening to hear what the Prime Minister or one of the Presidents has to say. They'll listen because it's a new form of entertainment in a life that's work, sleep, and little else."

"Oh, I think you're wrong there as well," Hynes said. "They'll want to know what Britain's getting out of this trade deal. We've been shipping them canned food for the last decade, so it's about time we got something out of the... I mean," she stammered, as if she'd only just registered Mitchell's accent. Changing tack, she said, "You know what I heard? It's petrol. I've got a two-pound bet on it."

"Whatever Britain's getting, it won't be gasoline," Mitchell said. "If they've enough resources to re-open the wells and build a new refinery, how are they going to bring it over here?"

"In barrels, I suppose," Hynes said.

"But if they can make barrels for oil, they'd be able to make cans for food, so what would be the point of us shipping it across the Atlantic? Besides the only cars we've got are rusting by the roadside or have long since been scrapped."

"Yes... well," the engineer muttered, clearly having had enough of the detective's cynicism, "we'll find out at the end of the week, won't we? Excuse me. I've got to go and... check the placements."

The woman stalked off towards an apprentice who got a tongue-lashing for being in the wrong place at the wrong time. Mitchell watched the carpenters and engineers at their work for a few minutes more, but found his gaze drifting towards the sea, and the rusting hulks beached along the coast.

He was one of the few people who knew how the ships really had come aground on the shore, and one of even fewer who cared. But they were the real reason Britain had recovered faster than anywhere else. The food had kept them alive as they'd dug the mass graves, learned to plough by hand, laid the railway lines, subdued the criminals who dreamed of becoming tyrants, mined the coal, and turned pleasure yachts into fishing boats. It had sustained them until they brought their first harvest in, and it was a good harvest, more than they could eat. They'd built the power plant, and then the factory to recycle rusting steel into cans. Then came the canneries and food processing plants. It wasn't easy. Death was their constant companion during those early years, but the stockpile had grown. Finally, fishing boats could be spared to discover what had become of the rest of the planet. Communication was slowly re-established with coastal communities around the world, and the sailors went, bearing gifts. As sail was replaced by steam – tinged with hopes of diesel – the shipments had grown until they'd become a highly divisive issue. It wasn't simply the inconvenience of rationing, but some people were questioning whether the mines, power plants, factories, and farms, only existed so that food could be sent overseas.

The broadcast announcing a trade deal between Britain and the three governments that called themselves the successors to the old United States wasn't a sign of recovery. It was symbolic. A political message to the isolationists who would keep the food in Britain, and to the technophobes who thought radio was the first step leading back to AIs and the final destruction of the planet. And as much as the broadcast was for Britain, it was a message to the separatists in America. The world might have stalled with The Blackout, but it hadn't changed. The American election was going ahead, and reunification would happen, no matter how much a small faction may wish otherwise.

Mitchell turned towards the cracked asphalt road that led down the cliffs to the beach. As he walked his old, familiar beat, the sound of sawing grew distant, and he began to relax. He always came to this spot when he could spare the time. The rusting ships kept the beach relatively isolated, and few people had made their homes in the apartment blocks and seafront hotels nearby. That had changed with the construction of the antenna. Not only had they extended the railway line from Christchurch, but they were planning on electrifying the entire district. Of course, being Britain, that had led to letters to the newspaper complaining that local rents were going up.

No, the broadcast wasn't progress. A newspaper with complaints in a letters page and sports results printed on the back, almost lost amidst advertisements, *that* was worth celebrating. The results were for soccer, and the adverts were mostly for the powdered tea substitute the chemical works produced, but it was a promise of what was to come. However, it was the broadcast that would be the first chapter in the new history books, and that summed it all up. There would be history books again, and time for people to study them, but there wouldn't be a single one that recorded the name of Henry Mitchell.

His hand went again to his arm, this time deliberately brushing against the sergeant's stripes. The demotion was his own fault. Policing had changed in the time he'd spent wandering the wasteland. They even had an academy now though the students spent more time studying maths and geography than forensics and law. Being given the new unit, however, seemed like an insult. Even the name was a joke. Serious Crimes. There were no *serious* crimes. Of course, all crimes were serious to the victims, but if a wagonload of cattle went missing, you looked for the butcher selling off-the-ration meat. If a wife was found murdered, you looked for the husband who'd not turned up for his shift at work. Serious, but not so complicated that they needed a new unit to deal with them. There were few thefts, and certainly no large ones, because in their twisted Utopia they all had so little.

Maybe the commissioner was right. Mitchell had come to England on what was meant to be a working holiday, but had fallen into a harsh life of brutal justice. Both of those worlds were gone. Since The Blackout, he'd come to love and hate Britain in equal measure, but it wasn't home. His home was twenty years ago, a foreign country he could only visit in wistful dreams.

That left the question of where he would go in three months' time. Not back to America. There was nothing there for him anymore. No, but there was Isaac. It was six months since they'd last spoken, but Mitchell knew the man would offer him a home. His hand went to his pocket and the note in it. Isaac had come to the city and wanted to speak. It wouldn't hurt to go and listen to what the man wanted to say. There was the girl, of course. He would have to stay a sergeant in the police for the next three months, but after that he could... he could... could...

There was something wrong about the man standing by the row of old beach huts. He had a white streak in brown hair that didn't quite cover the missing half of his ear. That was nothing unusual. Most people had some reminder of those savage early years. No, it was his entire attitude that was wrong. The man was trying too hard to look nonchalant.

"Evening," Mitchell said, as he walked past. The man grumbled something in reply. Mitchell raised a hand to his cap, stealing a brief glance beyond the half-eared man. There were two other men standing in the gap between a pair of huts. Mitchell kept walking and didn't look back until he knew he was out of sight. He ducked behind the wall of a wooden cafe that had been shuttered long before The Blackout and climbed up the steep grassy slope behind. He pulled off his cap, dropped to his knees, and then to his belly, crawling until he was close enough to see the three men.

Yes, something was wrong with them. It was the clothes. The sentry and one of the other two men were dressed in the same mix of patched, overly washed jeans, faded T-shirts, and cracked boots that most people wore. But over the top they had jackets that were far too warm for the weather. The third man, however, was wearing a well fitting, cream-coloured suit. Either he'd paid a scavenger to search the ruins for clothes his exact size, or he'd paid a tailor to make him something new out of old-world linen. Whichever it was, it meant the man had money, and that meant he had an office, a home, and plenty of other places he could conduct this meeting. So why do it here? Of course, there could be an innocent explanation, but for each that Mitchell could think of, there were a dozen far more sinister ones.

He looked around, gauging whether he could get close enough to hear what was being said without being seen. No. That left him with only one course of action. Whatever he might do in three months' time, wherever he might go, here and now he was a copper. He crawled back down the hill and towards the path. He didn't run, he didn't saunter. He *did* pause to adjust the bulletproof vest and check his pistol was loose in his holster. Then he walked off the path and onto the beach.

The huts were level with where a cruise liner had come aground. A storm in the first winter had torn its stern anchors free, twisting the ship until it was parallel with the shore. The spring tides had pushed it onto its side. The sand was now littered with debris spilled from the ship and stained red from where it had been left to rust. Mitchell picked an erratic path through the detritus, waiting until he was thirty yards from the hut before raising a hand in greeting to the sentry. The man nodded back.

Mitchell changed direction, walking casually towards the man. The sentry turned away from Mitchell just as the other two men came into view. He could see their mouths move in urgent conversation, but couldn't hear the words over the sound of the crashing surf. They stopped talking to watch his approach. For the briefest of moments, Mitchell thought his suspicions were unfounded, and then the sentry bolted, sprinting off down the path.

The other raggedly dressed man pulled out a gun. Mitchell dived forward as a bullet whistled through the air above his head. He landed hard, his elbows jarring on a section of hull plate buried beneath an inch of sand. Ignoring the pain, he dragged himself towards a stack of cabin doors that someone had piled up on the beach. There was another shot and the sound of a bullet pinging off metal.

A feral grin spread across Mitchell's face. After the paperwork, politics, and uncertainty of the last few months, this was a situation with which he was familiar.

"Police!" he yelled, adding under his breath. "Like you didn't realise that." He reached for his gun. Not the standard issue revolver at his belt, but the old-world 9mm he kept strapped to his ankle. Glass shattered a dozen yards in front of him.

"Three," he whispered, counting the shots as he darted a quick glance around the edge of the thick doors. The man in the suit was crawling along the path, away from the gunfire. Mitchell couldn't tell if he'd been injured or was just too terrified to stand. Mitchell ducked back into cover just as a bullet ricocheted off the metal doors behind which he was hiding.

"Four," he said as he raised his pistol and fired off an unaimed shot of his own. The man replied. A bullet thudded into the sand a foot to his left, another into a hunk of driftwood two feet to the right.

"Six," Mitchell said, and stood up. His hunch was based on a momentary glimpse of the man's weapon but he was certain it was a revolver. He was right. The man stood between the huts, fumbling cartridges into the chamber.

"Drop it!" Mitchell barked. The man didn't, opting instead to dive behind the relative cover of the hut's wall.

Mitchell took a sweeping step to the left, and another, trying to get a clear view. "You run, I'll fire," Mitchell called. The man had the grass slope to one side, the path to the other. "Throw out the gun and come out with your hands above your head. Do it!"

He took another step. His heartbeat echoed in his ears. It always did at this moment. Knowing one of his bullets would easily pass straight through the wooden wall of the hut, he shifted his aim. Slowly, he tightened his grip. He was about to squeeze the trigger when there was a shout from behind the hut.

"All right," the man yelled. "I'm coming out."

"The gun first," Mitchell shouted back.

There was another pause, one that was almost too long, before a revolver clattered onto the path. Mitchell untensed, but only fractionally.

"Now you," Mitchell called. "Slowly!"

An arm appeared, and then a shoulder, a head, and… the other arm was held low, behind the man's back.

"Don't—" Mitchell began, but it was too late. The man spun around, the arm came up. In his hand was a second pistol, but before he could bring it to bear, Mitchell fired. The bullet struck. The man flew backwards. Mitchell ran across the sand, but he knew the man was dead long before he reached him.

He kicked the gun out of the lifeless hand and suppressed that familiar wave of nausea he always felt after he brought more death into the world. He looked around for the man's two companions. The one with half an ear was long gone, but the suited man was still trying to crawl along the path, barely sixty yards away.

Mitchell jogged towards him. The man heard, pulled himself to his feet, and started to run. Mitchell started to sprint. He pounded down the sand-swept path. Twenty yards. Ten. Five. Three. Mitchell dived, knocking the man down.

"Stop," Mitchell growled. "And stop moving. It's your own damn fault." He dug a knee into the man's back. "Stop," he said again. The man did.

Mitchell grabbed the handcuffs from the pouch at his belt, and cuffed one hand, and then the next.

"Where's the other guy going?" Mitchell asked. "Where?"

His prisoner said nothing. Mitchell looked around, but there was no sign of the half-eared man.

"What's your name?" Mitchell asked.

"I don't have to tell you," the man said.

"Strictly speaking, that's true," Mitchell said. "But it doesn't mean I'm not going to find out. I've got you for attempted murder."

"You can't arrest me, I've got diplomatic immunity."

"Yeah, right," Mitchell began, and was about to add a mocking laugh, but there was something about the accent and clothes that gave him pause. "Are you serious?"

"My papers are in my inside pocket."

Mitchell pulled the man to his knees and searched his pockets until he found something he hadn't seen in decades: a passport. The front wasn't stamped with the name of the country but with the words 'Office of the American Embassy'. Mitchell flipped it open and stared at the photograph. The picture was of such poor quality it could have belonged to almost any male between the ages of twenty and fifty.

"It says your name is Lucas Fairmont and that you're the principal secretary to the ambassador himself."

"Which means you've got to let me go," Fairmont said.

"Where are you from?" Mitchell asked. "Iowa?"

"I'm not saying anything more," Fairmont replied.

"Fair enough," Mitchell said. He began a far more thorough search of the man.

"Hey! You can't do that!" Fairmont protested.

"And yet I am," Mitchell said. There were no weapons, only a thick envelope hidden in a deep pocket concealed in the coat's lining. "What's this?" he asked, waving the packet in front of the man's eyes.

"Diplomatic correspondence. Which means you can't open it," Fairmont said.

14

"Does it? Let's see." Mitchell tore at the seal, pulling the envelope open.

"No! You can't read them! It's against the law!" Fairmont protested.

This time Mitchell said nothing as he examined the contents. There were seven sheets of paper. On the left-hand side of each page was a list of names and addresses, with an esoteric collection of details next to each; an elementary school, the colour of the mailbox, the name of an aunt, a name of a business, the address of a lawyer... He turned to the next sheet and found it was much the same.

"What does this list mean?" Mitchell asked.

"I'm not saying another word," Fairmont replied.

"Yes, you said that before," Mitchell said. "But why did you bring them out here? Were you selling them? Is that it? Have we devolved to espionage already?" He waited to see if Fairmont would say anything. He didn't.

"Don't say I didn't give you a chance," Mitchell said. He hauled the man to his feet and pushed him back along the path, towards the dead body.

"Stay here," he said, pushing the man down to his knees, five yards from the corpse. "I'd suggest you tell me what was going on and in return I'd get a few years shaved off your sentence. But I don't think you'll take a deal, will you? No, I thought not."

Mitchell backed away from the man until he could see both Fairmont and the corpse. He picked up the gun the man had thrown out. It was a revolver, of the same make as the one holstered at Mitchell's belt. Hopefully it was stolen. The armoury in Scotland manufactured rifles for hunters, shotguns for farmers, and revolvers for the police. Only the Navy used old-world firearms; assault rifles with barrels modified to take the new ammunition made at the powder works in Loch Creigh. Everything from Uzis to AK47s had come to Britain with the waves of immigrants who'd passed through the Channel Tunnel. Fortunately, after surviving the horrors of mainland Europe, few people had any ammunition left. Creating a standardised cartridge of a calibre too large to fit in the most common of old-world weapons, and whose sale was restricted and taxed,

15

was a crude form of gun control. One that clearly hadn't worked. He pocketed the revolver and picked up the other gun. It was an old-world snub-nosed pistol with four cartridges in the magazine. He weighed it in his hands, thoughtfully.

"Do you think he planned to shoot you with this?" he asked Fairmont. The man said nothing.

The sergeant turned back to the corpse. His bullet had entered through the man's cheek, flying diagonally through the man's head, blowing out an eye before taking off the top of his skull. He didn't recognise what was left of the face, but that didn't mean much.

"You want to tell me who he is?" he called out to Fairmont. The man glared back.

The dead man had little in his pockets. There were four loose rounds for the revolver, two one-pound notes and four penny-stamps, a clasp knife with a five-inch blade, and a coin. Mitchell examined it closely.

All currency was printed. Denominations from fifty pence to twenty pounds were issued as notes, smaller currency was printed as stamps. Even the rarest of metals could be scavenged from the ruins of the dead cities, but electricity was scarce. Forging a printed, paper note was far more difficult than building a stamp to press out a metal coin. This coin, however, had never been used as currency. One side was stamped with what looked almost like a large backwards 'L'. Around the face was an inscription, THE TRUTH LIES IN THE PAST, with each word separated by five stars. It felt like silver, but that was so common as to be worthless. It was certainly an odd thing to carry after the man had clearly gone to the trouble of emptying his pockets. There was no ration book, no handkerchief, no scraps of paper, and no keys. The man's clothing was worn, but well repaired. The boots were old and clean but not polished. Boot polish wasn't cheap, but it was certainly cheaper than black market government-issue ammunition. The coin was the real clue. Someone had gone to the trouble of creating it, and that meant there was a meaning to it. If he found the meaning, he'd find the answers to the other questions. Of course, first he would have to secure the scene, call the coroner, report the shooting to the commissioner, and begin the tedious mound of

16

paperwork that would then ensue. He looked at Fairmont. Or perhaps not.

"Get up," he said, hauling the man to his feet.

"You have to release me," Fairmont said. "I've got diplomatic immunity."

"That's not how it works. How old are you?" He opened the man's passport. "Thirty-six. If that's close to the truth then you're too young to remember. What your piece of paper means is that I have to take you to the embassy. I'm sure they have a cultural attaché who'd be interested in speaking to you."

"Cultural attaché?" Fairmont asked, clearly confused.

"You see? That's what I mean. You're too young." He dragged Fairmont along the path. There was probably someone from the embassy at the antenna. If not, he could send someone to fetch one. Hopefully what he'd stumbled across counted as a diplomatic incident and that would make it the business of the SIS - the Secret Intelligence Service. It certainly wouldn't be a matter for Serious Crimes, and that meant Mitchell could ignore the paperwork and get busy solving the case.

Chapter 1
A New Cadet
17th September

Police Cadet Ruth Deering stared at the handwritten sign on the door
to the small cabin. Serious Crimes. She looked at the slip of paper in her
hand. There it was, in slightly smudged black and white, Serious Crimes. It
was her first assignment as a police officer, and it would be where she
worked for at least the next three months. She couldn't say this was the
last thing she'd wanted because she'd never heard of the Serious Crimes
Unit until yesterday. As much as she'd wanted anything, it had been a
placement somewhere outside of Twynham. Instead, as most of her class
had hurried off to catch the trains that would take them to the far-flung
corners of Britain, Ruth had gone home. She'd pressed her new uniform
and tried to convince herself that it could have been worse. Looking at the
building, with its chipped paint, rotten felt roof, and rusting metal ramp,
she wasn't sure how.

The cabin was hidden behind what was now the stable, but which had
been a swimming pool in the days when Police House was a school. The
cabin wasn't even a proper bricks-and-mortar building, but one of those
temporary structures about the size of a shipping container and with just
as much charm. Ruth reread her assignment one last time, but wishing
wasn't going to change the handwritten words. She straightened her cap,
smoothed down her jacket, made sure the belt with its truncheon,
revolver, and handcuffs, was square, and raised a hand to knock. She
stopped. It had been her idea to join the police. For good or bad, it was
what she'd wanted, and now, as her adoptive mother said, she had to own
the decision. She pushed the door open and stepped inside.

"This isn't a storeroom anymore," a man said. "You'll have to dump
your records somewhere else." He spoke without lowering the newspaper
from in front of his face, nor his feet from the one square foot of desk
that wasn't covered in a mountainous stack of folders. His accent was

American. Different to Ruth's mother's East Coast twang, but similarly tempered from decades of living in Britain. From the stripes on the uniform jacket hanging on the back of his chair, she guessed he was the Sergeant Mitchell to whom her papers told her to report.

"Cadet Ruth Deering reporting for duty, sir," she said, snapping to attention.

"Cadet?" the sergeant growled, dropping a corner of the newspaper just enough for a bloodshot eye to glare at her. "Reporting? What do you mean?"

"Sir... to Serious Crimes," she stammered. The eye continued its unwavering stare. Not sure what else to say, she thrust her orders out towards the man. The newspaper was lowered another inch, and now there were two baleful eyes giving her the most searching look she'd ever known. The sergeant folded the paper, slowly running his finger down each crease in turn, before gently placing it on top of a precariously balanced box. In one surprisingly swift movement, his feet came off the desk and his hand came out grabbing her orders.

"Let me see that," he said.

No longer hidden behind the newspaper, and his attention no longer on her, Ruth was finally able to get a proper look at her new commanding officer. He had grey-flecked hair and a frost-pocked face, with a slight paunch around his waist that wasn't helped by a shirt that looked a size too small. He was around forty, she guessed, and going by the bloodshot eyes and stained uniform, he was still living the lifestyle of a much younger man.

"Well, that's Commissioner Wallace's signature," the sergeant said. "So, they've really sent a cadet to Serious Crimes?"

Ruth heard the inflection, but wasn't sure what the actual question was. She was saved having to guess by a voice from behind her.

"What did you do?" a woman asked.

Ruth jumped in surprise and received a soft mocking laugh in return. She turned around to see a woman of around thirty, wearing the uniform of a detective constable, standing in the doorway.

"Do?" Ruth asked. "I'm sorry, I don't—"

"The fact you're here means that you've done something wrong," the sergeant interrupted. "Or you failed to do something wrong when asked. Which is it?"

"I... I..." Ruth stammered, completely at a loss.

"Did you cheat on your exams?" the constable asked. "I bet that's it, but your parents are too important for you to be kicked out."

"What? No. I didn't—" Ruth stopped, remembered who she was, where she was, and to whom she was speaking. "I didn't cheat," she said, "and I resent the insinuation."

"You do, eh?" the sergeant said. "Then maybe there's hope for you. I'm DS Mitchell, that's Detective Constable Riley." He glanced down at Ruth's orders once more before handing them back. "Welcome to Serious Crimes."

Ruth took the slip of paper and waited for the sergeant to continue. She realised he'd finished.

"Thank you, sir," she said. There were no lights on in the small cabin though that wasn't uncommon. There were no candles either, but since most of the room was full of boxes overflowing with paper, that was probably a blessing. Other than a few desks and chairs, and a row of cupboards against the far wall, the room was empty. There was no crime board, no sketches of suspects, no indication of any police work at all. If anything, the cabin looked like a dumping ground for forgotten files. "What is it that... I mean, what does Serious Crimes... um..." The sergeant gave her another look, shook his head, and picked up his paper. Ruth guessed that she'd failed some unknown test.

"You want to know what Serious Crimes does?" he asked. "Well, so do we." With a flourish the paper was unfurled, and his face disappeared from view.

There was a long, awkward silence broken by Riley. "We were set up a week ago," the detective constable said, her tone clipped. "Technically we're to deal with inter-jurisdictional overlap."

"I'm sorry, what's that?" Ruth asked.

20

"You know how the police is structured?" Mitchell growled. "Each city and town has its own police force. Three officers in a market town, more in a city, too many in Twynham. There's the Secret Intelligence Service, who are misnamed for many reasons, but who are charged with investigating crimes against the state. The railways have their guards, the mines their provosts, the docks and border towns have the Marines, yes?"

"Yes," Ruth agreed.

"Right, so if you've been paying attention you'll have realised there is no overlap. This is a dead-end unit, cadet. Welcome to Purgatory. The eleventh circle to which Riley and I have been sent because we refuse to go away. If you insist on asking more questions, I'd suggest you start by asking yourself who you crossed to end up here."

Ruth opened her mouth. She closed it again.

"If we're keeping her," Riley said, "can I use her for witness statements?"

"Knock yourself out," the sergeant mumbled. "Just do it quietly."

"Do you know how to write a report?" Riley asked.

"Yes, ma'am," Ruth said.

"I'm not ma'am," Riley said. "You call me detective when we're in front of civilians, Riley when we're not. You can have this desk." She lifted a pile of files off a rickety chair and dumped them on an equally large pile on the desk.

"Yesterday evening there was a fight at the docks," Riley said. "Fifty-three sailors were involved. Go through the statements and find out who started it."

Ruth searched around for an intelligent question. The best she could come up with was, "If this was at the docks, and they were all sailors, doesn't that make it the Navy's jurisdiction?"

"It should do," Mitchell said. "Tell her why we got landed with the paperwork, Riley."

"Because," the constable said, in a singsong sigh as if she was parroting something repeated to her many times, "a good police officer knows to pass off the paperwork any time they can."

"Yes," Mitchell said, "but tell her why it got passed on to us."

Riley threw Mitchell a venomous look which, due to the newspaper, the sergeant completely failed to notice. "Because," Riley said, this time as if the words were being dragged out of her. "I went to help the Marines break up the fight. It was at that point the captain of the SS Nile reported a cargo of oranges was being unloaded when the fight began. He claimed four crates had been lost over the side of the wharf."

"It's the next part that's most significant," Mitchell said. It sounded like he was smiling. "Go on, tell her what you did."

"What anyone would do," Riley said. "I jumped in to retrieve the crates."

"She jumped in," Mitchell repeated. "Cadet, why did she do that?"

The unexpected question caught Ruth stumbling for a reply. She thought quickly. "Um… because the laws of salvage mean those oranges would have been hers?"

"See," Riley said. "She gets it. Just like any normal person would."

"A normal person would think twice before jumping into the sea," Mitchell said. "Tell the cadet what you found."

"Nothing," Riley admitted. "There were no crates."

"Then the fight was a way of covering up the theft?" Ruth guessed.

"Precisely," Mitchell said. "And what does that tell us, cadet?"

"Um… That sailors can't be trusted?" Ruth said.

"Not quite, and a good copper avoids such bald generalisations," Mitchell said. "It tells us that the Marines were not complicit in the crime. If they'd been bribed, there would have been no need for the diversion. Honesty is a rare treasure, to be prized when it is found. That there are some trustworthy guards at the dock is a piece of information worth the cost of a uniform and a week's worth of paperwork. Have you ever eaten an orange, cadet?"

"No, sir," Ruth said.

"Nor have I, not for the last twenty years. As you go through those reports, carefully reading line after line, imagine the orange sitting on that desk. That's your motivation. Now, find me someone I can charge."

Ruth opened the first report and didn't look up until she'd finished. Mitchell was looking at his newspaper though Ruth didn't think he was actually reading it. Riley was sitting at her own desk, a battered novel in her hands. Neither were paying her any attention. In fact, they both seemed to have forgotten she was there. For the moment that was how she liked it. She turned back to the report.

Ignoring the four-letter invective, there were scant few details. All the participants in the brawl came from the same ship, the SS Nile, which had been on a survey mission to Gibraltar. The oranges had been collected from a wild grove on the Spanish coast. According to what she'd read, the fight had begun when Lemuel Evans, a stoker, had hit Donald McCormack, the purser's mate, with a boat hook. She reread it to make sure, but it seemed cut and dry. Suspecting it couldn't have been as simple as that, she turned to the next report. It gave a completely different account. Franny Winters, the ship's carpenter, had instigated the brawl by hitting Jimmy Lim, a sailor second-class, with an uppercut that had broken two teeth. She read on, statement after statement, and found that each participant blamed a different mariner for starting the fight.

As she turned to the tenth account, and was silently cursing Constable Riley for jumping into the sea, the door to the cabin opened. A man in rolled-up shirtsleeves but still wearing the green hat of a railway messenger entered.

"Is this Special Crimes?" he asked.

"It is," Mitchell said. "Who are you?"

"Taylor, messenger." He held out a slip of paper. The man's face was grim. When Mitchell read the piece of paper, his own dropped to match it.

"Have you ever seen a dead body, cadet?" Mitchell asked.

"In the morgue, sir. During autopsy class."

"You're about to see one in the wild. There's a train waiting for us?" he asked of the messenger.

"There is," Taylor said. "But they can only hold it until half past."

"That's barely ten minutes from now," Riley snapped, as she took the message from Mitchell. "Tell them to wait for us, or they'll rue it."

The hapless messenger backed out of the door.

"Rue it?" Mitchell remarked as he pulled his jacket on. "Did you get that from your novel?"

Riley shrugged. "You said I needed to be more loquacious."

She didn't treat Mitchell like her superior, Ruth thought, more like a brother or a—

"Cadet, there's a crime-kit over there," Mitchell's voice cut in on her thoughts and his hand waved towards the back of the cabin. Ruth took the hint and hurried over to the kit. The box wasn't made of laminated pine like the modern ones she'd used in the academy but of faded old-world plastic and was twice the size. Fortunately, it was on a trolley. Again it was unlike the newer ones she remembered from training. This was all angular aluminium tubes and almost-perished rubber straps.

"There are evidence bags in that box on the counter. Ten should do," Mitchell said.

"And don't forget the sign," Riley added. "You need the sign. You know why?"

Ruth picked up the wooden sign with the word 'Police' painted in white on a blue background. "By law all crime scenes must be marked with them," she said.

"But why?" Mitchell asked.

She thought quickly. "Because interfering with a crime scene carries an automatic five-month light labour sentence. Coming within ten feet of the sign counts as interfering. In the academy they said it's an easy way of making someone commit a crime so you have leverage over them."

"They taught you that, did they?" Mitchell asked. Again, Ruth felt she'd failed another unknown test.

She grabbed ten paper evidence bags from the box, stuck them in the crime-kit, balanced the sign on top, and hauled the trolley to the door. It clattered into a desk and then the wall as she hurried outside. Mitchell and Riley were waiting patiently at the foot of the cabin's ramp. The sergeant gave her a long, thoughtful stare.

"Let's go," he said, setting a brisk pace as they left Police House and headed towards the train station. "Riley, what do we know?"

"The note informs us that a body's been found two miles north of Ringwood Junction," Riley said. "It was spotted just after dawn by a guard on a goods train heading north. Word was telegraphed back when the train reached its next stop, and then passed along, up, and around, until it reached us."

Riley finished at about the same time as one of the trolley's small wheels got caught in an old steel grating. Ruth heaved it back onto the road and then had to run a few paces to catch up.

"Any thoughts, cadet?" Mitchell asked.

"I suppose the obvious one is why are we involved. Is this something Serious Crimes is meant to handle?"

"I told you before, Serious Crimes isn't meant to handle anything," Mitchell said. "We're to sit in our cabin, file paperwork, and neither be seen nor heard."

"Then why are we going?" she asked.

"Good question. Who signed the note, Riley?"

"R.C.," Riley said.

"You know who that is?" Mitchell asked.

"No, sir," Ruth said.

"That's Rebecca Cavendish. Or *the* Railway Company as she likes to think of herself. She's one of the original drivers who brought the engines down from the museums during the first few weeks after The Blackout. You know that story?"

Ruth shook her head.

"What did they teach you?" Mitchell muttered. "The old power stations were destroyed during The Blackout. What little oil there is in Britain was too deep for us to drill. The few solar panels and wind turbines that still worked were too large to be moved. But there's coal. Rebecca, and people like her, kept old steam engines running for fun. If you can maintain a century-old locomotive, you can build a new one. They became the blueprints for our new engines, and for the coal-fired power stations. But the coal is in the north, in Wales, Scotland, and Northern England, and the food was here in the south. The roads were made impassable by millions of stalled cars, so the railways became our lifeline.

We'd all be dead if it wasn't for her, and some of us honour our debts. When she asks, we do, because there's probably a reason why she sent for us."

"Oh." Ruth tried to think of a polite way to frame her next question, but there really wasn't one. "What I meant," she said, "was why aren't the railway police dealing with the crime."

"Probably because Rebecca thought Mister Mitchell could do with some fresh air," Riley said.

Mitchell gave a grunt halfway between agreement and annoyance as he nimbly sidestepped a delivery cart. Ruth managed to haul the trolley out of the way just before the horse lashed out with an angry hoof. The working day had long since begun, but the roads were far from empty. There were carts delivering to the market, messengers taking mail and telegrams to the homes and businesses in the centre of town, and labourers hurrying to construction sites.

A woman wrestled a squeaking old-world pushchair out of the door of a greengrocer's and threw the police officers a glare when they didn't stop to help. Next to it was a bookstore with a sign out front reading 'New stock from Hay now in.' Beyond that was a clockmaker, the window full of mostly new timepieces, all of which told her that…

"Sir, it's been nine minutes. Shouldn't we run?" Ruth asked.

"They'll hold the train," Mitchell said.

"They will?" Ruth was genuinely surprised. The railway timetable was considered as reliable as the winter sugar ration was scarce.

"Rebecca wouldn't have sent us the note if she wasn't prepared to keep the train waiting for us," Mitchell said.

Ruth doubted anyone was that powerful but, when they arrived at the station seven minutes after it should have left, the train was still waiting for them. The driver saw them, raised a hand, and stepped into the cab of a highly polished engine. There was a whistle, a burst of steam, and the sixteen old-world carriages started to move.

"Passenger cabin's the third car from the end," Mitchell said, and he finally broke into a run. Riley bounded after him, easily keeping pace. Ruth gripped the handle of the trolley and hauled it along in their wake. She kept her eyes fixed on the guard standing in the open doorway. Mitchell stepped on board. Riley jumped in after him. The train began to accelerate.

"Hurry!" the guard yelled.

Ruth put on a burst of speed, heaving the trolley in front of her, and holding it out towards Riley. The constable leaned out further, grabbed Ruth's collar and bodily hauled her, trolley, and crime-kit, onto the train.

"Thank you," Ruth hissed, as the guard slid the door closed.

It was a refurbished old-world carriage with scratched windows that hadn't been designed to open. There were seats at the rear and front, but they'd been removed in the middle section and replaced with a set of narrow cages either side of an equally narrow walkway.

"Is that the mail?" she asked the guard.

"It is," he said. "The telegraph's good for letting the mine know the train's on its way, but it can't send a pair of socks to someone working an open seam. Vital work, the railways, it's what's kept our country going." He turned to Mitchell. "We'll get to Ringwood Junction in about half an hour. We'll slow there, but we won't stop. You'll have to jump."

"I wouldn't have it any other way," Mitchell said.

The guard walked down the swaying carriage, past the cages and the handful of other passengers, and disappeared through the door at the end.

Mitchell and Riley had taken up station at the pair of window seats nearest the door. She had her book out, he had his eyes closed. Ruth stayed standing for a moment taking in the passengers at the far end. She wondered who they were, and how far they were going. If she hadn't been assigned to Serious Crimes, she could have been sitting there with them, on her way to somewhere exotic. Or just to somewhere far, far away from Twynham. She sighed and sat down.

"Describe them," Mitchell said, without opening his eyes.

"Who?" Ruth asked.

"The other passengers," he said.

She glanced along the aisle. Now seated, she could only see the back of one head and the front of a different knee. "There are seven people," she

27

said. "Two men with a boy and a girl. I would say they were both around fifteen years old. From the luggage nearby they're relocating to the north."

"And?"

"And a man in a dog collar sitting opposite, with two women in the chairs behind."

"And?" Mitchell prompted again.

Ruth thought. "The two women are of a similar height, hair colour, and have similar features. I'd say they were sisters, perhaps cousins, but they are related. About twenty-five to thirty years old, maybe a little older. The man, woman, and two children don't look like a family."

"They don't?" Mitchell asked.

"Well, they don't look alike, not that that means much, but the children aren't sitting close. They're more… sort of upright. Like they're sitting at attention. I think the man and woman are two masters, the children are their apprentices."

"Which would make them how old?" Mitchell asked.

"Right, of course, so they're at least seventeen. Probably tailors, going by the clothing."

"Probably. Anything else?"

"Um…" she hesitated and did it too long.

"The priest is wearing a crucifix around his neck, not a cross," Mitchell said, opening his eyes and fixing them on hers. "But he *is* wearing it around his neck. The green book on the seat next to him is a Latin primer. Taken with the fact there was a conference at the New Priory last weekend, I'd say he's a Catholic. The two women are miners. You can tell that from the coal dust that's embedded under the skin. It makes them appear older than they are. I'd say they were in their early twenties. From their clothing you can tell they're returning to work after a short stay in Twynham. It's comfortable clothing, not showy. If they were in mourning they'd be wearing black. Since they're not, they didn't come here for a funeral. However, travel is expensive unless you get a warrant. Miners get those for births, deaths, and marriages of immediate family. It's unlikely to be a wedding, as who has enough free time to get married in the middle of September? Therefore it's a birth. Probably of a niece or nephew. Taking in their age, and that they've chosen to work in the mines, that tells us that the family was recently in need of money. The mines are dangerous, but they pay well. I would say that they chose to change careers due to the imminent arrival of the child."

"How do you know they changed careers?" Ruth asked.

"Riley?" the sergeant prompted.

"It's the clothes," Riley said, lowering her novel. "They're very good quality and handmade. It suggests they were tailors, or training for it."

"They could have bought the clothes," Ruth suggested.

"Not when you consider the looks they were giving the two master tailors and their apprentices," Riley said. "They're not looking at the people, but what they represent. It's wistful regret at the life that they could have had. But it's not resentful, and that suggests that out of whatever tragedy has forced their change of career, something good has come out of it. A child."

"That's impressive," Ruth said.

"It's a theory based on observation," Mitchell said. "Didn't they teach you that in the academy? They should also have taught you that I could be completely wrong. Perhaps they're a couple sent to the mines as part of a prison sentence who came to Twynham on a compassionate furlough. The priest might be a vicar, and the crucifix an heirloom. We look at people, and weave a story around that which we can see, but you must remember that it remains a story until facts confirm it as truth." He closed his eyes. "Or not."

Ruth had heard something similar from one of her instructors at the academy. At the time she'd filed it away as interesting but not important. Mathematics, geography, history, English, and everything else had to be learned by rote and was tested on a weekly basis. Failure in those tests led to expulsion. By contrast, the lectures on policing were seen as an opportunity to doze as much by their instructors as they were by the students.

She fixed her gaze on the landscape beyond the scratched windows. They'd long since passed the sheds and loading yards around Twynham. The view now was of fields filled with cows, interspersed with occasional abandoned houses. But they sped by too quickly for her to tell if the roofs had been broken by missiles during The Blackout, or by weather and time in the years since.

"It's so fast," she murmured.

"You think this is fast, you should have tried flying," Mitchell said. "Have you never been on a train before?"

"Once," Ruth said, her eyes glued on the trees rushing by. "In the academy."

It had been during their survival training, and that journey had been made at night. The recruits had been dropped in the middle of nowhere and told to find their way back before breakfast. Ruth had, but five of the other recruits were still missing by lunchtime. When they were found, they were dismissed. That was her lasting memory of the academy, of one person being expelled after another.

The fields gave way to a hamlet where smoke belched from chimneys tacked onto houses built in the age of central heating, and then to woodland. They passed a horse and cart on the wide road that had been dug along the railway line. Then a trio of bicycles, laden with... but they went by too fast for her to tell.

"It's about another mile," the train's guard said, interrupting her reverie ten minutes later. "We'll slow the train, but we won't stop."

"Yes, you said." Mitchell stood. "And coming back?"

"When we stop to take on water and Marines for the journey north, we'll have word passed along the line. Just signal a train and get ready to jump on."

A few minutes later, the train gave a sudden violent jolt. The whistle blew, the train slowed, and Mitchell opened the door.

"Keep your knees bent," he said as he jumped out.

"Don't forget the trolley," Riley said as she followed him.

The trolley clutched awkwardly in one arm, Ruth jumped from the train. She remembered to keep her knees bent, but staggered as she landed. Riley caught her collar, pulling her away from the accelerating train.

"Thank you," Ruth coughed through a mouth full of smoke.

There was a woman standing by the side of the tracks, wearing the green livery of the Railway Company.

"The driver of the 06:34 spotted the body," she said, speaking quickly, and backing away from the three police officers. "I was on the 07:10. I've been with the body ever since. That path through the grass to the south is the one I used to check he was dead." And with that, she turned, grabbed the handrail of the rearmost car, and pulled herself onto the departing train.

"Could it be a coincidence?" Mitchell said, as Ruth cleared the last of the smoke from her lungs. "Such things do exist, though they're not as common as most people think."

"Is this where…?" Riley asked.

"It is," Mitchell said.

Ruth followed their gaze. Both officers were staring at the twisted wreckage of an aeroplane. To her eyes, it looked no different from any of the dozens that littered the landscape near the city. No, she realised, they were looking past the plane at the forest beyond.

"Sir?" Ruth asked, unsure how to frame the obvious question.

"I remember this spot, cadet," Mitchell said. "I've been here before." He walked over the stained asphalt and crossed onto the tracks, peering at one tie, and then the next. "They all look the same now," he said. "But it could be this one. Perhaps not." He straightened. "I helped lay this railway line, many years ago. The old tracks run through the New Forest, and that was controlled by bandits. That's what we called them. Slavers would be closer to the truth. Cannibals wouldn't be far wrong. We lost a lot of cargo, and two locomotives, before the Prime Minister decided that it would be too costly trying to dislodge them. Instead we built a new line, here along this old road." He stepped off the tracks and back onto the asphalt. "I wasn't the only one to disagree with her, but we were, and are, a democracy. In the end she was proved wrong. We had to go in and clear the forest, and then we came back to bury the bodies that had been on the plane. What was left of them." He shook his head as if ridding it of an unpleasant memory.

"Of course," he continued, slightly more loudly than necessary, "these roads weren't built for the constant weight of all these goods trains. The tracks have to be constantly re-levelled. Take that as a reminder that the path that seems easiest usually isn't." He paced another step along the tracks, bent to look at another rail, and then stood and faced her. "Now, cadet," he said, "the first lesson is gloves. The second is to take stock of where you are."

Ruth pulled the kidskin gloves from her belt and put them on.

"There's blood here," Riley said, kneeling eight feet further down the road. "Not much. A few drops. Direction suggests he came from the tracks."

"Any sign of a fight?" Mitchell asked.

"Not on the road. I think he was on a train and got off here. But speaking of signs," Riley added, "where do you want to put that one up, cadet?"

Ruth picked up the blue and white police sign and looked for a suitable spot to place it. Then she understood. They were in the middle of nowhere.

"If you put it by the tracks you could arrest anyone on a passing train," Riley said.

Ruth blushed and put the sign back on the trolley. Trying to cover her embarrassment, she looked along the train tracks, at the road running alongside them, and finally at the fields on either side. The only sign of life, or at least of human life, was the disappearing plume of smoke from the train. There were no farms, no houses. The fields had grown wild and were choked with weeds, long grass, and occasional saplings. It wasn't quite the middle of nowhere, but it was close. She looked at the two sets of tracks leading down the embankment. Both the slightly curving path taken by the railway guard and the other, more erratic route, ended at the body of a man. He wore a dark suit and lay on his back with his eyes open. It was almost as if he was looking up at the sky.

"It was at night," Ruth said.

"What was?" Mitchell asked.

"That he died," Ruth said. "If the driver of the first train this morning saw the body, and if it was here before dusk, then surely someone would have seen it yesterday evening."

"Good. Keep your eyes on the ground," he said, and headed down the embankment, towards the corpse.

Ruth tried to follow his instruction, but as she drew nearer, and the smell grew more pronounced, she found her eyes drawn to the body. She'd seen corpses in the autopsy lectures, but those had been more about anatomy than forensic pathology, and the smell had overwhelmingly been one of disinfectant. Before that, the only bodies she'd seen, or that she remembered having seen, were two withered skeletons found in the basement of a house a mile from her home. The building had been destroyed during The Blackout, and the couple had been found as the rubble was finally being removed. That had been just before nightfall, so the bodies were left there, to be taken away for burial the next day. That evening, curiosity had got the better of sense, and Ruth had snuck back to the ruined house. It was the scratch marks carved in the cellar wall she remembered most clearly. Some were thin lines, others deep gouges from where the couple had tried to dig their way out, first with scraps of metal, and then their own fingernails. Those bodies had been almost mummified, the skin a papery leather, the odour dark but not as pronounced as the copper and earth smell coming from this victim.

"Male," Mitchell said as he reached the body and waved at the flies hovering around the corpse's slightly open mouth. "Twenty-four. Twenty-six. Not much older, nor younger." He picked up a hand. "Blood on the palm, from where he held the bandage in place. From the pattern of callouses, he wielded a shovel or axe, but not in the last few months. No bruises on the knuckles or on the face. Cadet, tweezers. Cadet? The tweezers; they're in the box."

Ruth was grateful for the excuse to turn her back on the body. She opened the crime-kit. There were some instruments she recognised, but a lot she didn't. They all must have some purpose, but as a whole it looked like a collection of junk. She found the tweezers and passed them to the sergeant.

"It's not a bandage," Mitchell said, pulling a red-stained swatch of cloth from the man's side. "It's a handkerchief. Bag?"

Ruth pulled a paper evidence bag from the kit and held it open as the sergeant dropped the handkerchief in it.

"Doesn't look like a knife wound," Riley said, peering over the body.

"No," Mitchell said. "It's a bullet wound. Small calibre. Perhaps a revolver."

"You don't think…?" Riley began and again stopped with the question half asked.

"Possibly," Mitchell said. "Cadet, have you seen a bullet wound before? Step closer."

She did, glancing at the wound, but found her gaze drawn to the man's face. With his eyes open, his expression was oddly serene. "He must have died looking at the stars," she said.

"And there are worse things to have as your last sight on Earth," Mitchell said, turning to look at her. "But he could have had another forty years looking up at the night sky. We have to find out why those were taken away from him. Remember the face, but don't dwell on it. Look at the wound, the body, find the evidence that will lead us to his killer."

"There's something else there," Riley said. "Under his shirt. A belt?"

"Let's see… yes, a belt. Of a sort. A money belt, I think, and well concealed." He gently peeled the shirt back, revealing a stained belt with a blood-clogged zip. Mitchell tugged the zip until the pocket opened. He reached inside and pulled out…

"Banknotes," he said. "They all seem to be twenty-pound notes." He passed them to Riley. Mitchell ran a hand along the man's waist before rolling the body onto its side. "No exit wound," he muttered. "A bullet will tell us the calibre, and we can run it against the guns. Perhaps it's a match." More loudly he added, "Cadet, hold him."

Swallowing, she reached down.

"Not his arm, his side. Here," Mitchell said, pointing. Ruth adjusted her grip. The body felt disconcertingly warm and soft. She told herself that was because of the sun, but found herself once more looking at those lifeless eyes. The victim wasn't that much older than her though, being born before The Blackout, he would have had a very different childhood. Perhaps he remembered the old world. He would certainly have remembered the years after. The hunger and suffering, the fear and despair that Maggie had told her about. A wave of sorrow washed over her, lasting until a bluebottle fly landed on the man's eye, when it was replaced with an equally strong wave of nausea.

"There," Mitchell said. "Got it." He unclasped the money belt and pulled it free. "Six pouches in total," he said, pulling open another zip. "Twenty-pound notes in this one, too. And… and if you're going to throw up, cadet, don't do it on the body! Let him go. Take a step back."

Gratefully, she did, turning her back on the corpse as she sucked in huge mouthfuls of air.

"Twenty-pound notes in each one," Mitchell said.

"There's about ninety in this stack," Riley said.

"That means there's over ten thousand pounds here," Mitchell said. "That's an absurd amount of money. Nearly five years' salary."

It was more than five years of Ruth's salary. As a cadet, she would be paid one hundred pounds a month. In three months, at the earliest, she might qualify as a probationary constable, and it would rise to a hundred and thirty. A detective like Riley was on two hundred. Mitchell earned around two hundred and fifty.

"The belt looks handmade, and very crudely done," Mitchell said. "White canvas. Probably hemp. Each pouch is just large enough for the stack of notes. Or, to put it another way, each pouch is full of as many notes as it will hold. Cadet, what do you make of his clothes?"

"The clothes, yes, right." Ruth took one last deep breath, and turned around, this time forcing herself not to look at the man's face. "They're old-world make," she said. "The shirt's been mended a couple of times, but it was in good condition. The collar isn't frayed. The jacket's a little short, and the trousers are a little long, but it's good quality clothing. Only a couple of moth holes in the jacket."

"Hmm," Mitchell grunted. "Always start with the boots. You can tell a lot about someone from the shoes they wear, and this man's boots were made to measure. Look at the soles near the heel. You can still see where the leather was scored. I'd say these have had about three months of wear. Probably cost him twenty pounds. Maybe thirty. He has money now, and he had money a few months ago, but not enough to buy clothes that fit. That is interesting. It's possible that his death is unrelated to the money, but that would be one coincidence too many for my tastes. No, I think it's the reason he died. Perhaps he's a thief, or a courier, or a gambler who had a stroke of monumental good luck before one ultimate piece of bad. Either way, he wasn't shot here. Nor was he shot on the train, or the killer would have followed him off. That suggests he boarded the train to escape. Exactly from whom or what can be added to our list." He bent down and began searching the man's pockets.

"Twenty years ago," he said, "we'd look for a driver's licence and call up the DMV, or what did you call it over here? The DVLA? There would be a phone with the contact details of parents, the photographs of friends, and the address of where he worked. We'd have a record of every text conversation and email he'd recently sent. It would take a few minutes and we'd know as much about him as he knew about himself. There would be GPS data that would tell us exactly where he was last night. We could see what other phones were in the same area and use those to track our killer. We'd run a trace analysis on his clothing. We'd collect every skin tag and foreign fibre. But this is now. We have no phone, no driver's licence, and while there may be DNA, what use is it without a database? So, what do we do? We fall back on our eyes. String," he said, passing it up to her. She placed it in an evidence bag. "Matches. A slip of paper with... nothing on it. A clasp knife. A stub of a pencil. Not exactly enlightening. No ration book, no keys."

Ruth watched as the sergeant began to search the body again, this time more slowly.

"Are you looking for something?" Ruth asked.

"I don't know," Mitchell said, "but it's not here. Get me the thermometer," he added, before she could ask what he meant.

She rooted around in the crime-kit until she found it.

"What's the formula?" Mitchell asked as she handed it to him.

"I... um... what formula?" she asked.

He gave that increasingly familiar disappointed sigh. "A body loses around one and a half degrees Centigrade every hour after death until it…" He bent over the corpse. "Until it reaches ambient temperature. We have to make an assumption that his body temperature prior to death was thirty seven and a half degrees and this…" There was another pause. "Yes, and this tells us that he died around midnight. Unfortunately, that's a very rough estimate. It could be three or four hours either way. In short, it confirms what the lack of rigor mortis and your observation about the train guard already told us. Namely, he died late last night or early this morning. You see," he said, standing up, "that's the problem with the academy. It's nothing but an overgrown high school, there to make sure you can read and write, and tell left from right, if not right from wrong. Police work, real police work, is something else entirely. It's about asking questions until there are so many that some turn into answers. Who was he? Why was he killed? Where did the money come from? Where was he going? We'll begin with those."

"Do you think he alighted from the train because of the plane?" Ruth asked, more to show willing than because she thought the answer would be yes.

"I doubt it," Mitchell said, "but there's no harm checking. Why don't you go and see if there's any sign anyone has been there recently. Look for tracks through the grass."

"Yes, sir," Ruth said, glad she had something that would take her away from the corpse.

There were tracks through the overgrown grass, but all were too small to be human. They probably belonged to a fox, she thought. There were stories of ferocious beasts that had once been held captive in giant parks so people could see them up close. Why anyone had wanted to do that baffled Ruth as did much of the old world. Maggie had said it was because she lacked the context of having grown up in a time when those things were normal. It was the sort of non-answer that Maggie often gave.

There was a flash of movement in front of her. She jumped back just as she registered it was a squirrel that had been perched in the bramble-covered cowling of the plane's engine. No, she told herself, the stories of those beasts were tales told to frighten a child. There were no hippos or tigers, not around here. But there were wild dogs, feral cats, and hogs living in the New Forest. She looked again at the narrow paths through the grass and told herself not to panic. It was the corpse that was making her nervous. It was a brutal sign that the peace of the classroom was finally over.

She picked up her pace, her brisk walk almost turning into a run by the time she reached the broken wing and clambered up. The door had been jammed open long enough for a whispery fern to take root in the hinges. She gently brushed it aside as she stepped through the dark portal. Light streamed through the broken cabin windows, adding a metallic gleam to the skeletal frames of the seats. The padding and material were all gone, as was the carpet, though she didn't realise it at first. The floor under her feet was soft, but matted with a layer of dark green moss. It was that, she hoped, that gave the place its musty smell.

Behind her was a cargo space as empty as the passenger cabin in front. There was no obvious reason why anyone would choose to come to this old wreck unless it was as a reminder of something from the old world. The victim could have been a passenger, but it would take days to search the plane. Judging by the decay, any search would be a fruitless one. She raised a foot and, without intending to, found herself turning around and going back outside. The sergeant was right; she was unlikely to find anything on the plane. As she walked back along the wing, looking at the distant figures of the two detectives, she realised that the sergeant had known that. Mitchell and Riley were deep in animated conversation, but Ruth was too far away to hear what they were saying. She sighed. Mitchell had wanted to get rid of her so the two of them could talk in private. Presumably about that incident they'd half discussed back near the tracks.

A swatch of colour behind the engine caught her eye. She'd noticed the flowers as she'd climbed the wing but had dismissed them as another patch of weeds. From above, she saw they were roses, planted six feet apart. The nearest was entwined around a wooden cross. Now that she knew what to look for, she saw other crosses, and solitary posts where the horizontal bar had fallen away. It was a graveyard, presumably for the passengers. She looked back towards Mitchell. He'd said that they'd buried the bodies. *What was left of the them.* Digging the graves was one thing. Going to the trouble of planting the roses was something else.

Ruth knew the story of how the world had nearly been destroyed. Looking down at the graveyard brought new meaning to those words. People had created computers, each more powerful than the last, always with the intent that the next one would make life easier, better, safer. It never did. The computers became more powerful as successive generations of scientists searched for their holy grail. Like that old legend, it was one that never truly existed. Finally, someone created a computer that was so powerful it came alive. That was how Maggie had explained it to Ruth. In that creation, her mother had said, was the chance for people to become the best they could be, and that best would be better than anyone had ever imagined. But other scientists, jealous at not being the first, had rushed their own machines into existence. A few seconds after their first spark of life-giving electricity, those AIs had spread throughout the integrated networks of the world. They'd found each other, and like all children throughout history, they'd fought without considering the consequences of their actions. Maggie didn't know who launched the missiles. It might have been the remnants of a government trying to destroy the AIs, or the machines themselves in a final suicidal end to that brief conflict. Twenty years on, it didn't matter.

That was what Maggie had told her, but Ruth now saw the explanation for what it was: a story to be told to a child, like describing those people in the forest as bandits. They'd buried *what was left* of the bodies. Ruth knew what that meant and wished she didn't.

She climbed down from the wing and headed back to the two officers. As she approached, Riley moved away, heading towards the railway tracks and an approaching train.

"It was night," Ruth said, as she got nearer to Mitchell. "He wouldn't have been able to see the plane."

"Then why did he alight here?" Mitchell asked in reply.

Ruth shrugged.

"You remember how the train jolted just before we jumped off?" Mitchell asked.

"I thought that was the brakes," she said.

"No, it was the uneven tracks. I expect the victim was half unconscious from blood loss, but that jolt woke him. It tells us that he was coming from somewhere to the south, exactly where we'll know when we find the train he was on. And that," Mitchell said, bending down over the corpse once more, "is a line of investigation we'll have to leave to the Railway Company." He pulled off one of the man's boots, and then the other. "The autopsy will give us the bullet, the time of death, and perhaps some other details that will tell us more about the man. But for that, we have to wait for the coroner." He placed the boots into a large evidence bag and then picked up the other bags. "We'll take the money to the Mint, and they can confirm whether a sum this large has been withdrawn in recent days, or if there's been some robbery."

"Wouldn't we have heard?" Ruth asked.

"I would hope so, but we should still check."

"And the boots?" she asked.

"They will lead us to the shoemaker, and that will give us a name, and perhaps an address. At the very least we will learn when they were made. But," he added, as Ruth walked over to the trolley, "you'll have to wait here. Someone has to stay with the body until the coroner arrives."

Ruth watched the sergeant walk up the embankment. The approaching train slowed, and he and the constable jumped on board. She kept watching as the train disappeared off into the distance.

Chapter 2
Happy Birthday

At first, Ruth stood by the body, waving her hands in an attempt to keep the flies away. After half-an-hour, the futility of the task, the smell that worsened as the day warmed, and irritation at her new colleagues made her give up. She stared at the blue and white police sign. Making her bring it all the way out here had been a joke and not a very good one. It wasn't as if she'd known that the crime scene was in the middle of nowhere. Riley and Mitchell had. She carried the sign over to the shade of a young oak growing halfway up the embankment and sat down on it.

"Some birthday," she muttered, shrugging off her woollen jacket. That it was her birthday was no secret. It was on her birth certificate and would have been in her personnel file, which, since he clearly hadn't been expecting her that morning, the sergeant hadn't read.

She brushed her hand through the thin carpet of dry leaves until she found a pebble.

In truth, it almost certainly wasn't her birthday. The seventeenth of September was the date on which Maggie Deering had found her wandering alone and abandoned through the immigration camp. That wasn't in Twynham, but in Kent, near the entrance to the Channel Tunnel. That camp was gone. The occupants had been wiped out during the SARS epidemic that Ruth assumed had killed her real parents. She wasn't even sure that Ruth was her name, just that it had been embroidered on a singed ribbon around the neck of a toy bear she'd been clutching that fateful day. Ruth had become her name, the seventeenth her birthday, and Maggie had been her mother ever since.

She found another pebble and placed it next to the first.

Her memories of the camp were an indistinct nightmare of monstrous shapes and terrifying colours that swamped any true recollection of her early life. When Maggie had found her, the only word of English Ruth had known was 'five'. Taken with her malnourished height, Maggie had decided that was probably her age. That had been eleven years ago. Ruth doubted she'd turned sixteen at some point today, but she almost certainly wasn't eighteen, and that was the minimum age requirement of a police cadet. Lying about her age wasn't an auspicious start to a career in law enforcement, but the lie had begun as a way to get into university.

"Not so I could end up here, like this," she said. Her gaze fell on the corpse and she immediately regretted her petulance. She'd gambled and she'd lost, but it could be a lot worse.

The lie had been Ruth's idea. Maggie was a teacher and Ruth had been an eager pupil, sucking up every morsel of knowledge she could. It was the lessons on probability that had been her undoing.

Unless you were bright enough for some professor to sponsor you for a scholarship, entry to university was by examination. Anyone who would be between seventeen and eighteen years old on the first day of term could sit those exams, but only once. They lasted a week, and everyone who got more than ninety-percent was entered into a lottery for one of the two hundred places at the university. After three months of study, the professors allocated each student to a course best suited to their aptitude.

Ruth knew that she could pass the exams, but the problem lay in the lottery. There had been a boom in the birth rate during the third and fourth years after The Blackout. But, because of a meningitis outbreak during the second year, there would be no more than a thousand applicants for the class that had begun just over a year ago. It came down to probability, a one-in-five chance of getting a place set against a one-in-fifty. All it required was lying about her date of birth. Maggie had been against it, and it had taken weeks for Ruth to persuade her.

Like most children, she had no official birth certificate. As Maggie had been her only teacher since the day she'd rescued her from the camp, there was no one to contradict the lie. Having sent in an application with her date of birth listed as the seventeenth of September 2021, she'd sat the exams and waited impatiently for the results. She'd passed, but she didn't win the lottery. What made it worse was an announcement they'd made a week after she'd begun her training at the academy. The number of students being taken at the university was being increased for the year she should have applied.

"Just my luck," she muttered, brushing the dirt off another pebble.

She'd been left with few choices. Professions like law, medicine, and teaching were filled with those who'd worked in that field before The Blackout. When a vacancy did occur it was taken by a miner or farmer too old to wield a pick or hoe. It was for that reason that Ruth couldn't simply join Maggie in the classroom. Conversely, trades like tailoring and candle making were usually reserved for those who'd learned them from their parents. She could apply, but she'd be starting ten years behind everyone else. Of course, first she'd have to find a trade she wanted to learn. Then she'd have to wait another year, because she'd been so certain that she'd get a place at university, she'd missed the deadline for applications.

That left mining, farming, or factory work. They paid well, far better than policing, but it would be a job for life. She didn't want to spend the rest of hers stuck to a workbench or coal seam. She wanted to see the world because she was sure there had to be more to it than she'd ever known. There were the Marines, of course. Thanks to widespread malnutrition, her entire generation suffered from stunted growth, so she didn't think anyone would have questioned whether she was old enough to join the military. She herself had doubted that she'd make it through the physical training. That left the police. At first Maggie had been adamantly against it, more so than she'd been over lying about Ruth's age. Then, a week before the deadline, she'd relented. Ruth had applied, and she'd got a place.

"And now look where I am."

She counted out the pebbles. There were sixteen in a rough circle, with two more in the middle. "Happy birthday, Ruth, however old you are."

There was a loud 'caw', as a raven landed in the field ten feet from the corpse.

"Shoo!" she shouted, picking up a pebble and throwing it at the bird. It hopped a few paces out of the way and cawed at her again. She sighed, and went to stand closer to, but upwind of, the body.

After half an hour, a second raven joined the first, and no matter what Ruth did, neither would move more than a dozen yards from the victim. When a train's whistle pierced the early afternoon air, she couldn't remember being more relieved.

Unlike the train that had brought them to the scene, this one came to a complete stop. It consisted of an engine, a tender, and a single carriage. A man and woman, both wearing off-white coats, jumped out. They grabbed a stretcher from the train and ran down the embankment towards her.

"The body's over—" Ruth began.

"We can see it," the woman snapped. Ruth stared at her for a moment, but decided that nothing she could say was worth the risk of having to walk back to the city. She grabbed the crime-kit, briefly considered leaving the sign where it was before she balanced it on top, and pulled the trolley up the embankment.

"Sorry," a bearded man standing in the doorway to the carriage said, though from his tone he didn't mean it. "Coroner's only in this carriage. You'll have to ride with the driver."

Ruth nodded, more to herself than to the man, and headed to the front of the train. The driver helped her on board.

"You look hot. 'ere, 'ave some water," he said, passing her a ceramic jug.

"Thanks," she said, and took a swig.

"What was it?" the driver asked. "An 'unting accident? I 'eard it was a gunshot."

"I'm not sure," Ruth said. "I don't think it was an accident, though."

"Really?" the stoker asked. "A murder, then? Go on, give us some details."

Ruth looked again at the distant haze that marked the city. It was definitely too far to walk.

"Well," she began, and gave a highly expedited summary. She focused more on the blood and flies than on the bullet and made no mention of the money. It seemed to keep the two men entertained, at least until the orderlies had loaded the stretcher, and it was time for the train to leave. A whoosh of steam, a shriek from the whistle, a jolt, and the train shunted backwards towards Twynham.

"Four minutes, twenty seconds," the stoker said, his voice rising to carry over the sound of pistons and steam.

"Until what?" Ruth called back.

"Until we 'it the three-fifteen coming the other way," the driver yelled, as the train picked up speed, reversing along the tracks.

He didn't seem worried, so Ruth followed his example, and craned her head around the side of the train. There was a tap on her arm.

"You better hold onto your hat," the stoker said. "This is going to get fast."

And it did. Ruth let the wind whip through her hair as the train kept accelerating. As they hurtled back towards the junction, she couldn't imagine even that wrecked plane ever moving at such a speed.

By the time the train pulled into a siding at Twynham Central, Ruth's face and uniform were covered in soot, but her earlier gloom was gone.

"The coroner has the body, sir," she said when she returned to the cabin in the yard behind Police House. The clock on the wall said it was four o'clock. She was surprised it wasn't far later.

Mitchell raised his head from the map he'd been peering at and looked at the clock. "It's unlikely they'll start the autopsy before tomorrow morning, which means we won't get the bullet until the evening." He glanced over at her, and his lips curled in an attempt not to smile. "That's an interesting look for you. Do you have a mirror?"

"No, sir," she said, looking around the cabin in the hope of seeing one.

"If you're going to ride in the cab of a steam train, you need a mirror." He returned his gaze to the map.

Not sure what she should do, Ruth dragged the crime-kit back to where it had been at the beginning of the day.

"Should I take these to the evidence room?" she asked, picking up the evidence bags containing the victim's meagre possessions.

"No, leave them with me for now," Mitchell replied.

"And the tweezers? Shouldn't they be washed?"

"I'll deal with that."

"Oh. Right. Um… were there any robberies of large sums of money last night?"

"Hmm? No. Not that have been reported. Or there weren't an hour ago. You might as well go home. There'll be more than enough work tomorrow."

"Thank you, sir," Ruth said. Her eyes caught sight of the desk, and the pile of statements she'd been wading through that morning. "I, um, I'll finish these first."

"The shift's over, cadet, be grateful for it."

"What I don't do today," she said, "I'll have to do tomorrow."

"Ah, the young," Mitchell said. "When you get a bit older you'll learn that what you put off today is someone else's problem when you retire. And I can't do that, even if it's only for the night, until I've locked up. Go home, and then I can do the same."

"Good night sir," she said, and headed out the door.

She collected her bicycle from the rack on the other side of the stables and began the long ride home. The trains didn't run to where Ruth lived. The Acre wasn't a slum, not quite, and it was far larger than an acre. Situated on the site of an old refugee camp, it was next door to the newer immigration centre. Other than the name, Ruth couldn't see any difference between the two. Nothing but a wide road separated the two old-world housing developments once occupied by retirees seeking the warmer weather of southern England. Nor was there much difference between the refugees with whom Ruth had shared Maggie's classroom and the immigrants who filled it now. Some came from Ireland, but most had found a way of making the perilous crossing from continental Europe.

The Acre and the new centre next to it were very different from the camp in which Maggie had rescued Ruth. That was a place of tents, scant rations, and growing demand as every day brought a flood of new refugees through the Channel Tunnel. As Ruth understood it, after the great die-off, small groups had banded together throughout Europe. They'd lived off old-world stores of food as much as from farming. When ships began surveying the European coast, they'd made landfall to collect water. News of Britain's recovery began to spread by word of mouth. After successive waves of disease cut through the barely coping communities, the survivors headed west. They took disease with them. SARS, Maggie had said it was called. Antibiotics had stopped it spreading throughout Britain. They'd been made in the laboratories built during the nearly catastrophic meningitis outbreak a few years before. But there hadn't been enough doses, or there had been too many refugees in the camps around the Channel Tunnel's entrance, or the medicine hadn't been administered in time. Or perhaps it was all three. Ruth's family had died, but she'd survived.

After that, the flood of refugees turned to a trickle, and not all made it as far as a camp. Increasingly, fishing vessels or the growing Navy picked up those who came by boat. Those refugees often found work, and a home, with them. As more farmland was reclaimed, there was employment in Kent for those who made the more treacherous land crossing through the pitch-black nightmare of the Channel Tunnel. Without an employer as a sponsor, no ration book was issued, no healthcare was provided, and no schooling was found for the children. Those refugees were relocated to The Acre. As the numbers had dropped, The Acre had become too big a site, and so the camp had been closed. The refugees were moved to a resettlement centre on the other side of the wide road. Maggie still taught, but she was paid based on how many pupils passed the pro-forma exams. As they often moved on after only a few months, her salary had shrunk.

The Acre, and all the buildings that stood on it, were now the property of Mr Foster. Officially – and it had been very official – the government gave Foster the land in exchange for a similar sized plot the man had owned before The Blackout, and on which the main railway depot had been built. From the moment the first judge had been sworn in, Foster had fought a protracted legal battle to have that land returned to him. Ruth didn't know if he'd been a bitter man in the old world. After fifteen years of legal wrangling, and with the prize of a few dozen houses at the wrong end of the metropolis, Foster was certainly bitter now. The newspaper coverage hadn't helped. During those early years there had been little news that wasn't full of gloom and despair. Updates on Foster's legal battle had become a regular fixture, prompting letters and opinions from anyone who could find pencil or pen.

The Acre was too far inland to be home to any fishers. It was too far from the factories for the salaried commuters, and it was far too far from the electrical grid to appeal to those with higher incomes. It was a place for the poor until they could afford something better. The new rents were low, but as high as Mr Foster was allowed to charge. As such they were more than most tenants could afford to pay. Especially Maggie and Ruth.

As she passed the new watermill that marked the boundary of the old town of Christchurch, exhaustion overtook Ruth, as did many other workers cycling to the shops before the evening rush. Soon the houses she passed were as often partially dismantled shells as they were occupied. The roads emptied, and she was alone except for an occasional rusting car deemed worthless even as scrap.

The sun was low on the horizon when she finally caught sight of their home. It was a rambling double-fronted semi that would have been completely detached if it wasn't for the joists and props holding up the house next door. Maggie had put those up herself and used the ground floor as the schoolhouse.

The wooden gate squeaked as Ruth pushed it open and wheeled her bike into the garden. Maggie paused from digging over the potato patch at the front of the house.

"Evening," Ruth said.

"What on Earth happened to you?" Maggie asked.

"It's from a train," Ruth said. "I rode in the engine."

"I could guess where the soot came from. I meant your jacket. Is that blood?"

Ruth glanced down. She'd not noticed before, but there was a stain around her sleeve and another across the waist.

"It's not mine," she said.

"Well, whose is it?" Maggie asked.

"I don't know his name. Let me change, and then I'll tell you all about it."

"That's about it," Ruth said, a brief wash, a change of clothes, and half an hour of conversation later. "Serious Crimes doesn't seem to have any real responsibilities, and I'm stuck there for the next three months. Probably longer."

"Well, you have to be somewhere, and that's the best I can do," Maggie said, hanging the uniform jacket up to dry. "A murder on your first day, that's something. Though I don't know whether it's worth celebrating or not."

"Except all I did was carry a trolley and then sit by the body until the coroner turned up."

The kettle began to whistle. "And what were you expecting?" Maggie asked, as she poured a splash of hot water into the teapot. "Chasing smugglers across the roof tops? Foiling conspiracies committed by criminal masterminds? You've read too much Conan Doyle and not enough history. Or would you rather have spent the day being shot at?"

Ruth threw a glance at the locked pine box in the corner of the room. Her revolver was now inside. Ruth had the key, but Maggie had made it clear she wasn't happy about the gun being inside the house.

"I suppose not," Ruth said. "It's…" She trailed off.

"I know, dear," Maggie said, throwing out the water from the pot. "You wanted to be somewhere else, but how would it be different from here? If you were in Shetland or some market town in Kent, you'd have spent the day doing paperwork or patrolling an empty street. They may have been streets you'd never seen before, but you'd have soon realised that concrete sidewalks look the same the world over." She opened the tin of powdered tea, added two heaped spoonfuls to the pot, and poured in the boiling water.

"Maybe," Ruth said. She was starting to think that Maggie was right, not just about her day, but about her joining the police, and that was a depressing thought in itself. She reached for the pot.

"No, dear. You have to let it brew."

Ruth shook her head. The label on the tin might read 'Satz! Assam' but it was a caffeinated substitute that no one who remembered the original thought tasted like real tea. Like the sweetener, pharmaceuticals, ersatz coffee, and so much else, it came from the chemical works on the River Avon. Ruth had never had real tea and didn't understand Maggie's need for the ritual. She even insisted on buying the 'black', unsweetened variety despite the tins with powdered milk and sweetener being the same price. Milk was available on points, but sugar was rationed, though today the bowl was nearly a quarter full.

"It sounds like it's a unit of troublemakers," Maggie said. "Put there to keep them out of harm's way."

"Yes, and the sergeant said I should ask myself why I've been posted there."

"A very good question," Maggie said, adding a splash of milk to the cups. "Have you come up with an answer?"

"No," Ruth admitted. "Unless they guessed that I lied about my age."

"If they cared about that, they'd have thrown you out," Maggie said. "No, the only reason I can think of is that you've been sent there to spy on them. Certainly, I imagine that's what your sergeant and that detective constable must think."

"But I'm not a spy," Ruth said.

"Not yet. But give it a few days and I expect someone will call you into their office and ask you to keep them informed. In exchange you'll probably be guaranteed graduating to constable in three months and passing your probation in a year."

"That doesn't seem too bad," Ruth said.

"It's a double-edged sword," Maggie said, finally pouring the tea. "If you inform on them, your colleagues won't trust you, and you need their trust. You were at a murder scene today, who's to say when your life might be in their hands? But if you don't obey an order from your superior, you'll be sacked. Or worse. This is the police after all. It's probably a crime."

"Then what do I do?"

"Be careful. Be cautious," Maggie said. "And remember you can always quit. Winter is on its way and summer always follows. You can apply for an apprenticeship."

"Maybe," Ruth said, not wanting to have the oft-repeated discussion that inevitably turned into an argument.

"Anyway," Maggie said, as if she'd had the same thought. "For now, just do your job and keep your head down. Let's forget about it. I've got something for you. I wanted to give it to you this morning, but there wasn't time." She walked over to the battered dresser and took out a small parcel. "Happy birthday, dear."

Ruth took the parcel and tugged on the bow holding the red velvet cloth in place. It was the same piece of material that had wrapped all of her presents for as long as she could remember. Inside was a small box, and inside that…

"A watch? Thank you."

"Every police officer needs one," Maggie said.

Ruth stood, and hugged her adoptive mother, as much for the words as for the gift. They were the first sign that, though she might not approve of Ruth's choice of career, nor how she'd attained it, she did accept it.

"There's a spring inside that will wind the watch as your wrist moves," Maggie said. "It's not as accurate as the other kind, but it's accurate enough. Now sit down, and I'll get your dinner. I made you a cake for dessert."

"A cake?"

"Of course, it wouldn't be much of a birthday without a cake. But light the candle, it's getting dark."

Ruth struck a match and lit the candle on the table, and another by the window. There was no electricity in The Acre, though they now had mains water via a tap in the front garden. When they'd chosen the site for the radio antenna, just a few miles to the southwest, there had been rumours that they would electrify the entire stretch of coast. It hadn't happened yet. Even if it did, Ruth knew they wouldn't be able to afford it for their home.

"Where did you get the ingredients for the cake?" Ruth asked.

"The eggs are our own," Maggie said, "but I've been saving up the coupons for the sugar and fat."

"For how long?"

"Oh, throughout the year," Maggie said, taking a large dish out of the oven.

"But they're only valid for a month," Ruth said.

"I've been trading the ones we don't need. With you getting your lunch at the academy, there's been a few to spare."

"Trading with whom? And for what?" Ruth asked.

"Ah, and isn't that the nosiness of a true police officer. Now, eat your dinner before it gets cold."

The meal was potatoes and vegetables from their own garden, seasoned with mustard and herbs, and with no trace of meat. Even with the coupons and price controls that was too expensive to be anything but a rare luxury. Ruth didn't mind. The meal was filling and had the comfort of familiarity that came from being what she'd eaten most evenings for as long as she could remember.

They were about to cut the cake when there was a knock on the door. It opened as Maggie was still halfway to her feet. Mr Foster, their new landlord, came in.

"Sorry to trouble you, and at dinnertime, too. I do apologise," he said, his voice dripping with insincerity. "I saw the candles and thought I'd pop in on my way home."

"You can't barge in here," Ruth said.

"Oh, I think I can," Foster said. "You owe me for the water rates."

"It's not due for another two weeks," Maggie said.

"No, in two weeks it'll be overdue," Foster said. "And then I'll have no choice but to evict you. I wouldn't want that, which is why I thought I'd come and remind you, in case you forgot. There's a lot of forgetfulness about at the moment. People leaving candles burning when they've gone to bed, that sort of thing. A lot of fires get started that way."

"That's a threat," Ruth said. "And those are illegal."

"Oh, no, it's not a threat," Foster said. "Just an observation. You see, I — here, whose is that?" He pointed at the uniform jacket hanging in the corner.

"It belongs to a friend of ours," Maggie said. "He got into a fight. I was cleaning it for him. You can still make out the bloodstain. Hard to get those out, isn't it, Mr Foster?"

"Huh," Foster grunted. He looked around the kitchen again, this time taking in the two sets of dinner plates and the lack of evidence that anyone else was in the house. "Two weeks," he said. "Not a day longer."

He turned, stamping his muddy boots on the step as he left.

"I should put that uniform back on," Ruth said.

"Oh yes, and what would you do then?" Maggie asked, as she pushed the door closed.

"I'd arrest him," Ruth said.

"What for? He made insinuations, but were there any threats you could take to a judge? The government gave him this land, he paid for the water to be put in, and we have to pay him for it."

"But it's not right," Ruth said. "We've been living here for years."

"It *is* right, though it might not be fair, but life isn't fair, Ruth, I've told you that often enough."

Ruth nodded as she grabbed the dustpan and started sweeping up the mud the man had trailed into their home.

"Where are we going to find the money?" she asked. "I won't get paid until the first three months are up, and it's not like we've ever had any to spare."

"Have you ever been starving? Have you ever not had a roof over your head? No. So don't worry about the money. Now, leave that floor alone, I'll deal with it later. Come and finish your cake, and you can tell me more about this sergeant. You say he's from America?"

"Originally, but his accent's different from yours."

"It is? How old is he?"

"Forty. Maybe older, maybe younger. You know how hard it is to tell," Ruth said. She went on to talk about Mitchell, Riley, and the rest of her day in more detail than before. Hours passed, the cake was eaten, and the candle burned low.

Chapter 3
Counterfeit
18th September

Ruth's sleep was plagued by visions of steam trains that morphed into monstrous flies circling the face of the dead victim. She woke frequently and was glad when the inky darkness outside her window faded to the soft pink of the new day.

She raked the stove and went outside to fill the kettle. The tap in the garden was an improvement on the pump down by the old petrol station. Before that, they'd had to trek back and forth to the river. However, the convenience of the tap wasn't worth the risk of losing their home. There were plenty of other houses, of course, though after twenty years of neglect most had little beyond roof and walls to offer. Many didn't even have those. Then there was the school. If Mr Foster evicted them, would Maggie have to find somewhere else to teach the children from the immigration centre? Probably. Would the government provide it? Possibly, though not quickly. Perhaps someone in the Ministry of Education would help simply as a way of avoiding the paperwork that would come with organising a new school building. Thinking of paperwork reminded her of Sergeant Mitchell and the question of why she'd been assigned to his unit. By the time she'd eaten and dressed, she still hadn't come up with an answer.

As she wheeled her bicycle along the lane, shooting frequent glances at the dark bloodstain on her sleeve, she hoped she might bump into Mr Foster. She wanted him to see her in uniform, but Maggie was right, what would she do then? What could she do? A million malicious ideas sprang to mind, but they were tempered by the memory of the dead man and his lifeless eyes.

According to her new watch, it was seven forty-five when she pushed her bike into the stand behind Police House. There were three-quarters of an hour before her shift officially began, but when she turned the corner of the stables, she saw Mitchell and Riley were already there. The detective constable stood in the doorway to the cabin, the sergeant at the bottom of the ramp, seemingly barring entry to two women. One wore the uniform of a captain in the SIS – the Secret Intelligence Service – the other was dressed in a distinctly civilian suit.

"There are few crimes *more* serious," Ruth heard Mitchell say as she got nearer. She slowed her pace.

"And treason's one of them," the captain said. "It's—"

"Forgery isn't treason," Mitchell interrupted.

"And this isn't a few coupons or some fake ration books. This is counterfeiting," the captain replied. Mitchell's tone was angry, bordering on enraged. The captain's voice was calm, with an edge that made it sound as if she was enjoying the confrontation.

"There's a threshold," the civilian said. "Of a thousand pounds, and you recovered over ten times that."

"But the amount doesn't matter," the captain said. "Just the method that was used to create the currency."

Now that she was closer, Ruth saw that the woman wasn't wearing a suit. The jacket had thin white piping along the seam that was absent on the calf-length skirt. They looked like old-world clothes, though ones that had hardly been worn. Ruth couldn't see any tears or repairs, and that meant they'd cost a good deal of money. Not as much as having a new set of clothes made by hand, but far more than Ruth herself could afford. She looked at the captain, but found her eyes being drawn back to the civilian. Then she realised why. It was the shoes. Both were black, but the buckle on the left was half the size of the one on the right. Whoever she was, Ruth imagined she must have been woken early, and dressed hurriedly in the dark to come here. As to why… she turned her attention back to the conversation.

"This is murder, Weaver. Murder!" Mitchell growled at the captain, his voice now dangerously low.

"And there are bigger issues at stake, *Mitchell*," Captain Weaver replied.

"Nevertheless," Mitchell replied. Ruth waited for him to go on. So did everyone else.

"Fine," Captain Weaver said, when it became apparent the sergeant had finished. "Then I'm pulling rank, *sergeant*. This is *my* case, and I want your notes and the evidence you collected. All of it. Now."

There was another long pause.

"Riley?" Mitchell finally said.

The constable went inside the cabin and came out a moment later with a thin file and half a dozen small evidence bags.

"That's everything?" Weaver asked as she took it from the constable.

"Yes, captain," Riley said.

Weaver eyed her, and then Mitchell.

"The law is the law, sergeant," Captain Weaver said.

"That has *always* been my point," Mitchell replied. He turned on his heel and walked into the cabin.

"Constable." Weaver nodded to Riley, turned, and headed across the yard. "Cadet."

Ruth snapped to attention as the two women walked past. She kept her eyes fixed ahead until she could no longer hear the soft clicking of the civilian's heels.

"What was that about?" she asked Riley.

"Not out there," Mitchell's voice came from inside.

Riley gave a shrug that spoke volumes though not in a language Ruth understood.

"Sir?" Ruth asked when she was inside.

"As you might have gathered," Mitchell said, pacing back and forth between the desks. "The money we found on the body was fake. Forged. Counterfeit. I took it to the Mint yesterday to find out when it might have been issued. They ran the serial numbers and discovered that they haven't been issued yet."

"They're certain?" Ruth asked.

"That woman was. Her name's Standage and she's the director of quality assurance. Apparently that means she's in charge of serial numbers for banknotes." He walked over to the door and peered outside. "That," he said, more quietly, "is what they're telling us. How much truth is in it, I don't know." He sighed and turned away from the door. "Call it forgery or counterfeiting or even treason, I don't care. Someone has been murdered. That is the serious crime. That is what we must solve because you can believe that *Captain* Weaver won't." He spat out the SIS officer's rank with venomous distaste.

"We're still investigating?" Ruth asked.

"Of course," Mitchell replied, as if he was surprised the cadet had to ask. He opened a drawer and took out a folder identical to the one Riley had handed to Weaver. "Cadet, what do you know about money?"

"Um… that there's never enough of it?"

"Quite. Do you know why we use paper money rather than metal?"

"No sir."

"The problem arose during that first winter when it was too cold to go outside," he said. "People huddled together for warmth, hoping the snows would melt, and dreading what the landscape would look like when it did. Those who could sew repaired clothes. Those who could weave a story told one. The doctors, nurses, and dentists had plenty of work, and the crudest of tools to do it. With little else to occupy their time, many were happy to labour for no reward except having some familiar task to fill their minds. Others weren't, and barter began. The problem with barter is that it's hard to tax. Without taxes the government can't pay police, and if the government don't pay us, you better believe the criminals would. So we needed a currency. We couldn't use gold or silver, as those could be found in any abandoned house, there for anyone strong enough to brave the weather to find it. Using batteries, candles, and other old-world goods could only ever be a temporary measure. We wanted a society that was building something new, not just looting the ruins of the old. Our first efforts were crude, but they had to be. We were limited by what we could physically make, and that was metal oblongs, two inches by five, each with an octagonal hole in the middle. You've seen them?"

"Yes, sir. We have a couple at home," Ruth said.

"And I bet you've thought you could make a few yourself? A lot of people did. As many as there were who sat down to sew cloth or skin by firelight, there were those who found rasps and saws. The metal was everywhere. Cars. Trucks. Buses. They littered the streets. We made the designs more elaborate, but that only resulted in our forgers becoming more skilled. That currency didn't last long. Scarcity is the key. Raw materials are not scarce in our world. Electricity is. Hence the printed, paper notes. You could forge one by hand, but there are far quicker ways of earning a living. To print a note, you need a computer for the design, a printer, paper, and ink. That suggests more than one person is involved, but we knew that since our victim was unlikely to have shot himself."

"Computers? That's why the SIS is involved, isn't it? Because of the risk the AIs will start up again?" Ruth asked.

Mitchell blinked, looked at her, and then gave a long drawn out sigh. "That's the trouble with your generation. You don't understand what an artificial intelligence is. Yes, the fact that this was done with a computer gives the SIS jurisdiction regardless of any other facts. No, it doesn't mean this has anything to do with AIs or The Blackout. The design isn't so complicated that you'd need a mainframe. A basic graphics package would do, and you'd find one of those on half the computers in the country. Therein lies the dilemma. Though electricity is scarce, computers aren't. Even after twenty years, I doubt it would take more than a day of searching to find one that hadn't succumbed to damp and decay."

"I don't understand. I thought you said it was harder to forge because they used computers," Ruth said.

"He means the electricity is harder to get hold of," Riley said. "Would you need a lot of it?"

"Yes," Mitchell said. "After you factor in the printer - and we're not talking about some deskjet or simple scanner-copier that—" He saw the expression on the two women's faces. "It doesn't matter. The answer is yes, you'd need a lot more than most people have access to. I've got a single light bulb in my place. Do you have electricity, cadet?"

"No, sir. Not yet."

"Well, you can't simply pull out a light bulb and plug in a computer. You'd need an adaptor and a transformer, and not an old-world one. And that's before we've addressed the issue of paper and ink, both of which, as you heard, were an exact match."

"Where do we start?" Riley asked.

"I have a meeting with Rebecca Cavendish. She sent me a note this morning saying that a bloody handprint had been found on a train. She didn't say which train, which means she wants a favour before she'll tell me." He grabbed his coat. "Armed with the probability that either our victim or our killer is a counterfeiter, continue following the boots. Find who made them, and when you do, find out whether our man bought them with a twenty-pound note. How many did you manage yesterday?"

"Four," Riley said. "I've three more on the list for Twynham. After that we'll have to try Wales or Scotland."

"And we will, if we have to," Mitchell said. "Weaver cares about the money. I care about the murder, and I will not have a killer running free in my city."

Riley opened the drawer to her desk and took out the large evidence bag.

"Are those are the victim's boots?" Ruth asked.

"They are," Riley said. She watched Ruth, and Ruth knew why. The constable was waiting for her to make some comment about them not having been handed over to Captain Weaver.

"Where exactly in Scotland?" Ruth asked. "Because I've always wanted to go."

Chapter 4
Boots

The roads were full of commuters, some on bikes and others on foot, all heaving their way to their various places of work. It was chaotic, and would have been cause for seeking refuge in a doorway if her uniform hadn't saved Ruth from the worst of the jostling crowd.

"Have you known Sergeant Mitchell long?" Ruth asked, in an attempt to make conversation.

"Long enough," Riley replied.

Silence descended.

"What about Captain Weaver?" Ruth asked. "Won't we get into trouble for continuing the investigation?"

"We won't. We're just following a line of enquiry given to us by our superior."

"But the sergeant will?" she asked.

"There's no trouble they can give Mister Mitchell that he can't find himself," Riley said. "But when this is over, we'll either have found the killer and they won't care, or we won't and no one will ever know."

Ruth didn't think it would be as simple as that, at least not for her. She tried a different tack.

"How will the boots help us?"

"Have you ever been to a tailor?" Riley asked.

The answer was no, but Ruth said, "Of course."

"They took your name and address, and told you they'd keep your measurements on file, didn't they?" Riley asked.

"I suppose."

"It's the same with boots. You can't get a pair like these made in a day. The man would have had to give the bootmaker a name and an address."

"Which might be fake," Ruth said.

"Almost certainly," Riley said. "But from the date they were made we'll know when he first came into money. That might tell us something."

"Like what?"

"Don't know," Riley said. "I went to four places yesterday. No luck. All made work boots and not much else."

Riley had an odd manner of speech, Ruth thought, using words as if they were as tightly rationed as meat.

"Drake Avenue is next on my list," Riley continued, waving a hand towards a side road on which the foot traffic was slightly thinner. "You grew up around here?"

"A few miles away," Ruth replied. She'd visited the market a few times, but it was a long way to come for stalls laden with the same food they grew in their own garden. It wasn't until she'd joined the academy that she'd spent much time wandering the city.

"You need to know the streets," Riley said. "The shops. The people. Who belongs. Who doesn't."

Drake Avenue didn't deserve the name. It was less than a hundred feet long, barely five feet wide, and filled with trestle tables. They clearly belonged to the pub halfway along the road. It was called The Golden Hind according to the freshly painted sign swinging in the gentle breeze and was doing brisk business judging by the staff. One waiter was clearing tables after the breakfast rush while another was sweeping the street. From the look of it, the pub's landlord was keeping the entire avenue clean. It was good for business, Ruth supposed, or perhaps it was a way of placating neighbours who would otherwise complain about late night noise.

The Golden Hind was such a dominating presence that Ruth almost walked past the shoe shop without noticing it. Situated three whitewashed houses down from the pub, Ruth first took the thick coating of grime on the windows to be grey paint.

"It looks closed," Riley said as she knocked on the door. "Odd."

"Why is it odd?" Ruth asked.

"They should be open for the passing trade as people go to work," the constable said.

Ruth peered through the nearly opaque window. "I can see shoes," she said, "on shelves against the wall and on a table in the middle of the floor."

"Odder," Riley said. "Why make them in advance?"

"I think it's old-world stock," Ruth said. "And I can see a shadow. Someone's coming."

"Detective's Riley and Deering," Riley said when the door opened. "And you are?"

"Xavier Collins," the young man replied. He was around five-eight and too young to pull off the clipped beard and moustache he'd attempted to grow.

Riley looked down at the list in her hand and then back at the man.

"No, you're not. You're not old enough," the constable said.

"You're looking for my father?" the man half said, half asked.

"I don't know," Riley said. "Does he own the shop?"

"Yes," Collins said with a sigh. "What's this about?"

"Does he make shoes?" Riley asked, pushing past the man to enter the shop.

"We did do repairs," Collins said, following her back into his store. "But we now specialise in premium old-world stock. Take these; they're new in from Birmingham." He picked up a lurid red and green pump from the centre table. "I'm selling them at five pounds a pair, but for our friends in blue, how about four pounds fifty?"

"I can buy a pair of trainers in the National Store for fifty pence," Ruth said. Her last pair had actually cost half that, but she didn't want Riley to know. "So why would I pay ten times that for these?"

"These aren't just trainers," Collins said with brittle enthusiasm. "Not only have they never been worn, but this brand wasn't even available for sale. They've come from the exhibition centre in Birmingham. There was a skateboarding expo due to start the day after The Blackout, and these were going to be revealed to the world for the first time. They've spent the last twenty years in a hermetically sealed vault. I couldn't believe it when I saw them. No moisture, no rodents, no insects got anywhere near them. Four pounds, and I won't be making a profit on them at all."

"Birmingham?" Riley asked. "You have a scavenging licence?"

"I... er..." he stammered, his eyes flitting between the shoes and the door in search of an answer.

"A tax receipt?" Riley prompted.

Collins's shoulders dropped a little. "Do I need one?" he asked.

"Tax is due on all old-world goods found in the wasteland and sold in the city," Riley said. "The exception is a scavenger who sells ninety-percent of the haul to the National Store. That remaining ten-percent is tax free, and can be sold to shops such as yours, in which case a receipt is provided. How long has your father been sick?"

"Sick? How did you know?" Collins asked.

"Because you don't know how to run a shop," Riley replied.

"He was fine when I left. He had a stroke when I was away," Collins said. His eyes flickered towards the door behind him.

"He's upstairs?" Riley asked.

Collins nodded.

"Stay here," she said, adding to Ruth, "Watch him." The constable disappeared into the back of the shop.

Collins stared at the floor. Ruth looked around the shop. She picked up one shoe, and then the next.

"Three pounds fifty?" Collins suggested.

Ruth shook her head.

"The girl?" Riley asked when she came back into the shop.

"That's my sister," Collins said.

"It's only the three of you?"

"Yes," he said.

"Do you know anything about repairing shoes?"

"I can glue and sew, but—"

"Can you resole a shoe?" Riley asked.

"Yes."

"And all this stock came from Birmingham?"

"Yes," Collins sighed.

"Your father didn't make boots?" she asked.

"No, he just did repairs."

"Put this stock in the back, somewhere it can't be seen," Riley said. "Clean that window, put a sign out the front, and start doing repairs again. I won't arrest you, not today, but I will come and check you aren't obviously doing anything illegal. And get your sister back in school. Sitting by your father's bedside won't help his recovery."

"You're not... thank you. Thank you," Collins stuttered. "Ah... can I offer you a pair each?"

"No. That would be bribery," Riley said, and she left the shop. Ruth followed.

"Why didn't you charge him?" Ruth asked.

"What would be the point? They used to say justice was blind. Sometimes police have to be blind, too, knowing when the punishment will do more harm than the crime. He clearly can't afford the fine, so he'd get three months light labour. Who'd look after the father or sister while he was dismantling scrap? Maybe he'll learn the lesson that what was valuable in the old world is worthless now. Maybe he won't, but he owes us. That's useful."

"Why? Does a cobbler make a good informant?"

"No more than anyone else, but someone who made it all the way to Birmingham and back does. Contacts. That's what you need in this job. Call them informants if you like, but it comes down to someone who'll tell you something because they trust you more than they fear anyone else."

Ruth weighed that up.

"Riley?" she asked.

"Yes?"

"What's skateboarding?"

The penultimate shop on the list was in Green Harbour Drive, situated in a visibly more affluent part of the city. Small cafes were nestled between workshops. The clientele sitting at the tables outside wore clothes that fit and which weren't dotted with patches and sewn repairs. They passed the Ministry for Exploration and Foreign Affairs and the far busier bakery next door.

"It's that one," Riley said, pointing at a small shop. It was nestled between a tailor's boasting the latest tweeds from Scotland and a pharmacy advertising more herbal remedies than chemical ones. There was no sandwich board outside, but a discreet sign read, 'Repairs done whilst you wait. Shoes & Boots made.'

"No mention of pricing," Riley said. "That's always a sign of expense. You take the lead. We want to know if they made the boots and when, and whatever they know of the man who bought them."

A small bell tinkled as Ruth pushed the door open. The sound of hammering came from the back, closely followed by the smell of warm leather.

"And they'll be ready this evening?" a man asked of the woman behind the counter.

The woman picked up a shoe, looked at it for a moment, and then put it down. "We can have it repaired in about an hour. It will take a little longer for the glue to dry. You can collect it at lunchtime."

"That would be perfect, thank you," the man said, and barely seemed to notice the two officers as he hobbled out of the store.

"How can I help you?" the woman asked.

"Um... yes. Do you make boots here?" Ruth asked.

"And shoes. I thought the police got issued with as many as you could eat," she said with a smile.

"Did you make these?" Ruth asked, taking the boot out of the evidence bag.

"Maybe," the woman said. "Hang on. Miranda?" she called into the back of the shop. The sound of hammering stopped. A moment later a woman in a thick leather apron appeared in the doorway behind the counter.

"What is it, Joyce?" Miranda asked. She saw the police. "What's happened?"

"Did you make these boots?" Ruth asked.

"Let me see." Miranda picked the boot up, turned it over, peered at the sole, and then nodded. "I did."

"Do you remember anything about the man who bought them?" Ruth asked.

"Why?" Joyce asked, as she opened a drawer below the counter. "What's happened?"

Ruth glanced at Riley. The constable nodded.

"Unfortunately, the man is dead. We're—"

"We're trying to identify him," Riley cut in. "There was no ration book, no I.D."

"He was robbed?" Miranda asked.

"It's—" Ruth began

"We can't say," Riley said.

"Here," Joyce said, holding up an index card. "Size ten, slight fallen arch on the right, wide toed, black leather. His name is Andy Anderson."

"I remember him now," Miranda said. "He's the one who said he was from Iceland."

"Iceland?" Ruth asked.

"Or his family were," Miranda said. "He told us that they fished off the coast, that's how they survived The Blackout. He said they took the boat south and landed in Scotland. Anders Anderson was his name, but he'd anglicised it to Andy. That was his story, but it sounded… well, it sounded as if he was making it up as he went along."

"Do you remember anything else about him?" Ruth asked.

"He was short," Joyce said. "About five-eight. Young. Of course you'd know that. What else… there was a slight Scottish burr to the accent, as if he'd grown up there, but there was no Scandinavian in it."

"How much did the boots cost?" Ruth asked.

"Sixty pounds, but that includes a ten year guarantee," Joyce said.

"It's still a lot," Ruth said.

"We pride ourselves on our quality," Joyce replied defensively.

"Did you keep a record of how he paid?"

"Up front, and in twenty-pound notes," Joyce said. "I remember that because the clothes he wore didn't suggest he'd be able to afford it."

"And do you have an address?" Ruth asked.

"Twenty-three Spring Close."

"And the date?" Riley prompted.

"The twentieth of July," Joyce said.

"There's a lot of wear on these boots for two months," Miranda said. "He must have worn them every day. Was it a bad end?"

"Good or bad, all ends are the same," Riley said. "It's the journey that offers variety. Thank you for your time."

"Andy Anderson? That's got to be fake, doesn't it?" Ruth asked when they were outside.

"Maybe," Riley said, "you never know. You did good in there, but next time ask fewer questions. Let people talk. That way they'll answer questions you didn't know to ask."

Ruth filed that away as another second-hand lesson from Sergeant Mitchell.

"Do we go to Spring Close?" she asked.

"First, we go back to the yard and speak to Mister Mitchell. What would you do if you were the killer?"

"Me?" Ruth asked. It wasn't the question she'd been expecting.

"You run a counterfeiting ring. You've shot someone who you caught stealing from you. Or maybe he was sent to deliver the money and never returned. Either way, what would you do now?"

"Move, I suppose."

"Me too. It's been over twenty-four hours, I don't think we're looking for the counterfeiters any more, but are looking for where they've been."

Chapter 5
Andy & Charles

"Back already? Did you strike out?" Mitchell asked. He stood by the wall on which he'd pinned the map that Ruth had seen him peering over the night before.

"We got a name. Andy, or Anders, Anderson," Riley said.

"That sounds fake," he said. "Anything else."

"The shoes were bought on the twentieth of July, with three twenty-pound notes. Anderson was wearing rags at the time. Slight Scottish accent. We've got an address," Riley said. "Twenty-three Spring Close. He told them his family escaped from Iceland after The Blackout, but they thought he was making that up."

"Spring Close? Let's see." Mitchell ran a finger across the map. It had the precise jagged lines of old-world printing, but with dozens of more recent pencil and pen annotations.

"Here." Mitchell pointed at a spot two miles north of Ruth's own home. "Can't tell much more than it was a housing estate. There's no water or electricity. It's a mile from the railway line, but it's another two miles to the nearest station. It's not a likely place for someone to live, though people do make their homes in the most unlikely of places." On the wall next to the map was a pin with a piece of red thread hanging from it. Mitchell took it down and placed the pin on the map.

"This is where his body was found," he said. He took another pin from the wall, stuck it in the map a few inches further to the west, and tied the loose end of string to it. "According to Rebecca Cavendish," he said, "as soon as they spotted the body they began searching the trains, mostly to make sure nothing had been stolen. A small pool of blood was found in the rear car of a tannery train. Due to the smell, the inspections on those trains can be best described as cursory, which is why they didn't find the bloodstain until last night. So, we now know that at 23:01 on the night of the murder, the train departed from the tannery at Holton." He pointed at the second pin. "About twenty miles west of here. Between 01:50 and 02:00 the train passed the spot where we found the body." He stuck a third pin into the map at a point just before the train tracks crossed the River Stour. He stretched the string around the pin until it was bent almost at a right angle. "It travelled around twenty miles east, and then ten miles north."

"It took three hours to travel thirty miles?" Ruth asked.

"The tannery train is a low priority service. It would have had to pull into sidings to let more time sensitive cargo, like milk, to overtake. Or to put it another way, except for the first few miles, it spent so much time slowing and stopping, that Mr Anderson could have boarded pretty much anywhere."

"But not Spring Close," Riley said. "That's nearly three miles to the east of that route."

"Yes, it was too much to hope he'd give the address of his hideout. Cadet, if you were the counterfeiters, what would you do?"

Ruth glanced at Riley. There was a shadow of a smile on her face.

"I'd move, sir," Ruth said.

"Exactly. It's possible that Anderson wasn't shot at the same location the money was printed. Let's assume he was. Who was he? A counterfeiter who was betrayed? Or was he a thief who was caught? We don't know, but whichever it is, the killer is unlikely to have stayed in the area. Do you remember what I said about computers? They need electricity. Where along here would they be able to steal the power?" He leaned forward over the map, tracing a finger along the train line from the tannery to the spot past Ringwood Junction where the body had been found. "Somewhere remote," he muttered, "where no one would notice people coming and going yet not heading to work. Somewhere the sound couldn't be overheard. Not a village. Not a town. Not a factory, at least not a large one… No, I don't think they would set it up inside a legitimate business. There would be too great a risk of the operation being discovered. Hmm. The printer is the key here."

"Could it be somewhere like the newspaper offices?" Ruth asked.

"No. Though you could find the computer in almost every house, the printer is something else. The one they use to print the newspaper wouldn't work at all. In fact, I would guess their printer was made from other machines, stripped down and adapted to the paper and ink that we have available. The ink… maybe… yes," he murmured, stepping back. "Whoever could build the printer could probably run a cable from a nearby building, stealing the electricity from the grid. The Electric Company keeps an eye on usage like, well, like people whose profits depend on it. So we are looking for somewhere a few thousand watts an hour wouldn't be missed."

"Not on this stretch to the west of the city," Riley said.

"Why not?" Mitchell asked.

"He got off the train because it jolted him awake," Riley said. "At that point it was travelling north. After he was shot, he would have intended to go to a hospital. He got off when he realised the train was taking him away from the city."

"A reasonable assumption. That leaves us with this section of line here." He pointed at a spot that the map marked as the old Bournemouth airport. "There's a house near this factory, just south of the power plant itself, another here near the warehouse for the National Store, and this one close to the aluminium recycling works. We'll check all three."

Riley nodded. It took Ruth a moment to understand what he'd said.

"Don't we need a warrant?" she asked.

"For a walk in the countryside? There's no point," Mitchell said. "I spoke to the commissioner. He was quite emphatic about this being Weaver's case, and she's still busy with the coroner. No, we'll go and take a look for ourselves. Someone has to, and it'll beat sitting around here. First, though, we'll go to Spring Close. Even if it's a false address to go with the fake name, there is a reason Mr Anderson chose it."

Her bicycle wobbling slightly due to the unbalanced weight of the crime-kit – though this time without the sign – Ruth followed the other two away from the centre of Twynham. The leaf litter carpeting the roads grew deeper until, by the time they were approaching Spring Close, it had turned into a thin loamy soil covered in weeds, moss, and occasional saplings.

The houses in this neighbourhood were mostly abandoned. A few had been boarded up. Others had been stripped even of their window frames. The area had become a builder's yard, the properties dismantled to form repairs on those closer to the coast or railway, but it wasn't completely deserted. Where there had once been a garden in front of a house, there was now a patch of dug-over earth dotted with canes and shreds of thin netting.

"I don't know why people live in places like this," Riley said.

"No taxes," Ruth said. That had been the saving grace of The Acre, at least until Mr Foster took over.

"Spring Close," Mitchell said pointing at a battered road sign pinned to a low wall. "Riley, you go around the back, the cadet and I will find the front."

The constable leaned her bike against a wall, and disappeared through a ragged hole where a door had once stood, and was soon lost amidst the rubble and broken timbers.

"Watch the windows," Mitchell said as they dismounted and leaned their bikes next to Riley's. "Look for movement and shadows." He slowly walked into the close, his head moving from side to side. "Anything that shines," he continued, "might indicate where metal has been recently abraded. Look at the soil in the gutters to see where bicycles, hooves, or feet might have disturbed it. Has trash been recently dumped in the street? Is there fresh manure? Is there a puff of steam from a chimney indicating where a fire has been hastily put out?"

The answer to those questions was no. The windows to number twenty-three were as dark as the rest of the curving row of terraced houses. Mitchell knocked on the door. There was no sound from within.

"Police," he called, though not loudly enough to carry more than a few dozen feet. He pushed the door. It swung open, and Ruth saw that the lock was broken. With his left hand, Mitchell pointed at the bright yellow splinters around the lock, while his right went to the revolver at his belt.

"Go back out into the road. Watch the windows," he hissed, and went inside.

Ruth backed slowly away, feeling a rush of gratitude that she didn't have to enter that dark and suddenly forbidding house. That was followed by a wave of guilt at her instinctive cowardice. She watched Mitchell disappear into the gloom, and only then remembered the gun at her own belt. She drew it, keeping the barrel pointing down as she looked from window to window.

She tried to count the seconds as they passed, but her racing heartbeat made her lose track. Then, in a window on the second-storey, she saw something. As instinct raised the revolver to point at the shadows behind the glass, she heard a voice from inside.

"It's clear," Mitchell called.

"Clear," Riley echoed a moment later and from a little further away.

Ruth holstered her weapon. Flexing her fingers in an attempt to stop them from shaking, she went into the house. The front door led onto a narrow hallway. There was a staircase on the left, with a door just before the first step and two more leading off to the right. At the end of the hall was a fourth doorway, in which Riley now stood.

"You smell that?" Mitchell asked as he came down the stairs.

"Damp?" Ruth asked.

"Mildew and rot," Mitchell said, "with a hint of smoke. Cadet, you take the front room, Riley, the kitchen. There is a reason why Mr Anderson gave this house as an address. Find it."

Judging by the sofa upturned against one wall, Ruth guessed it had been the living room. Whatever other furniture had once filled the space was gone along with the carpet and half of the floorboards. Those must have been removed in someone's search for... something. As she bent down to see what, there was a voice from behind her.

"Anything?" Riley asked from the doorway.

"Scavengers," Ruth said. "They must have taken the furniture and the carpet. Probably took the floorboards to burn, but they were after the pipes." She pointed down to where a section of copper piping had been sawn through. The exposed under-floor was covered in a thick layer of cobwebs and dirt, and a thinner dusting of metal filings.

"Probably during the first year," Riley said. "The furniture would have been burned, the pipes taken to make a still or repair some other house."

"Then no one has lived here for years?" Ruth asked. "Maybe Mr Anderson made up an address, and it's a coincidence that he picked one that actually exists."

"It's no coincidence," Riley said. She held out her hand. In it was a soot-blackened photograph. "There was a photo album in the oven. Looks like someone searched the house for any clues as to who lived here, and burned them. I bet it was Anderson. It was an electric oven, a sealed box with no chimney. As soon as he closed the door, the oxygen supply was cut off. Not everything was destroyed. You know what that means?"

"He was in a hurry." Ruth looked at the picture. It was a family portrait of a man and his four sons. "They all look a bit like him. The dead man, I mean. There's a definite family resemblance."

"Definitely. Mister Mitchell!" Riley called.

Mitchell came down the stairs, an evidence bag in his hand. "What did you find?" he asked.

Ruth handed him the photograph.

"Hard to say when it was taken," he said. "Jeans and T-shirts. Can't see anything in the background to give it a date, except… is that a world cup shirt? That would place it within a year of The Blackout. I'd say our Mr Anderson is one of the children."

"He's the youngest," Riley said.

"You can't really tell from the picture," Mitchell said.

"And his name is Charles," Riley added.

"You found something else?" Mitchell asked.

Riley grinned and led them into the kitchen. She opened the door to a floor-to-ceiling cupboard. The shelves were empty, but on the inside of the door, still faintly legible were a series of lines marking a height, each with a date and a name.

"Charles is five years younger than the next of his brothers," Riley said, pointing at the dates. "He was born here, you see, and that's the first one, on his first birthday. The body we found is certainly far younger than thirty. That means our victim is Charles."

"So he's twenty-five," Ruth said, staring at the picture. The youngest child bore the least resemblance to the man they'd found.

"Any clue as to his surname?" Mitchell asked.

"None," Riley said. "There are a few more photographs in which you can see one or two of the family. Nothing else."

"I think it was Charles who burned them," Mitchell said, holding up the evidence bag. "I found an empty can of tinned beef in the smallest bedroom, which now makes more sense. He came back here, stayed at least one night, and made an attempt at destroying any record of who he really was."

"So when he went to the shoemakers, and they asked for an address, he gave the first that came to mind?" Ruth asked.

"Probably, and that would mean that Anders Anderson was the first *name* that came to mind," Mitchell said. "Maybe Anderson was his surname, maybe it wasn't, but the name meant something to him. Cadet, what should we do now?"

"We should see if there's anyone called Anderson working in the Mint," she said. "Or anywhere else where they would have access to these kind of computers. If he survived The Blackout, maybe his brothers did. Maybe his entire family are the counterfeiters. We should see if we can find them."

"We could," Mitchell said. "But that's going to take time, and the trail is only getting colder. If the family isn't involved, any details they give us will be as out of date as anything we find in this house. And what if Anderson isn't his surname? Well?"

"Um… I suppose we could see if there's an address book in any of the neighbouring houses," she said.

"Or letters undelivered in the post office," Riley added. "Or see if the electoral role for this parish wasn't destroyed. A paper copy was kept at the town hall. But if the trail is cold why not spend our time doing that? It's what we're meant to do, isn't it?"

Ruth looked from her to Mitchell, her brain whirring as she tried to guess at the subtext.

"And what if another body turns up tomorrow?" Mitchell asked. "Because I doubt Mr Anderson's will be the last. This way is quicker."

"He's in the city?" Riley asked.

"He is," Mitchell said.

"Who?" Ruth asked.

"Come on, cadet," Mitchell said as he headed out the front door. "It's time you met Isaac."

Chapter 6
Isaac

"I'm staying outside," Riley said. "You should, too," she added, addressing Ruth.

They had come to a halt halfway down a long avenue near an old church, outside of which a man stood, watching them. He was at least six inches taller than Mitchell, and twice his width. There was something deeply sinister about the man, but curiosity won over caution.

"No," Ruth said. "I'll go in."

"It's not a good idea," Riley said, this time speaking to the sergeant.

"She'll have to meet him sooner or later," Mitchell said. "Might as well get it over with."

"Who is Isaac?" Ruth asked as she and the sergeant walked towards the church. The man standing sentry disappeared inside. "Is he a criminal?"

"He's worse than that," Mitchell said.

Though from the outside the church appeared intact, only the frontage had survived The Blackout unscathed. The altar was lost under a pile of rubble, above which nesting birds made their roosts in the fractured remains of the roof. The pews had long since been removed, but in the middle of the nave was a table. Behind it stood the man who'd been waiting outside and a petite woman made to look even smaller by comparison with the living mountain next to her. Sitting at the table was a man in a grey suit, a hat covering his head, shaded glasses over his eyes.

As their echoing footsteps caused roosting birds to flutter and flap around the rafters, Ruth squinted at the man, trying to tell whether she'd ever seen him before. So much of his face was hidden that it was hard to tell, but she was sure she would have remembered that slightly waxy sheen to his skin. He could have been a well-preserved sixty or a prematurely aged thirty. In part because of Mitchell's approach to examining Mr Anderson's body, she turned her attention to the clothes. It was a suit, but not of old-world make. There were more pockets for one thing, and the collar was far higher, suggesting it was worn for warmth more than style. The hat was very old-fashioned, but looked new. His suit, she realised, was of a similar colour and cut to the clothes worn by the man and woman behind him. It was almost like it was a uniform.

"Hello, Henry," the seated man said.

"Isaac," Mitchell replied. "I thought you were going to leave town."

"And yet this is where you came to look for me," Isaac replied. His tone was cultured, relaxed, almost amused, and somehow neither English nor American. "For the second time in forty-eight hours, I might add. What does that tell us?" He turned his shaded eyes towards Ruth. "Hello, Ruth. It's good to finally meet you."

Ruth found herself nodding in return, though more in reflex than in agreement.

"I thought you would have gone north, to check on that other matter," Mitchell said.

"Fortunately, or unfortunately if you prefer, there was no need," Isaac said. "I can find no record of that symbol in any of the databases to which I have access."

"None?" Mitchell asked.

"It seems as if there truly are some new things under the sun of our brave new world," Isaac replied. Ruth found her nostrils flaring in irritation. Isaac smiled. "But that isn't why you've come here. Not today. How is Maggie?"

"What? Fine," Ruth replied automatically. "Wait, do you know her?"

"Ignore him," Mitchell said. "He's trying to get under your skin by pretending he knows more than he does. He probably had you followed when he learned you were working with me. He has me followed, don't you Isaac?"

"Just to keep you safe, Henry."

"And doesn't that sound comforting?" Mitchell said. "But you'll note he didn't deny it, cadet. You see, his are the simple tricks of an honest charlatan."

The man behind Isaac let out a low growl.

"And I see you've got a new convert," Mitchell said. "One who doesn't know how the world works. You should tell him, Isaac, before he makes me do something that you'll regret."

"It's all right, Gregory," Isaac said, though he kept his head turned towards Ruth. "Henry is an old friend, cadet, or can I call you Ruth?"

Ruth shrugged.

"Ruth, then. I am Isaac, and I know that Henry will have told you very little about me, but I *am* pleased to meet you. As for you, Henry, you could try being a little more polite when you come looking for my help."

"What would be the point?" Mitchell asked. "You won't refuse me."

Gregory gave a rattling growl.

Isaac raised a hand. "No, Gregory. Henry is right. I won't refuse him. So, Henry, what do you want?"

"A body was found yesterday in a field two miles north of Ringwood Junction," Mitchell said.

"I know," Isaac said.

"Did you know that we found over ten thousand pounds of counterfeit currency on the corpse?"

"No, I hadn't heard that," Isaac said. "What was the quality of the forged notes?"

"Almost perfect reproductions," Mitchell said. "It was the serial numbers that gave them away. They haven't been issued yet."

"Wait," Ruth said. "How did you know the body had been discovered?"

"I hear things," Isaac said. "Eventually I hear everything, but what you're really asking is whether I had something to do with it. I didn't, did I, Henry?"

"No, he's not a suspect," Mitchell agreed. "Not in this anyway. A man is dead, Isaac, and I doubt he'll be the last. He used the name Andy Anderson to buy a pair of boots in July. The address he gave led us to the man's real childhood home, twenty-three Spring Close, and to a first name of Charles. We need to know his surname, what happened to his family, and—"

"And everything else. Yes. Do you have any of the fake currency?"

"No. It's all at the Mint. Weaver's leading the investigation."

"She is? That explains your presence here, not to mention your mood."

"How long will it take you?" Mitchell asked.

"An hour, a week. I can't say until it's done. Over ten thousand pounds, you say?"

"That's right," Mitchell said.

"It was inevitable, of course. Not the counterfeiting," Isaac added, seeing Ruth's expression. "I mean how crime would evolve. Or devolve, if you prefer. During the early years there was nothing to steal, and there were so many deaths that murders were rarely noticed."

"I noticed," Mitchell said.

"Indeed you did," Isaac said. "Now that wealth is re-emerging, greedy desire has awoken to stalk the land once more. People want what they don't have regardless of whether they need it. As wealth grows, the complexity of crime grows with it. Ten thousand pounds? It's only the start. I will send a message when I have an answer for you. Stay cautious, Ruth."

"Sir, about what he said—" Ruth began when they were outside.

"He talks in riddles as a way of adding to the mysticism," Mitchell said. "But he's a man who always speaks the truth. That makes him dangerous."

"But who is he?" Ruth asked.

"That's a good question," Mitchell replied.

"You should tell her," Riley said. "She's met him now, so she should know."

Mitchell looked at Riley, and there was another moment of unspoken conversation.

"Fine," Mitchell said, relenting. "It's hard to say who he is now. In a way it's the same answer to the question of who he's been since The Blackout. He's an outlaw, in that for the last twenty years he's lived outside every law except his own. Most people think he's dead, or a legend —"

"Tell her about the Tube," Riley interrupted.

Mitchell glanced over at her. His lips pursed. For a moment Ruth thought he wouldn't.

"In London," Mitchell said, "just before The Blackout, a message was sent to tens of thousands of people, telling them to take shelter in the underground railway tunnels. It was sent to their phones, do you understand? No, you don't. Despite the networks being down, this message got through. Perhaps it was sent to more people; it's hard to know how many ignored it. Those who believed the message took to the deep tunnels. That's how a lot of us survived the nuclear holocaust."

"And tell her what happened then," Riley said.

Mitchell looked up at the sky, more as if he was remembering than as if he was weighing up how much to say. "Isaac knew to come here," he said. "To this stretch of coast. He had a message on his phone, as anonymous as the ones everyone else received, saying that those ships would be here, run aground. The cargo ships, you understand, the giant bulk carriers with millions of tonnes of wheat, oats, rice, powdered milk, and all the rest. We found the ships just as Isaac had said we would. Some people tried to call him a prophet, and I'll admit that he didn't let them. Not then. Recently, he's changed. His current group of followers have a cultish obedience I find unsettling. He lives by his own laws and beyond the reach of ours. He'll kill, but he won't murder. He'll take, but he won't steal. He rarely gives a straight answer, but he never lies. That's what makes him truly dangerous."

"And tell her—" Riley began, but Mitchell cut her off.

"I think that's enough about him for now," Mitchell said. "We've three properties to investigate as to whether the counterfeiters might have been there. If we're quick, we should have it done before five. There's a nice pub near the power station. They do a wonderful game pie. Or they did. We can talk about Isaac and The Blackout then."

Ruth replayed what Mitchell had said as she followed the other two away from the town. Then she went back over what Isaac had said. Who was he? Who had he been before The Blackout? And had that mention of Maggie really been just a bluff? As the metres turned into miles, she decided those questions weren't nearly as important as those regarding what Sergeant Mitchell was doing now. Certainly he was carrying out an investigation against the orders of a superior. What Maggie had said the night before came back to her, and she wondered whether she should tell someone what he was doing. Captain Weaver, perhaps? There was nothing she could do about it. Not now. She decided that she'd see what Mitchell said in the pub at day's end and get Maggie's advice that evening. Having delayed the decision, if not made it, she tried to enjoy the day as they cycled through the rambling suburbs of Twynham and then beyond.

As they rode towards the industrial heartland, the smoke-filled clouds above them grew thicker and the train stations grew larger. The timber-framed platforms were increasingly lost amidst the brick and steel sidings where workshops loaded their finished products for shipment to the market. The road's surface changed from poorly repaired asphalt to a mixture of dirt and coal-dust as it detoured around a station far busier than the others. Labourers moved with glacial caution as they loaded wooden crates from the light bulb factory that sprawled around an ancient church. The track joined an old cobbled street as it went through a small park where rusting children's swings were lost amidst the precisely divided allotment plots. That was replaced by a field of wheat, and then with one empty of crops but full of farmers hacking at the soil with pick and shovel.

Riley and Mitchell, engrossed in muted conversation, ignored the workers they passed. Ruth couldn't. The looks they gave her weren't envious. If anything, they were smug. Theirs was a life of unionised hours, high pay, and allowances for clothing and accommodation. After five years toil, any farmhand could apply for a loan to start a farm of their own. Those were increasingly along the pirate-troubled coast of Kent, but it was *theirs*. It was a hard life, but a secure one with prices fixed and payments guaranteed by the government. And it was a life Ruth could have. Previously it had seemed too small and provincial an ambition, but now she wondered if her time in the academy had been wasted. Her mind turned back to Mitchell, and she realised that of course she had to report him. He was withholding evidence from Captain Weaver, and that certainly was a crime. Maggie's advice, that she could resign, rang in her ears until Mitchell pointed at a broken signpost.

"This is the turn off," he said.

At first, Ruth thought he was pointing into an impenetrable thicket of brambles, but there was a narrow path cut through the centre. It wasn't wide enough for them to walk the bikes, so they rode in single file. Her narrow, studded leather wheels bogged down in the rotting mulch. Woody stalks caught in her spokes, and thorny stems lashed against her legs as she awkwardly walked the bike through the barbed corridor. For once she was glad of her thick uniform and was gladder still when the track abruptly widened and she was able to dismount. Five hundred yards after that, Mitchell led them directly across a stretch of rough cropped pasture towards a thicket of new-growth trees.

Ruth glanced at the sun and then searched the sky for the dissipating cloud of smoke from the power station as she tried to gauge exactly where they were.

"Over there," Mitchell said, his voice low and his arm pointing through the trees.

"What?" she asked.

"Can't you hear it?" he whispered back.

She concentrated. There was something, and it was different from the rustling creak of the trees above them. It wasn't rhythmic, but nor was it a natural sound.

"What is it?" she asked.

"People," Mitchell said. "Doing what, I don't know, but it's coming from the direction of the first house I wanted to check. Leave the bikes here. Cadet, you stay ten paces behind Riley at all times. Understand?"

She didn't, but nodded anyway. Uncertainty of what lay ahead added a coating of fear to the doubts that had been plaguing her all morning.

Mitchell and Riley moved soundlessly through the closely packed trees. They'd done it before, Ruth thought. A lot. That begged the question of where in Twynham a city copper would— a branch cracked under her foot. She looked up to see Riley and Mitchell had stopped, hands poised over their holsters, not looking at her but scanning the trees to either side. She waited. After a moment, they continued. She followed, this time keeping her eyes and concentration on the ground.

The sound slowly resolved into that of hammering, sawing, and the clattering of metal. When she reached the treeline's edge, she saw hundreds of people swarming across the landscape.

"Are they putting up a factory?" she asked.

"A warehouse," Riley said.

More than one, Ruth thought. She could barely make out the house that had been marked on Mitchell's old-world map. The narrow track leading to it was still visible, but was now at the middle of a much wider road. A score of orange-clad labourers were grading and levelling the surface under the watchful eye of a pair of armed prison guards.

"Is that a work gang?" Ruth asked.

"Fulfilling a sentence of light labour," Mitchell said. "It looks like they're putting in a train line."

Beyond the gang were more workers, these dressed in that casual uniform of patched blue and black that most people called their everyday clothes. They scrabbled up scaffolding as they erected cladding on a building's skeletal frame. Behind the partially constructed warehouse was another that was nearly complete. Distant figures clambered across the roof putting guttering in place. Further back, there were more buildings, all seemingly finished.

"I think we can safely say that wherever Mr Anderson was shot, it wasn't here," Mitchell said. "You see the lamps? The mirrors? They must be at this night and day."

"But what is it?" Ruth asked. "What are they building?"

"Is it the National Store?" Riley asked. "That's what's over in the distance. Are they extending it?" She sounded as uncertain as Ruth felt.

"Looks like it," Mitchell said.

"But it's so big," Ruth said. "I mean... I suppose I should have realised."

Selling goods from an abandoned property was classed as looting and profiteering unless a scavenging licence was applied for, in which case, ninety-percent of the haul was taxed. That tax could be paid in money but was more usually paid in goods. These were stored by the government, and then sold at nominal rates in the branches of the National Store that each town, city, and large village had. There were exceptions and exemptions, but it made a life of farming, making, or mining, more profitable than a career in picking through the remains of the old world.

"Can there be that many frying pans in the country?" Ruth asked.

"And pots, pans, crockery, cutlery, clothes," Riley listed.

"Easily," Mitchell said. "What they're building is barely bigger than some of the large malls they used to have in the States. I don't know how much electricity is needed to make Teflon, but why bother when you can stockpile enough pots and pans for three generations? But I don't think that's what they're doing."

"And what's that?" Riley asked.

"They're increasing storage capacity. What they want to store, I'm not sure, but it has to be connected with the trade deal with the Americas. It looks like the buildings have thick walls and thin roofs, and that gives a clue, but not one connected with Mr Anderson's murder."

He moved back through the woods, towards where they'd left their bikes. This time he made no attempt to be quiet, nor did Riley, so when they spoke, Ruth was able to hear.

"There was nothing about it in the paper," Riley said.

"Which simply means they told them not to print it," Mitchell replied. "There has to be five hundred people working there, perhaps a thousand. You can't keep something like that quiet."

"But they're spending our taxes on it," the constable said. "We should know about that."

"An interesting point, especially coming from you," Mitchell said. "Why don't you ask your MP? You never told me how your date with him went, by the way."

There was something close to a growl from Riley. Mitchell chuckled in reply. Then there was silence as they collected their bikes and continued cycling along the edge of the overgrown fields.

"There's no one here," Mitchell said, stepping over a charred beam. Ruth thought that had been obvious from the first sight they'd had of the ruined house.

"You think this was where they were doing the printing?" the constable asked.

"I think so," Mitchell said, "and they destroyed the evidence by burning the building to the ground. They did a thorough job of it, too. Cadet, walk the perimeter. Look for wheel marks that would show where a heavily laden cart was driven away."

Ruth shuffled around the broken fence, scanning the ground, and then the surroundings. She tried to picture the house as it had been, not just a few days ago, but in the decades before that. Built by a road so narrow it didn't deserve the name, it was nestled amidst fields, yet it was too small for a farmhouse. Certainly there were no barns or outbuildings nearby. It was hard to say any more than that as only the rear wall of the house and a creaking few feet of roof remained. She wondered who would want to live in such a remote place. Though she suspected it was that isolation which had made it so attractive to the counterfeiters.

There was a loud rasping groan from the house, followed by a sharp crack. Ruth turned around in time to see Mitchell diving out from the house as one of the remaining roof beams fell. Ash, brick, and splinters sprayed outward as the last section of roof crashed down, bringing half the remaining wall with it.

"No printer," Mitchell said as he picked himself up. "No sign of anything that didn't belong in a normal home. Riley?"

"Can't see any cables," the constable called from the other side of the building. "If they were stealing electricity they must have laid them underground."

"Which is what I would have done," Mitchell said, brushing dust off his uniform. "There would be less chance of it being seen. Cadet, find anything?"

Guiltily Ruth glanced at the ground before answering. "No, sir, I haven't found anything," she said, which had the merit of being entirely true.

"Hmm. Well, arson isn't something I've much experience with," Mitchell said. "The ash is cold, but not damp. When did it last rain? Six days ago? Then the fire began in the last week, but not in the last twenty-four hours. If they had everything already packed up and a cart waiting, and if they burned the place down immediately after Anderson was shot, then it does fit our timeframe. Just. The factory is further away than I expected. You'd need at least a mile of underground cable to bring electricity into this place."

"What's the but?" Riley asked. "I know there is one."

"Finding the cable, bringing it here, and setting it in place would have taken time. But we can surmise from when Anderson bought those boots that this operation has been going on for months. Physically digging a trench between this house and that fence couldn't have been done without being seen, but they could print however much money the security guards asked for. They had time. They had money. If a problem can be solved with either of those two, then it could be overcome."

"Then we should go to the factory and ask when the fire was," Ruth said. "Surely someone noticed the smoke. Maybe they came out to investigate."

"Yes," Mitchell said. "We could do that. But if we did, anyone inside who's working with this gang would be alerted to our investigation. They'd disappear before we found them and we'd lose another lead." He paused and seemed to be weighing something up. "No," he finally said. "It's too great a risk, and this is too important. We have, I'm afraid, reached the end of our own investigation. Or this part of it."

"You want to tell Weaver?" Riley asked.

Mitchell glanced at Ruth again before answering. "I think so. This house needs to be searched, and it needs to be made safe before that can even begin. The factory needs to be surrounded before questions are asked inside. We can't do either of those and, frankly, I don't want to. This trail is cold, so it's time we looked for another. For that we need the autopsy report, and access to the bullet we found in Mr Anderson."

"You think it will match?" Riley asked.

"I don't know. Whether it does or not will give us more answers than sifting through these ruins. Certainly it will keep us occupied until we hear from Isaac."

"Why do you want the bullet, sir?" Ruth asked.

"What? Oh, yes. You don't know, do you? There was an incident the day before you joined us, but that is a story that can be told in far more salubrious surroundings than these. What time is it? Yes, we should make it to that pub before the rush when the afternoon shift finishes. I'll tell you there, cadet, and it might answer your questions about Isaac. It's about half an hour from here. I suppose, since we're going in that direction, we might as well look in on that last house."

By the time they next brought their bikes to a halt, Ruth was feeling somewhat better about her career. To their left lay a steep wooded hill. Beyond it was the third house. In an hour they would be sitting in a pub, eating game pie, and Mitchell would be explaining... not everything, probably not even enough, but that didn't matter. He was going to share some of the half-heard conversations he'd had with Riley. Better yet, he was going to inform Captain Weaver of what they'd found. Even if one of her superiors were to approach her that evening and ask what Mitchell was up to, what could she say that they wouldn't already know? It didn't answer the question of her future, but it did delay having to find that answer.

She tramped up the hill, enjoying the warmth of the day as she thought of the winter to come. Even when Riley and Mitchell reached the top, bent low, and then began to crawl along the ridge, she thought nothing of copying them. She reached the crest and found a spot where she was hidden by a sprawling fern.

Below them was a two-storey house with a one-storey extension at the rear. The windows on the ground floor had been boarded up, but the ones on the upper floor were unbroken and a few were wedged open. The roof looked intact, and other than being slightly run-down, the property appeared undamaged. There was no road leading to the house, just an unpaved, rutted track that went past a newly fenced pasture before disappearing down a dip. Just under a quarter of a mile beyond the house lay a fenced building, out of which jutted those ubiquitous smoking chimneys.

"Is that the aluminium works?" Ruth asked.

"It's basically a recycling plant," Mitchell said. "It turns old aluminium into new cans, before they're taken to the canning factories near the docks. Well, cadet, what do you think?"

From his tone she knew that was a trick question. She scanned the house, looking for whatever he'd spotted. The door was closed, but...

"The upstairs windows are open," she said.

"And?"

And? And what? There was no smoke coming from the chimney, nor was there any sign the garden had been tended in the last two decades. Then she saw it.

"The fence around the pasture is new," she said.

"It's not a pasture," Riley said. "Where are the animals? Look at the track. The ruts. It's a paddock for a horse that's currently out pulling the cart."

"And yet this land isn't farmed," Mitchell said. "There's no chicken coop, no vegetable patch. It's occupied, but not lived in."

"But by who?" Ruth asked.

"Let's watch, and wait, and see if we can find out," Mitchell said.

After half an hour, Ruth was about to ask for how much longer they would lie in the dank undergrowth when Riley raised an arm.

"From the east, at the end of the track," the constable hissed. "Do you see it?"

It was a high-sided scavenger's cart pulled by two horses and being led by a person in a wide-brimmed straw hat.

"Is that a woman?" Ruth asked.

"Think so," Riley said. "A scavenger, I think."

"Are those radiators in the back of the cart?" Ruth asked.

"And copper pipes," Riley said.

"Do you need radiators for counterfeiting?" Ruth asked.

Riley gave a snort.

"No," Mitchell said. "But there is a type of still you can make with them. I have a nasty feeling we've found out how that other house burned down, and it had nothing to do with the counterfeiters destroying evidence."

"A still exploded?" Riley asked.

"And they've been out to get the supplies to build another one," Mitchell said.

A man came out of the house, walked a dozen yards towards the track, and waited for the cart to approach. He had close-cropped hair that might have been silver, grey, or blond. There was something strange about his face, but he was too far away for Ruth to tell what. When the woman brought the cart to a halt, the two engaged in animated conversation. As the wind shifted, Ruth caught a few syllables but nothing she would call words. The man waved a hand towards the house. A moment later, a second man came out. He went to the cart and began levering a radiator off the back. The woman unhitched the horses and led them toward the paddock.

"What do you think, sir?" Riley asked.

"I think they've burned down one house, and are likely to do the same thing again unless we have a quiet word," he said.

"We're going to go down there?" Ruth asked. "Shouldn't we get backup?"

"I don't want to arrest them," Mitchell said. "I want to know if they started that fire. I don't want to tell Weaver that house is where the counterfeiters were if a quick sift through the ashes only turns up a melted still. But if they didn't destroy that house, they might have seen something."

"Won't they run?" Ruth asked as she followed the sergeant through the bracken and back down the hill.

"If they do, then we've broken an illegal distillery. That'll please the commissioner, though it will mean we spend the rest of the week filling in the paperwork."

Ruth wasn't reassured. They collected the bicycles, wheeled them around the hill, and towards the track. What was even less reassuring was what Mitchell said as the roof of the house appeared over the horizon.

"Stay behind me," he said. "Do what I say, and nothing more. Understand?"

She nodded.

"If there's any sign of trouble, fire your gun in the air," Mitchell said. "They'll run."

"Probably," Riley added.

Ruth's sense of anxiety grew as they walked nearer. The rest of the roof, then the upper windows of the house, and then the head of the man on the back of the cart came into view. He spotted them a moment later and shouted a warning to the others. The woman returned from the paddock. The first man, the one Ruth thought of as the leader, stood watching them. Mitchell raised a hand. The leader stepped away from the cart. He was holding a suitcase. Presumably he'd brought it out from the house. Ruth wondered why. The woman stayed where she was, her body shielded from view. The second man was... he was backing away from them, Ruth realised. Not fast, and he wasn't heading towards the house.

That sense of unease finally boiled over. Something was wrong. Very wrong. She couldn't say why or what. Riley must have seen it too, because for each forward step the constable took, she was taking one to the right. She was angling toward the further side of the track, close to the fence. Ruth understood that it meant Riley was planning something, she just wished that she knew precisely what.

"Lovely day for it!" Mitchell called out.

Ruth turned her attention back to the two figures by the cart. The woman was young, in her early twenties. The leader was older, and there was something strange about his face.

"Can we help you?" the woman called. The man put the suitcase down.

"We've had a report from the recycling plant," Mitchell said. "They're concerned because of a fire in another property not far from here."

They were fifty yards away now. The woman's lips were curled up at the edges in an approximation of a smile. The man was staring at Mitchell. Ruth kept her eyes fixed on him. He wasn't smiling. Or perhaps he was. Now that they were closer, she could see his face properly and saw that it was distorted by a mass of scars. He looked like he'd fallen through a plate glass window only to land on a fine metal sieve.

"We're looking for pipes," the woman said.

"Then I'll need to see your licence," Mitchell said. They were thirty yards away, close enough for their voices to carry without the words being shouted.

"Of course," the woman said.

The man abruptly waved at the house. "Do it!" he shouted.

And then it all seemed to happen at once.

Ruth was looking at the woman and saw surprised confusion spread across her face. At the same time, there was a loud noise, and something hit her, knocking her down to the ground. Before she had to time to register that it was the sergeant, he was half rolling her, half dragging her into the ditch on the far side of the track.

The sound had been a gunshot. Someone was shooting at them. As if to underline that too-slow realisation, there was another shot. Acting on instinct, because it certainly wasn't out of volition, Ruth raised her head.

"Get down!" Mitchell hissed, pushing her back into the ditch. "And stay down. Don't move."

His face was almost immobile with tension, but his eyes raged. He pulled out a gun, not the revolver in his belt, but a small, sleek, black pistol from a holster on his ankle. He raised his hand and fired off two shots towards the house.

"Riley?" he called, and Ruth realised the constable wasn't in the ditch with them.

"Here," she called from somewhere on the far side of the track and a little closer to the house.

"One shooter. Single shot rifle. Second storey. Southeast corner. Remember Guildford? The bridge?" Mitchell yelled.

"Understood," Riley replied.

"Listen," Mitchell hissed. He raised his gun and fired again. "Riley is going to run to the—" There was a shot from the house. "Riley is going to take the right," he continued. "I'm going to run to the house. I want you to stay here. Understand?"

Ruth nodded.

"Say it."

"I'll stay here," she said.

"On five," Mitchell called out loudly, and he fired again.

Ruth began to count. She'd only reached three before Mitchell pushed himself out of the ditch.

Suddenly, she realised her revolver was still in its holster. All thumbs and no fingers, she fumbled with the button. She drew the revolver for the second time that day, and for the second time in her life that she hadn't been cleaning it or practicing on the range.

There was a shot, and then another, but they sounded as if they came from different guns. Ruth forced herself up, raising her arm. Mitchell was running towards the house, firing off shot after shot. There was no sign of the scarred man or of the woman. The second man, the one who'd been helping to unload the radiators, was running towards the paddock. Riley was chasing after him. Focus, Ruth told herself. The barrel of her revolver was weaving left and right. She tried bracing her left hand on her right wrist. Though that steadied her aim, it did nothing for her wavering vision. Any shot was as likely to hit the sergeant as it was the house.

There was another shot from inside the building. She saw Mitchell stumble, trip, and fall. He'd been hit.

Ruth was out of the ditch and running towards the house before she'd had time to think. She reached the cart as she saw Mitchell stagger to his feet and stumble into the house. There was more gunfire, this time from inside. Muffled by brick, she couldn't tell whether it was from a rifle or pistol. She ran off the track, onto grass, and then over worn paving slabs. Sprinting up the drive, she reached the porch just as there was a percussive, single shot from inside, followed almost instantly by an even louder moan.

"Sir! Sergeant!" she called.

"Upstairs is clear," he called back from somewhere above. Any relief that he was still alive vanished the moment she stepped into the house. Revolver held in two hands, elbows bent, she rolled around the doorway to the front room. Levelling the gun, sweeping left and right, she frantically tried to remember her training. There was a monstrous machine, made of grey plastic and black metal, in the middle of the room, but there were no people. At the far end was a doorway, with two paint-chipped doors pushed wide open. She went through them and into a kitchen. The windows were covered with thick felt curtains that had been pulled aside. Through the glass she saw both the scarred man and the woman running across the meadow behind the house.

Without thought, she pushed open the kitchen door, and ran after them. The man was in the lead, almost two hundred yards away. From his easy stride, Ruth doubted she'd catch him. The woman was sixty yards closer, but running as fast as Ruth. She didn't care. They were angling towards the wire fence of the recycling plant. There was no escape there. She ran straight, running parallel to the fence, slowly gaining ground.

The scarred man seemed to realise that freedom didn't lie in front or to his right. He changed direction, heading towards the same woodland from which Ruth had spied on the house half an hour and a lifetime ago. The woman copied the man and changed direction. Now Ruth really was gaining on them.

The man turned his head. He saw Ruth. He shouted something. The woman turned. Ruth locked eyes with her. The woman started to run faster. Ruth tried to find some last burst of energy but found her reserves dry. She wasn't going to catch them.

The woman suddenly fell.

"Emmitt!" the woman called.

Ruth kept running.

The woman was on her hands and knees, pulling herself back to her feet. She managed another pace before she collapsed again.

"Emmitt!" she called.

Ruth grinned. The woman must have twisted her ankle. There was no way she would escape now. She threw a glance towards the scarred man. He seemed a lot closer than before, but the woman was closer still.

Still running, she holstered the revolver, and pulled out the handcuffs. Ten yards. Five. The woman was crawling away from her. Ruth's grin turned feral as she leaped, using her weight to push the woman down to the ground. She pushed her knee into the woman's back as she cuffed one hand, and then the other.

"You're under arrest," she said, and the words seemed strange in her ears. She pulled the woman to her knees, and only then remembered the scarred man. Hoping to get some sight of which stretch of woodland he'd disappeared into, she looked up. He stood fifty yards from her. Something dull and metallic was in his hands. It was a rifle, she realised. Though it was far squatter than those sold for hunting.

Drawing her revolver, she took a pace towards him. The man fired. Ruth's training took over. Her arm raised, her finger curled on the trigger. The gun clicked. She pulled the trigger again. There was another shot though not from her. The revolver clicked. Click. Click. Click. Click. The scarred man slowly lowered his gun. He watched her for a moment, as she ineffectually pulled the trigger, before he ran for the treeline.

Ruth's hands fell to her sides as she watched him go. She let out a ragged breath and turned to her prisoner. The woman had been shot, twice, in the chest. Blood still pulsed out of the gaping wound, but she was dead. Ruth took a step towards her, and then a stumbling step back, barely managing to turn her head before she threw up.

"Are you hurt?"

It was Mitchell, and his voice seemed to come from a thousand miles away. Hands roughly gripped Ruth's shoulders, forcing her to straighten. Then he raised a hand to her chin and gently turned her head from left to right.

"Look at me," he said. "Look at me. You're okay. Do you understand?"

"I… yes."

"What happened?" he asked.

"I forgot," she said.

"Forgot what?"

She raised her hand, but the revolver wasn't in it. "To load it," she said, blinking as she tried to focus on the long grass around her as she looked for her weapon.

Mitchell followed her gaze, bent, and picked up the gun. He reached to her belt and pulled out six cartridges. He quickly loaded the revolver and fired off six shots in the direction of the woodland.

"He fired at your prisoner," he said. "You returned fire. You missed."

"I didn't fire," she said. "I forgot."

"No," he said patiently, "you fired six shots. He ran. You didn't pursue because it was more important to secure the scene. Repeat it."

"I fired six shots. I didn't pursue because I had to secure the scene," she murmured.

"Good enough," he said, and handed her back her gun. Then he jogged off across the grassland in the direction of the woods. She assumed he was going after the man… Emmitt? Was that what the woman had called him? Ruth looked down at the body, and then quickly away and found she was looking at the house. There was no sign of Riley. What had the sergeant meant by secure the scene? Did he mean the house? Why? When she looked back towards him, she saw that he'd stopped, about fifty yards from her, and was looking at the ground. He bent and picked something up. A pace further on, he did it again. Then he started walking back towards her, throwing an occasional glance at the trees.

"Old-world make," he said when he reached her. In his hand was a casing. "From what I saw from the house, I'd say it was a military grade rifle."

"You mean the Marines?" she asked.

"No. I mean old-world military. And I don't think it was British," he said, examining the casing. "High velocity. That's about as far as I'm willing to guess." He looked at the dead woman. "Two good shots. Either would have killed her, so the second must have hit when she was on the ground. That tells us a lot."

"It does?" Ruth asked, curiosity cutting through shock.

"You've heard the expression, there's no honour among thieves? Sayings like that only last because there's a grain of truth to them. Now, there's a time to think about what just happened, but it isn't now. I've got a suspect handcuffed to the sink, Riley is missing, and that man could come back."

"I think his name is Emmitt," Ruth said.

"Then let's see if our suspect will confirm it. Come on, she's not going anywhere."

Ruth let herself be led away from the body. Walking helped clear the fog from her mind.

"I thought I saw you get shot," she said.

"I was." He pointed at a tear in his shirt. "Bulletproof vest," he said. "Stopped the bullet, but I'll have a nice bruise tomorrow. They're not standard issue, and you want to know why not?"

"Why?"

"When I came back to Twynham and saw the uniform they told me to wear, I asked. Most of us wore them when I left, you see. They're all different styles and designs depending on whether they came from the armoury in a ship, a provincial police station, or a military base. That means they're not uniform, therefore they can't be issued as such. Damn stupid bureaucracy."

"Oh." It was unimportant. The sergeant was alive. She was alive. "Wait. Riley is missing?" she asked.

"The man she was chasing got on a horse. The last I saw of Riley, she'd grabbed the other one, and was riding after him."

"Riley can ride?" Ruth asked.

"When I met her she was with a group of horse traders from Ireland. That's what they claimed to be. What they were… well, that's a story for her to tell you. Yes, she can ride. But if this man, Emmitt, comes back, I'd rather have some cover to hide behind."

"Do you think he will?"

"He might," Mitchell said, "when he realises we're alone. On the other hand… I don't know. None of this quite fits."

"What do you mean?" she asked.

They'd reached the house.

"Didn't you notice?" he asked. "See for yourself."

She followed him inside, throwing one last look at the treeline. There was no sign of Emmitt. No sign of anyone. She couldn't even see the body of the dead woman. Ruth went through the kitchen and back into the main room. There wasn't much light until Mitchell pulled the boards down from the room's bay window. Then she saw. The room was full of banknotes. Some were stacked neatly. Some stacks had been knocked over, spilling the currency down to the bare floorboards. Other notes were still stuck together on sheets of paper slightly smaller than an unfolded newspaper.

Mitchell picked up a stack of bills held together by a thin strand of off-white string. It was about four times the size of that which had been in one of the pouches of Anderson's money belt.

"Buy yourself the best house in the country," he said, placing the stack on a small table next to the hulking great machine, and picked up another. "Buy yourself a ship." He placed them next to the first. "And a crew." He placed a third next to the first two. "Provision it." A fourth stack. He picked up two more. "And what do you do with the rest? Buy a factory? Buy *every* factory?"

Ruth turned slowly around as she tried to work out how much money was in the room. She gave up when she reached a hundred thousand.

"How much," she asked, and was surprised by how weak her voice sounded.

"Here, sit down," Mitchell said, righting a wooden chair and placing it next to the large machine. He went into the kitchen and came out again with a stone jug. "It's water," he said, passing it to her.

Her hands shook as she took a sip, and then a gulp.

"It's millions," Mitchell said. "Exactly how many, I don't know. In many ways it doesn't matter. In the old world it would have been a small fortune. In ours it's a larger one than anyone could dream of earning."

"Is that the computer?" Ruth asked, jerking her thumb towards the massive grey machine.

"That's the printer. I'd say three copiers have been stripped down and rebuilt, combined with… I don't know. Perhaps those rollers were built specially for this job. We'll have to find out. But this," he said, picking up a small silver folder, "is the computer." He opened it. One half held a keyboard, and the other half was a screen that suddenly changed from mirror-black to a brightly lit image of a twenty-pound note.

"That's a computer?" she asked.

"You haven't seen one before?"

"In pictures," she said, her mind still foggy. "Phones, and those boxy things that go under desks."

"And that's the problem, isn't it. Everything was digital, so the pictures that have survived since before The Blackout are often a decade out of date. But this printer was built, not found, and exactly who constructed it is a question for our prisoner. Excuse me."

The sergeant disappeared upstairs.

Ruth realised that she was staring at a twenty-pound note lying by her foot. It was the answer to her and Maggie's problems, a way of getting Mr Foster off their backs at least until she was paid in three months' time. Surely there was no way to know exactly how many notes had been printed? Even if there were, it was reasonable to expect Emmitt or the other man had taken some with them. No one would notice one more was missing. She grabbed the note and stuffed it into her pocket.

Walking into the kitchen, she realised her heart was racing once more. No one would miss it, she told herself. But what if the bank started checking all the twenty-pound notes that were deposited? It wouldn't matter. Foster would spend the money. But what if he didn't? What if he took it to the bank and remembered exactly who'd given it to him? And even if he did buy something with it, sooner or later that note would end up at a bank. Ruth pulled out the banknote, intending to drop it to the floor.

"Anything in there?" Mitchell asked. He was handcuffing a man to the chair she'd been sitting in.

"Um…" She looked around the kitchen. "Some canned food," she said. "Something electrical. A stove, I think. A small one."

"Makes sense. If they're stealing the electricity for the printer, there's no reason they wouldn't take a bit extra to make their lives comfortable. Let's start with that," he said, turning to the prisoner. "Where's the power coming from? What are the names of the people working with you inside the factory?"

The man shook his head.

"Is that your way of saying you're not going to talk? Look at my colleague. Look at her. You see that blood on her face? It isn't hers. It belongs to that woman who was working with you."

Ruth found her hand moving to the side of her face. Then she remembered it still had the banknote in it. She turned away, thrusting the note back into her pocket.

"We didn't kill her," Mitchell said. "It was the man with the scarred face who did that. He shot her just after my colleague got the cuffs on her. Think about that for a moment. He killed her so we couldn't arrest her. Now, what do you think will happen to you when you get to prison? Do you think he'll be able to get to you on the inside? Or will he shoot you from a distance when you're out on a work gang?"

"I've got rights," the man mumbled.

"Yes, and I'm supposed to read them to you, but it seems a waste since you're going to be dead within a month. You see, your problem isn't that we've caught you, it's that you fired at us. Forgery carries a five-year sentence. Counterfeiting is an automatic fifteen. I don't know exactly which of those two you're guilty of, but you know what? It doesn't matter. Attempted murder of a police officer is an automatic sentence of life without parole. You're young. The years are going to be heavy. Sooner or later you'll talk. That scarred man knows that, and he won't risk it, so he'll kill you."

"And what? You're going to let me go?" the man asked.

Mitchell laughed. "I'm going to give you a chance. Forgery is five years hard labour, but you don't have to serve that sentence in a prison or on a work gang. You can opt for a life at sea. Believe me, it will be a lot harder than breaking asphalt, but you'll live, and at the end of it, maybe you'll have found a new career. This is a onetime offer. You tell me everything you know, right now, or take your chances. Start by telling us your name."

There was silence, broken by the soft clink of the handcuffs on wood as the man stretched and squirmed and looked around for some other way out.

"I was hired to guard the house," the man finally said. "And shoot anyone who comes near. I was... I wasn't thinking."

"Ah, there, you see?" Mitchell said, turning to Ruth. "He wasn't thinking. It was an accident. Now what's your name?"

There was another long pause. "How can I trust you?"

"Take my word or don't, you've no other choice. Your name?" Mitchell said.

The man breathed out. "Turnbull," he said, exhaling as much as speaking. "Josh Turnbull."

"See, that wasn't hard. What's the name of the man with the scarred face?"

Another pause, this one longer. "Emmitt. I don't know if that's a first name or a surname, but it's the only one he ever used."

"And the woman," Ruth asked, "the one that Emmitt murdered, what was her name?"

"Hailey Lyons."

"And the other man?" Mitchell asked.

"That's Marcus. Marcus Clipton. He was in charge. This was all his idea."

"It was? Then what was Emmitt's role?"

"He kept the machines working," Turnbull said.

"And how did you come to be in Mr Clipton's employ?" Mitchell asked.

"He hired me and Hailey. Just to guard the place. To make sure that no one came near it during the daytime. That's all."

"And did anyone come near?"

"No. Not until you lot showed up. Honest," Turnbull added. Ruth thought he was lying.

"I'll ask again, tell me how he hired you," Mitchell said. Turnbull hesitated. "Come now, this isn't the time to be coy," Mitchell said. "You've told us enough for Mr Clipton and Emmitt to want you dead, you might us tell us the rest."

"All right, fine," Turnbull said. "It was at the Marquis, the pub by the docks. This was in June. I can't work the fields during the summer because of my skin. I need something indoors. Marcus approached me.

He'd heard I was a good worker. Reliable. Asked if I'd like to do a bit of guard duty."

"How much were you paid?"

"Twenty pounds a day," Turnbull said.

"In counterfeit notes?" Mitchell asked.

Now Turnbull laughed. "N'ah. In tenners. A hundred pounds up front, the rest when it was over."

"And when was that going to be?" Mitchell asked.

"I… I don't know. Soon. But I don't know when."

"And Ms Lyons was hired at the same time?"

"That's right," Turnbull said.

"And that was in June?" Mitchell asked.

"Yeah, and we've been here ever since. Hailey went out for supplies. Only her. Marcus and Emmitt would come and go. I don't know where to. I had to stay here. Sleep at night and keep watch during the day. Listen, this is the first time I've ever done anything like this. I've never broken the law before—"

"And what can you tell me about counterfeiting?" Mitchell cut in.

"I dunno. Paper goes in, banknotes come out," Turnbull said with a shrug.

"What about the electricity?" Mitchell asked.

"They brought a guy in to do that."

"Describe him," Mitchell said.

"I can't. I didn't see him," Turnbull said. "There was this other guy, Charles; he was doing odd jobs for Clipton."

"Like what?"

"I dunno. I think he might have helped them find the parts for the machine."

"Describe him," Mitchell said.

"He was short. Twenty-five, maybe. Cropped hair. Sort of squinted a lot. Marcus shot him. This was a couple of nights ago. He thought Charles was stealing, so he killed him."

"You saw this with your own eyes?" Mitchell asked.

"Yeah. It was out in front of the house."

"That's interesting," Mitchell said, "because—" He stopped and spun around. The pistol appeared in his hand almost as if from nowhere, but it was Riley in the doorway. She had a shallow gash across her forehead. The constable lowered her revolver as Mitchell holstered his own.

"What happened?" he asked.

"He got away," Riley said. "That's a lot of money," she added. "Are these the counterfeiters?"

"They are. This is Josh Turnbull. The man you were pursuing was Marcus Clipton. The woman was Hailey Lyons. She was shot by a man called Emmitt, who has also escaped."

"Huh," she grunted.

"Do you think you can make it to the factory?" Mitchell asked.

"Of course," Riley said.

"We need to send word for a search party, and for people to secure the building," Mitchell said.

"Weaver?" Riley asked.

"No. Send the message to the commissioner. You go with her," Mitchell added, speaking to Ruth. Then he turned to Turnbull. "You lied to me. I'm going to give you until my colleagues return to tell me the truth."

"I didn't lie," Turnbull said.

"You did. You said this was the first crime you'd been involved with, yet you were hired because Clipton had heard you were reliable. Then you said you saw Marcus kill Charles, except we know he escaped. How do you think we found you? Now, start at the beginning, but don't lie to me again."

"You chased after him on a horse?" Ruth asked as she and Riley headed back towards the track and where they'd dropped their bicycles.

"What? Yes," Riley said.

"And your forehead?" Ruth asked.

"What about it?"

"It's bleeding," Ruth said.

"It is?" Riley raised a hand, wincing as she touched the gash above her brow. "Oh. Must've been a low branch. I got knocked off the horse. What about your face?"

"It's not my blood," Ruth said. "It's the woman's. Hailey Lyons. She was shot by that scarred man."

And as she remembered the moment, and saw herself uselessly pulling the trigger of the unloaded gun, the obvious question came to her. "Why didn't he kill me?"

"Be thankful he didn't," Riley said, staggering as she bent to pick up her bike. Ruth caught her arm.

"Are you all right?"

"Fine," Riley said. "It's been a long day, that's all."

Nevertheless, Ruth had to steady the bike as the constable climbed on to it.

"Maybe you should stay—" Ruth began.

"I said I'm fine," Riley said, setting off unsteadily. "Tell me what happened."

Keeping her eyes on the constable in case she were to fall, though feeling no less unsteady herself, Ruth did.

"Usually when you find the criminals you get answers, but not this time," Riley said when Ruth had finished. "This time it's nothing but more questions. Did you take any?"

"Any what?" Ruth asked, though she knew what Riley meant.

"Money," Riley said.

"No. Of course not."

"Good. It's not worth it," Riley said. "That's what criminals don't understand. They don't weigh up the risk against the reward. Except this time. This time the reward is… it's too big. It doesn't make sense."

"No," Ruth said, though her mind was once again on the banknote in her pocket.

They didn't go to the factory, but to the railway station, and sent a message back to the city via telegram. It was only as they were heading back to the crime scene, this time walking the bicycles, that Ruth was struck by a thought.

"We should go back and ask the station master if he saw anyone matching Clipton or Emmitt's description coming through there in the last hour. Or at least give him a description in case they go through soon."

"No point," Riley said. "Trains go to the cities, and neither of them will want to go there. If they were to board a train and jump off in the middle of nowhere, the guards would notice and report it. No, they'll keep running until nightfall, and then find somewhere remote to hide until it's all quietened down."

"Are you sure?" Ruth asked, because she wasn't.

"We're nearly at the house," Riley said by way of answer.

As they approached the building, Mitchell came outside to meet them.

"There's been no sign of Emmitt," he said.

"Did you think he'd return?" Ruth asked.

"Not really, but it says a lot that he didn't. Reading between the lines of what Turnbull said, it sounds as if Emmitt was the one running the operation, not Clipton."

"Did he say anything else?" Ruth asked.

"A few details that might help us, but he doesn't know much more than we can gather from looking around. Did *you* want to have another look around the house, cadet?"

"No, I…" Ruth began. There was knowing understanding in Mitchell's expression. "I would like another look at that printer," she said.

Turnbull was still handcuffed to the chair. He looked up as she entered and dropped his head when he saw it was her.

"Who were you expecting?" she asked. The man didn't answer. Ruth walked around the room, waiting until she was hidden behind the printer before she pulled the banknote from her pocket and let it drop to the floor. Then she walked through the house again, looking in the kitchen, and then the rooms upstairs, though she didn't take in any details. All she could see was Hailey Lyons's face, followed by Emmitt, and his expression after he lowered his rifle. He could have killed her. He should have.

When she went back outside, she found Riley sitting on the porch with her eyes closed. Mitchell sat nearby, his eyes on the distant trees.

"Did you learn anything?" he asked.

"Not really. I mean… um… I don't really understand what we've found."

"To summarise," he said. "Turnbull and Lyons were recruited by Clipton in June. By that stage Emmitt, and perhaps Mr Anderson, were already working for him, or with him. Lyons took the cart out to buy supplies. According to Turnbull because it was less suspicious for a woman to do that. I get the feeling the real reason was that they didn't trust Turnbull to do it. The printing was done at night, and the notes were taken away, in the cart, by Clipton." He gestured to the suitcase that Emmitt had been carrying to the cart when they had arrived. "Emmitt was in charge of the machines, and he would fix them when they broke. However, he wasn't here all the time, and if they went wrong while he was away they would have to wait for his return. From what Turnbull says there is almost certainly at least one guard in the recycling plant on their payroll. There is also someone who laid an underground cable from there to the house. Since that involved digging a trench and then filling it in, I'd be surprised if anyone on the factory's security detail hasn't taken a hefty bribe. As to where the money went, Turnbull doesn't know. Nor does he know the identity of the guards, or of this electrical engineer. He doesn't know Anderson's real surname, or precisely what the man's role was in the operation. What is telling is that he called him Charles. Why is that significant, cadet?"

"When he got involved with the gang he didn't realise he would need a fake name?" Ruth answered.

"Or they already knew what his real name was," Riley muttered.

"What about the radiators in the cart?" Ruth asked.

"They're junk. Camouflage," Mitchell said. "But I did find a scavenging licence inside the house that had Hailey Lyons's name on it, and that is interesting. If they'd shown it to us we might have gone away."

"Instead they shot at us," Ruth said.

"No," Riley said. "Emmitt signalled to Turnbull to shoot at us. Did he recognise you?"

"I didn't recognise him," Mitchell said. "And with a face like that I'm sure I would. But it's possible. Certainly there's some reason why he decided not to brazen it out. I did get Turnbull to admit that there are two bodies buried in the paddock. There may be more. From what he says they sound like people who were in the wrong place at the wrong time. We'll know more when we've exhumed the bodies. I'm starting to regret offering him a deal."

"Can you really do that?" Ruth asked. "Offer him that kind of deal, I mean?"

"Technically? No. But I can ask a favour of the people who can. I was being honest about his chances if we place him in a cell. I doubt he'd make it to trial. And now, cadet, we brace ourselves to answer a lot of questions." He pointed towards the plume of dust approaching along the track. It soon resolved into a column of Marines running almost at a sprint towards them. At the front, easily keeping up, was Captain Weaver.

"She got here fast," Mitchell said.

"We have a suspect inside, another dead in the field over there. Two other men got away," the sergeant said, speaking more to the major than to Captain Weaver. "A man named Emmitt took to the woods on foot. He's armed with an automatic rifle. Old-world. Optical sight. Another escaped on a horse, heading in that direction. His name's Clipton. He's about—"

"Emmitt and Clipton. You've got the descriptions?" Weaver cut in.

"Yes ma'am," the major said, and went to deploy his troops.

"You know what they look like?" Mitchell asked.

"What do you think I've been doing with my time?" she snapped. "You said Turnbull's inside?"

"That's right," Mitchell said.

"Fine." She pushed open the door. "No," she added. "You three stay out here."

Ruth looked at Riley, she at Mitchell. He stared at the ground, his mouth chewing on nothing, as if he was eating the words he desperately wanted to shout. After a few minutes there was a yell.

"Mitchell! Inside."

"Excuse me," the sergeant said, and pushed open the door.

Ruth watched the Marines as they split into three groups. One deployed in a loose ring around the house, another ran towards the woods, the third double-timed it across the paddock in the direction Clipton had gone.

"Maybe they'll catch them," Ruth said.

Before Riley could answer, there was a fusillade of swearing from inside the house, followed a moment later by Mitchell barging through the door.

"Come on. Time for us to go," he said.

"Sir?" Riley asked.

"That…" Mitchell began. He shook his head. "We're…" he tried again, but words seemed to escape him. He shrugged and stormed off towards the track. Ruth helped Riley to her feet, and they followed the sergeant.

They'd reached the point where the track joined the old road before Mitchell brought his bike to a halt and threw himself off it. Ruth pulled on her brakes a dozen paces from the sergeant, watching as he paced up and down, fists clenching and unclenching. Finally, it was Riley who spoke.

"Is it that bad?"

"She wouldn't honour the deal. Turnbull stopped talking," Mitchell growled. "I'll have to spend the evening finding someone to persuade her to get off her vertiginous horse. In the meantime, Clipton could be halfway to the Thames. I'll admit we might have stumbled across the place by accident, but…" He took a deep breath, and Ruth thought he was going to scream. He didn't. "It is what it is." He picked up his bike and began walking it towards the train line.

"You want to go after Clipton?" Riley asked.

"Emmitt is the one in charge. Or is he?" Mitchell stopped again. "Would a man like that allow someone like Clipton to order him around? Certainly Clipton was the frontman, the one who hired Lyons, Turnbull, Anderson, and whoever else. Emmitt has skills, we saw that. Not just with the rifle, but with the printer as well. There would have had to be a lot of money involved for him to take orders from Clipton."

"Well, there is, isn't there?" Ruth asked. "I mean, he could have printed however much Emmitt wanted to charge."

"Well, that's the point, isn't it?" Mitchell replied. "You saw how Emmitt killed that woman. If he wanted fake currency for himself, he would have shot the others long ago. There was so much money, too much, in fact. If it were to enter the market, it would completely devalue the currency, destroy the economy, and so make itself worthless. Whatever this is about, it isn't money."

"Why would it devalue the currency?" Ruth asked.

Mitchell turned to face her. His expression changed. "I'm sorry," he said.

"I asked why would—"

"No, I heard the question. I mean that I'm sorry. I made an assumption about what those people were up to, I was wrong, and you almost paid the price. I apologise."

"Oh. Right. Um… that's… okay," Ruth said uncertainly.

"No, it's not," Mitchell said. "You could have died."

"So could I," Riley muttered.

Mitchell waved that away. "When I—" he began and stopped. "This isn't what—" Again he stopped. He sighed. "Let's get back." He started walking again. "When I saw the dead body, I assumed this was going to be a simple case. I imagined it was the idle fantasy of some group of ageing physicists who saw it as an easy way of getting rich. They'd teamed up with a younger crowd and, inevitably, they'd turned on each other. Had I known then what we know now, I would have left you at Police House."

And again Ruth was at a loss as to what she should say. "I'm glad I came," she finally said. "I mean, I know I wasn't much use—"

"You arrested Lyons," Mitchell said. "That was impressive."

"For all the good it did," Ruth said, as an image of the dead woman's face came back to her. "But why didn't Emmitt shoot me?"

"A good question. One of many. Let us be thankful that there are enough to keep us busy for some time."

"Then we're still investigating?" Ruth asked.

"Of course. When they start shooting, you know you're on the right track. The question is what line of enquiry we should follow next."

Ruth waited to see if he would go on, but though the sergeant's lips moved, he kept his thoughts to himself.

They reached the old main road, along which the new train line had been laid, and turned their bikes towards the city. Ruth was still running over the events of the afternoon when a whistle pierced the air behind them. Mitchell stepped onto the tracks as a train approached. It came to a screeching halt, but not before the sergeant had to jump out of the way.

"What do you think—" the driver began, but stopped his angry tirade when he saw Ruth's face, still covered in dried blood.

"Tell the train to stop," Ruth heard Mitchell say. She opened her eyes, and only then did she realise she'd fallen asleep.

"We don't stop until we get to the main station," the driver replied.

"I said stop the train," Mitchell said, his voice tempestuously calm.

As the driver applied the brakes, Ruth looked around, trying to spot what Mitchell had seen, but it looked like they were in the middle of nowhere.

"This is as close as we get to your house, cadet," Mitchell said. "Go home. Get some rest. Tomorrow will be a busy day."

She nodded, climbed down, and watched the train disappear. As she walked her bike down the road towards The Acre, she wondered how the sergeant had known where she lived. She supposed he must have looked at her file the previous evening. That was something, she supposed. As was Weaver's arrival at the crime scene. There was no need to inform anyone as to what Mitchell was up to now. That led her to wonder how Weaver had arrived at the house so quickly, and with so many Marines who knew what Emmitt and Clipton looked like.

Chapter 7
The Mint
19th September

"Early again!" Maggie said as Ruth opened the door. "If I knew you were going to finish at this time, I'd have asked you to pick up the— what happened to your face?"

Ruth half raised a hand before she remembered it was covered in blood.

"It's not mine," she said. "I… I better wash."

The woman's screams woke her. Ruth sat up, listening. The screams were still there, but only inside her head. She wondered whose they were. There was a vague memory of a face, not so much a shape she could see but an echo that she could almost feel. Then it was gone, replaced by that of Hailey Lyons, Charles Anderson, and then of Emmitt, their faces going around and around like some twisted kaleidoscope. She shook her head, trying to clear it.

She was in her room. The world outside her window was dark, though there was a soft, flickering glow coming from around the bottom of the door. She sat up and swung her legs off the bed. She recalled going to wash, and at some point she'd changed, but she couldn't remember what had happened after that. Had she eaten? Her stomach growled no. She stood and opened the door.

The light was coming from the kitchen. Maggie was sitting in her chair by the fire, a candle in the window, another on the table. Next to it was a teapot and two empty cups.

"You're awake, then," she said. "And probably hungry. I'll make you something."

"Two cups," Ruth said. "You had visitors?"

"Sergeant Mitchell came round."

"He did?" Ruth asked.

"He was worried," Maggie said. "He told me what happened. I can't say I'm happy about it. This is not what I thought you'd be doing when you joined the academy. It was meant to be knocking on doors and filling in forms. It was meant to be safe. Not dead bodies, and people being shot in front of you."

"It is what it is," Ruth murmured.

"You got that from Mitchell," Maggie said. "And you've not known him long enough to be copying his mannerisms. I don't suppose there's any point trying to talk you out of going back?"

Ruth caught the inflection. "I don't know. I mean, no, there's no point trying to persuade me. But I don't know." She shook her head, trying to turn illusive emotions into coherent thoughts. "I have to go in tomorrow. There'll be an enquiry, and I'll have to give a statement. After that, well, maybe the choice won't be mine."

Maggie sighed. "It's today, dear, not tomorrow. Dawn's not far off."

"It's not?" She looked at her watch. It was coming up to half past four.

"Why don't you tell me what happened?" Maggie said. So Ruth did, finishing at the same time as dawn properly arrived.

"It's big, isn't it?" Ruth asked. "I mean, there have to be more people involved."

"Which means it's not over. From what you've said, it's barely begun. If you're going in, then you better leave now. But I'll say this. Work out why and you might get a better idea of who."

Which, Ruth reflected as she wheeled her bike down the road and away from the house, wasn't very helpful advice. She turned her mind to the bigger question of whether she wanted a career in policing. The simple answer was the same one that she'd had since she'd applied: no. She'd gone to the academy because joining the police had seemed like the easiest way of getting out of the city and seeing some of the world. The only reason to stick with it now was the paycheque she'd get in three months' time. She thought back to the forged twenty-pound note she'd taken and almost regretted not keeping it. Did that mean she wasn't cut out for policing? Certainly she wasn't motivated by any grand notions of law and justice. At the same time, she didn't want to stop, not until they'd caught Emmitt.

When Ruth entered the cabin in the yard of Police House, Mitchell was already there.

"Sleep well?" he asked.

"Some," she said. "You came to the house last night."

"I did," he said. "I wanted to check you were okay. Ours is a violent job, cadet. By its nature we see people at their worst and see the worst they are capable of. You shouldn't take that as a model for what the world is truly like. Try to find some small act of kindness that you've witnessed and make it the last thing you think about before you go to sleep."

She nodded politely and then took a proper look at the sergeant. He'd changed his uniform, but hadn't shaved. "Did *you* get any sleep last night?" she asked.

"Some," he said, echoing her own reply with a trace of a smile. "Riley and I went to the Marquis. The pub by the docks that Turnbull mentioned, you remember?"

"Vaguely," she said. "I thought she had a concussion."

"When she gets it into her head to do something, nothing can stop her, which is why I went with her."

"I could have gone with you, too," she said.

"To the pub? No, you're too young. You'd have got too much attention, and of the wrong kind."

"Oh. Did you learn anything?"

"In a way. A lot of regulars have stopped coming in over the last few months. Possibly they've gone away, gone straight, or just stopped going to that pub, but perhaps they were hired like Turnbull was. Riley is following up on some of those."

"What happened to him?"

"Turnbull? He's in the cells somewhere. Or he was when I got in a few hours ago."

"Shall we go and question him?" she asked.

"We'll have to wait until we're invited by Weaver," Mitchell said. "I've put in the request, and maybe it'll be granted. Maybe."

"Well, should I go and help Riley, then?"

"You wouldn't find her," Mitchell said, "and when she's done she'll go home to sleep. Besides, I'm afraid you have an appointment with the commissioner."

"What? Why?"

"Don't worry. The commissioner is, technically, to whom Serious Crimes reports, and that means he's the one who takes the official statements. I doubt he'll actually do it himself. It'll be a secretary or someone. Tell them the truth though I'd ask that you don't mention Isaac. If Weaver gets wind of it, she'll go looking for him, and I'd rather she focused on the job in hand. You fired six shots, remember."

"Yes, sir," she said.

The commissioner had an office in what had been the headmaster's study when the building was a school. Ruth nervously presented herself to the secretary and was shocked when she was ushered into the commissioner's private study. Commissioner Wallace was a man of average height, grey hair, and a kindly face that was currently peering at a sheaf of papers on the desk in front of him.

"Ah, Deering, please come in. Sit down."

Ruth looked around. There were two leather armchairs by an unlit fire, and another chair in front of the desk.

"Over there," the commissioner said, pointing towards the armchairs. "Can I offer you some tea? Or coffee?"

"No, sir. Thank you. Sir," Ruth stammered.

"If you're sure? Fine, just give me a moment." He turned his attention back to the papers on his desk.

As she perched on the edge of the chair, Ruth tried to remain at attention. She'd seen the commissioner before, of course, and most recently at the graduation ceremony, but she'd never spoken to the man. She'd never considered it, let alone dared.

"There, done," Wallace said. He crossed the room to sit opposite her. "If I'd known there was so much paperwork involved, I would never have taken the job. I thought that it would be all catching villains and foiling plots. Ah, but I was wrong. It seems, however, that is exactly what you have been up to these past few days. Relax, please, you're not in trouble. No one is. You've managed to expose a particularly dangerous plot, but we have formalities to follow. Tell me what happened."

So, for the second time that morning, and excluding the part about Isaac, Ruth did.

"Excellent," the commissioner said. "That matches Mitchell's account closely enough that we can call it the official version of the events. I've something for you to sign to that effect."

He stood, went to his desk, and came back with a piece of paper and a pen. He handed them to her. It was a typed account of the events of the previous day which broadly matched the story she'd just told him. Starting to feel as if she was at least a few hours behind everyone else, she signed her name at the bottom.

"That's one more piece of paper to be filed away and probably never read," the commissioner said. "Have you seen the newspaper this morning?"

She shook her head. He took a copy from his desk. On the front page were two sketches, one of Clipton, the other of Emmitt.

"They're not as good as photographs, but it's close enough," he said. "We started running them in the evening edition yesterday. I doubt it will do much beyond keeping the two men away from the train stations, but hope springs eternal."

Ruth focused on the headline above the pictures.

"It says they're wanted for murder," she said.

"We had to tell the newspaper what was really going on, damn free press and all that, but they won't run the real story. Not yet. You know why?"

She thought back and remembered something Mitchell had said. "It would destroy the currency?" she said.

"Precisely. Or it would destroy all confidence in it, and that would do as much damage as if the notes had been scattered about the countryside, there for anyone to collect. Ours is a fragile economy, cadet, tied to a standard of goodwill and expectation. The last thing we need is people rushing to the shops to convert their currency to canned food and candles and all the other more reliably tradable goods. But would you like to know the great irony in this?"

"Um… yes?"

"If we were to tell the populace that we'd broken up this counterfeiting ring, their response would be to withdraw their savings en masse. Since the Mint doesn't have enough currency on hand, we would have to use those forged notes to meet demand. I pointed that out to Mr Grammick. He wasn't amused. No sense of humour, that man."

Not knowing to whom he was referring, Ruth wasn't sure if she should agree, so instead she asked, "How much of the counterfeit money is in circulation?"

"Ah, we don't know. Not yet. They've begun sampling the notes that come into the bank, and we should have a better idea over the next few days. But, that isn't why I wanted to speak to you. Do you know why Mitchell is only a sergeant?"

"No sir," she said.

"Well, firstly, he wasn't always a sergeant. He was one of the original police officers before we had ranks and when our only laws were those ancient ones that dictate the difference between good and evil. But a few years ago he went wandering. I don't know why, or where he went, but he came back. He was made a captain, and then… suffice it to say that he has made some new enemies to add to a long list of old ones. I created the Serious Crimes Unit in the hope that a few years behind a desk might mellow him. I thought he might realise that the world has changed, that policing had changed. We have an academy. We have courts and trials, appeals and paroles. We have ranks and procedures. There is no place for his brand of rough justice. Not any more. I hoped he would realise this was something to be welcomed, but some people can't change. He is a good detective, I will grant you that, but he is reckless and has no regard for the chain of command. His greatest problem, however, is that I will be leaving soon, as will a number of others who owe him favours. Some are retiring whereas I will be returning to Parliament. The Prime Minister is standing down. I know that every summer there are rumours that she'll resign by Christmas, but this time it will happen. She's only waiting until the trade deal with the Americas is signed. When she leaves, I will take her seat in the House. I was a political appointment, here to bring some order to the law, as the law brought order to our nation. When I'm gone, there will be no one left to cover for Mitchell. This isn't a threat, cadet. It's a warning that I've already given him too many times to count. He won't change, nor will he change what he's planning to do. Regardless of what I say, he will continue with his own investigation. You were lucky yesterday, but luck never holds. Keep me informed, and I will keep a platoon of Marines ready to support you the next time he plans anything like the events of yesterday. When he does, come and tell me first. Agreed?"

"Yes, sir," she said. She didn't have an alternative.

"Very good. And take a message to Mitchell for me. Mr Grammick of the Mint wishes to see him at ten o'clock this morning. They're conducting their own investigation and have some questions they'd like answered. It's a formality, of course, but accountability is the difference between a police force and a street gang. Hmm. Yes…" He walked back to his desk, sat, picked up a pen, and wrote that line down. "Dismissed," he added, his eyes on the piece of paper.

Ruth saluted and left. She walked stiffly out of the office, past the secretary, along the corridor, and outside. She couldn't decide whether she wanted to slump with relief or despair, but the courtyard was too busy for her to do either. A trustee, a woman with hair so golden it looked almost white, was collecting leaves from around the drain. A few yards from her, three officers were loading five prisoners into a cart. One of the officers raised a hand in greeting. It was Simon Longfield, another in her class in the academy who'd been stationed in Twynham. In his case, it *had* been because of his parents. They were something important in industry and had ensured he got a relatively safe posting in Police House.

Ruth was about to raise a hand in return when one of the prisoners began yelling obscenities at the trustee. The woman baulked, shying away until she was cowering against the wall. Simon turned back to his charges, hurrying them onto the cart.

Ruth sighed. Simon was a friend, and though he would have had questions of his own, he might have been able to answer some of hers. Almost reluctantly, she headed back to the cabin.

"You look like you're still in one piece," Mitchell said. "How did it go?"

"I'm…" Ruth hesitated. She considered lying, but though she could play one side off against another, there was only so long she could stay in the middle. "I'm to inform on you," she said. "Or to keep the commissioner informed of whatever you're planning to do. He thinks you're going to keep on investigating, and that's going to end up with you being kicked out of the police."

"He said as much to me. Said I was antediluvian, and that I should be put out to grass. I hope you said you'd spy on me for him."

That wasn't the response she'd expected. "I did," she said. "And he said that he'd keep some Marines ready in case we need them."

"Good. He's a decent man. Too much of a politician for me to call him a friend, but he's always struck me as honest. That's as rare in policing as it is anywhere else. Now, the real question is whether you learned anything of use to the investigation."

"Have you seen the newspaper?" she asked.

"I did. Two murderers on the loose." He picked up his own copy. "Pretty good likenesses."

"Which means Captain Weaver must have been close to catching them," Ruth said.

"Not that close. I spoke to some of the Marines. They said she'd had them on standby but didn't know where to send them. The commissioner didn't let slip how Weaver knew what they looked like?"

"No, sir. But he did say you've a meeting at the Mint at ten a.m. They're conducting an internal investigation and want you to answer some questions."

"Or they want someone to answer some questions, and the commissioner thinks this will keep me busy. Well, why not. I'm free now, and you are coming with me."

"I am?"

"Until Riley comes in, or we hear from Isaac, or Weaver deigns to allow us to speak to Turnbull, we've no leads to follow." He swept his jacket from the back of the chair and marched outside. Ruth followed.

The Mint, like Police House and most of the other government departments, was in the centre of the old town of Christchurch. Like the others, it had been established in whatever buildings had been left undamaged after The Blackout. In the case of the Mint, it was an old bank and the supermarket next door. The bank part was still used as that, and Ruth had even been inside once. She'd queued up with Maggie as her mother waited to withdraw her teacher's salary for that month.

As she followed the sergeant through the leaf-blown streets, Ruth tried to remember when that had been. Seven years ago? Five? Eight? She wasn't sure. It was around the time that the first sets of paper banknotes were issued. Not the ones they had now, but the larger, cruder types. She remembered being excited about the idea. That had dissipated as they'd queued for a teller and then had to wait as Maggie's pay book was checked. Then there was an almost interminable delay while a paltry few notes were counted, recounted, and counted again. Ruth's overwhelming memory was of an anti-climax, made worse when she'd seen the goods for sale in the indoor market opposite. She thought that had been around Christmas, but in her memory the day had been warm. Since then, another branch of the bank had opened near the fishing quay, and it was there that Maggie cashed her cheque.

Inside the doors, beyond a pair of unarmed security guards, were two queues, one for deposits, another for withdrawals. Behind the tellers, Ruth could see scores of people with heads bent low over desks. She couldn't even guess at what they were doing.

"Cadet?" Mitchell prompted.

In the far corner, a young man sat at a desk that blocked the entrance to a set of doors behind him.

"Sergeant Mitchell. Officer Deering. We have an appointment with Mr Grammick."

"Yes of course," the man said without glancing down at the ledger in front of him. "But you're rather early. You'll have to wait."

"I don't think so," Mitchell said. "I have an autopsy in thirty minutes. Have you ever seen a corpse on a slab, the body cut open from neck to navel?" He leaned forward and pressed a finger against the man's throat and then drew it down his chest. "The sound of the rib cage cracking is something you never forget."

"I'll... I'll just... Excuse me." The man hurried away.

"Knowing how to communicate is essential to good policing," Mitchell said, a gleam in his eye.

The lines in front of the tellers shrank as customers were served and grew as more came in. There seemed to be more deposits than withdrawals. Presumably it was from the previous day's trading. Money was something that they'd never had much of while Ruth had been growing up, and so it wasn't something to which she'd ever given much thought. She watched as a trader passed a thick envelope to the teller. The woman's head nodded, and her lips silently moved as the money was counted, then recounted. She gave a firmer nod in agreement at the amount, before something was passed across the desk, signed, passed back, and countersigned. The trader took her receipt and left, but not without a few uncertain glances back at the teller.

"One more minute, and we're going," Mitchell said. "Time it."

The door opened, someone came in, someone went out, and the lines concertinaed again. Twenty, thirty, forty seconds. Ruth heard a noise behind her. The clerk was holding the door open for the same woman who'd come with Captain Weaver to the cabin the day before.

"Ms Standage, isn't it?" Mitchell asked.

"Mrs. Mrs Standage," the woman replied.

She wore the same outfit as the previous day, and her hair was almost out of place. She looked as if she'd not slept.

"And is our appointment with you?" Mitchell asked.

"With Mr Grammick, he'll be with us in a moment. This way, please."

Her tone was distracted. No, Ruth thought, not distracted, the woman was alert, and her posture was rigid, but she seemed preoccupied. So did everyone else whom they passed. Some rushed one way, some the other. Presumably it all stemmed from the discovery of the counterfeiting, but was there a purpose to it, or was everyone simply trying to look busy? Then Ruth noticed the woman's shoes. They were the same odd pair she'd been wearing the day before.

"In here." Mrs Standage indicated a small, windowless room with a table and four chairs. "Please, have a seat."

Mitchell took one facing the door. Ruth sat next to him. Mrs Standage sat down with obvious reluctance.

"You're in charge of quality control, is that right?" Mitchell asked.

There was a pause. "Yes," Mrs Standage finally said.

Ruth thought the sergeant would ask her to clarify what that meant. He didn't.

"Do you have children?" he asked instead.

"Yes," she answered immediately. "A... a son."

"How old is he?"

"Six." It came out in a whisper.

"That's a good age," Mitchell said. "When they're still asking questions but are old enough to understand some of the answers."

There was a slight curl to Mrs Standage's lips, as if she was about to smile, but the door opened before she could.

"Ah, detectives!" a ruddy faced man barked as he came into the room. Behind him was another clerk, this one holding a tray with two cups. The tray was placed on the table.

"Is that coffee?" Mitchell asked, taking what must have been an involuntary sniff.

"It is. It is," the man said. "The real stuff. I thought you might like a cup. A taste of home. You're from America, aren't you, sergeant?"

"A long time ago," Mitchell said, eyeing the steaming cups. "And you are Mr Ian Grammick, deputy director of the Mint and special advisor to the Chancellor."

"Ah, so you've done your homework, too," Grammick said. If anything, his smile grew wider. "That will be all, Bailey," he added. The clerk left. "Yes," Grammick continued. "I have special responsibility for inflation, or seeing that there isn't any. As such, any matter that threatens the stability of the currency comes into my remit. As for the Royal Mint, I am in charge of circulation, so counterfeiting is very much my bailiwick."

The *Royal* Mint, Ruth noted. Britain had been a monarchy, and technically it still was, though there had been no head on which to hang a crown for the last two decades. No one bothered with the word, whether it was for the Mint, the Marines, or the Mail. Similarly, no one remarked on the portrait of a long dead monarch on the reverse of the banknotes, or how all ships were christened as 'HMS' but referred to as 'SS' from the moment the gangplank was raised. No one Ruth knew, anyway.

"Is there much counterfeiting?" Ruth asked.

"Oh, people try all the time, but it's rare for us to find false currency actually in circulation. Please, do try the coffee. It was a gift from the American ambassador. It's from Puerto Rico, or Costa Rica. I don't recall which. They've started cultivating the wild plantations there."

"Really?" Mitchell asked. "I'm surprised they have the resources."

"It's for trade," Grammick said, clearly pleased at being able to demonstrate his knowledge, and thus his proximity to the centre of power. "It's part of the deal they'll formally sign at the end of the week."

"We're getting real coffee in exchange for food? That doesn't seem like a fair trade at all," Ruth said.

"Ah, this is only part of it. A small part, and really the most insignificant, but as a symbol it will be the most tangible."

"I'll believe that when I see it in the shops," Mitchell said. "How many forged twenty-pound notes have you found in circulation?"

"What? None," Grammick said. "That's right isn't it?"

"Yes, sir," Mrs Standage said. "I… as I understand it, the criminals were stockpiling the currency, not spending it."

"That's not strictly true," Mitchell said. "We know of at least some notes being used to purchase clothing in July."

"Really? In July?" There was a crack in Grammick's bombastic demeanour.

"Deering, why don't you tell Mr Grammick what we've discovered?" Mitchell said as he picked up a cup and took a sip.

Ruth went through the events of the past two days again. She kept the explanation brief. Even so, Mitchell had finished the first cup and had started on the second before she'd reached the point where they'd arrested Turnbull.

"Well, broadly, that is the account we had from Captain Weaver," Grammick said when Ruth had finished. "And from what you say I doubt more than a very small amount of forged currency has entered circulation. I don't think we need to worry. Do we?" He looked to Mitchell for an answer.

The sergeant took a long gulp, draining the second cup before answering. "That's really for you to determine," he said.

Grammick turned to look at Mrs Standage.

"I don't… I have some questions," she said.

"Go ahead," Mitchell said.

She glanced at a sheet of paper before speaking. "Do you think there could be more than one printer?"

"Person or machine?" Mitchell replied. "It doesn't matter, the answer's the same. There could be. You'll have to ask Captain Weaver. She's in charge of the investigation."

"But what do you think?" Grammick asked.

"Why not?" Mitchell said with a shrug. "Certainly, if I was you, I'd assume so."

"Yes. Yes, I suppose you would," Grammick said. "Well, we were planning on issuing new notes, and we're bringing those plans forward. We should have most of the currency replaced by Christmas." Again he looked to Mrs Standage for confirmation.

123

"By the first of December," she corrected him.

"I hope that will be soon enough," Mitchell said. "Did you have any other questions?"

Mrs Standage looked blank, as if she'd forgotten the list of questions on the table in front of her. "Did you..." She looked down. "Did you see any evidence as to where the paper came from?"

"Anywhere other than the official mill, you mean? No," Mitchell said. "Do you think it was stolen?"

"Possibly," Grammick replied. "There was a flood about six months ago in which a lot of stock was destroyed. Or we thought it was destroyed. Was it six months ago?"

"In April," Mrs Standage said.

"That's the theory we have at the moment," Grammick said.

"How much paper do you keep on hand?" Mitchell asked.

"Enough to meet the needs of every depositor," Grammick said.

It wasn't really an answer, Ruth thought, and surely paper might be ruined in a flood, but it wouldn't disappear. She was about to ask that, but Mitchell spoke before she could.

"What about ink, how much is missing?" the sergeant asked.

"That, I don't know," Grammick said. "You'd have to ask someone at the chemical works."

"You don't do the printing here?" Mitchell asked.

"Oh, we do. Downstairs. But the ink is delivered once a week. We only receive what we need, and we always use it all."

"It's delivered on Fridays," Mrs Standage said, almost automatically.

"Can't you just recall all the twenty-pound notes?" Ruth asked. "I mean, that was all they seemed to be printing."

"We can't do that," Grammick said. "People will ask questions, and we won't be able to give them an answer that won't result in them trading the money for goods. Without confidence, the currency will collapse, and so will this trade deal. That is critical. I can't say any more than that."

"I see. Well, I think that covers it," Mitchell said. "For now. Thank you for your time, and the coffee. If you've more questions about the investigation I suggest you ask Captain Weaver. If we have any more, rest assured, we'll be in touch."

He stood and held out his hand.

"I… but…" Grammick began, the smile slipping from his lips for a fraction of a second. "Of course," he said, standing. He shook Mitchell's hand. "Thank you."

"Not a word," Mitchell said as they left the Mint. "Not yet."

He peered at the doors for a moment, then at the buildings on the other side of the increasingly busy street. "This way."

He led her down the road that led along the south side of the Mint. They followed the wall until they reached a wide iron gate at the back of the building. Inside was a loading bay from when it had been a supermarket. Outside, watching them with bored interest, were two armed Marines.

"Morning," Mitchell said. "Are you usually on duty here?"

The two sentries looked at one another.

"Let me rephrase that," Mitchell said. "Were you deployed here yesterday? You can just nod if you like."

The Marines exchanged another look. Finally, one answered. "Yes. There's someone on duty night and day."

"And inside as well? I thought so. Do the staff use this door?"

"If they did, they don't anymore," the sentry said.

"They just use the front, the one for the bank?" Mitchell asked.

The Marine gave another nod.

"Interesting. Interesting," Mitchell muttered. "Thank you for your time." He continued walking, and Ruth continued biting down on the growing number of questions until they'd looped the building and were back on the main road.

"The market," Mitchell said, and then proceeded to lead her through it to a doorway between two stalls, both selling nearly identical cuts of venison. The door led to a branch of the National Store, this one selling nothing but crockery in every colour of the rainbow, alongside a few that weren't.

"Dmitri," Mitchell said, addressing the stout man behind the counter. He glanced around the shop, checking it was empty. "Do you still keep that room upstairs?"

"It's only temporary," Dmitri said. "There's a problem with the drains at—"

"Don't care. We need the room. No questions." Mitchell pulled a one-pound note from his pocket and placed it on the counter. It disappeared immediately and was replaced by a key.

"This way." Mitchell led Ruth up a rickety staircase and along a dark corridor to a chipped door. He unlocked it, and they stepped into a surprisingly large and well-furnished room.

"Dmitri's been living here since they got electricity in the shop," Mitchell said, by way of explanation. He dragged an armchair close to the window and pulled back the curtain. "That's got to be at least eight years ago, but it's always only temporary, until some emergency repair is finished on his house. Yes, there's a good view of the Mint from here. You can see the door, and anyone who comes out. Good. All right, cadet, tell me what you made of that little meeting."

"Um, well, Mr Grammick didn't seem to know very much."

"No. Maybe he's very good at something, but it isn't paying attention to the fine details. What else?"

"I don't think they know where the paper or ink went missing from."

"It's probably been stolen from right under their noses. I doubt Grammick's ever heard of stock control. Anything else?"

Ruth thought. "You suspect someone there of being involved, don't you?"

"I know it," Mitchell said.

"It's Mrs Standage, isn't it?" Ruth said.

"Why do you say that?"

Partly it was because Ruth didn't think it was Grammick, and that didn't leave many other people for Mitchell to have become so suddenly suspicious of.

"It's the clothes," she said, "specifically the shoes. They're the same odd pair she wore yesterday, and that means she didn't go home."

"She has a six-year-old son," Mitchell said. "I could believe that she hasn't had much sleep, but she has to have slept somewhere, if only for a few hours. Yet she didn't go home. While there are plenty of innocent explanations for that, the truly villainous one is more believable. Forget the paper and ink. Those could have been stolen by one of a hundred different people, perhaps someone who took the job purely for that purpose. Think about the designs, and the image on the computer back in that house. Someone stole that. Now think about how they discovered those notes were forged. The serial numbers had yet to be issued. Someone with access to the designs should have realised that. Had they used old numbers no one would have known unless they had the original and forgery side-by-side. No, I think that the insider wanted the forgery to be discovered. I fear this crime has taken a sudden dark twist, so I will sit and watch and wait, and then I will follow. If Mrs Standage didn't go home last night, perhaps she won't tonight." He took out his pad and scrawled a note. "This is Riley's address. If she's not there try Police House. Bring her back here, but I want you both out of uniform."

"Sir, the commissioner said I should keep him informed."

"Yes, but at the moment there is nothing to tell him. When we do have something, rest assured, I will send you for his Marines. But not yet."

Chapter 8
Self-defence

"Scone?" Riley asked, offering the bag to Ruth. She shook her head and kept her eyes fixed on the door to the Mint. Almost as soon as she and Riley had arrived at the small apartment opposite the Mint, Mitchell had disappeared on an errand of his own. That had been... she glanced at her watch. Two hours ago. In that time, along with customers coming and going to the bank, some employees had left the Mint, but Standage wasn't among them.

Ruth wondered if she'd made the right decision. Time would tell, and that was what was worrying her. Riley's address in hand, she'd left Mitchell, but she'd not gone to the constable's home. She'd returned to Police House and gone to speak to the commissioner. He'd been surprised to see her. She couldn't tell how much of that was due to how quickly she'd returned and how much to that she'd returned at all. He'd asked she keep him informed, and barely two minutes after she'd stepped into his office, she was out again, finally heading towards Riley's home.

The constable lived in a small cottage on the far side of the old priory. From what Ruth could see, she had the entirety of it to herself. Riley had taken the message in her stride. She'd made coffee – the ersatz kind – washed, dressed, and packed a bag with food almost before Ruth had changed into the set of borrowed clothes.

Ruth shifted in her seat, trying to find a position where her revolver, now holstered at her back and hidden under a calf-length coat, didn't dig into her spine. The borrowed clothes seemed to be both too large and too small at the same time. She supposed that was a blessing, or she would have fallen asleep long before.

"It's important to eat," Riley said, pushing the paper bag almost under Ruth's nose.

"Thank you," she said, taking a scone. "They're very nice," she added after taking a bite. They tasted identical to every scone she'd ever had. "Did you make them yourself?"

"A gift from the baker. I don't have time to cook. Don't see the point. Not when there are people who spend their lives learning how to do it properly."

Ruth nodded, but couldn't think of anything else to say. It wasn't that she didn't have questions – like how a detective constable could afford a cottage that had both mains water *and* electric lights – but those didn't matter.

Had she done the right thing in going to the commissioner? Ruth wasn't sure. She wasn't sure of anything except that a year of training had in no way prepared her for the job she was now doing. What she wanted was some simple, mundane task that would keep her hands busy while her brain could focus on her future.

"You all right?" Riley asked.

"I was thinking about yesterday," Ruth said, and it was a quarter true.

"Try not to."

"How's your head?" Ruth asked. Riley was wearing a baggy cap, the edge of a thin bandage visible underneath.

"I've had worse."

Silence returned.

"Did you find anything at the pub? The Marquis?" Ruth asked after another tedious hour had passed.

"Possibly," Riley said. A minute went by. Just as Ruth had decided to give up on any further attempts at conversation, Riley continued. "There are between twelve and fourteen criminals who haven't been seen in over a month. They're the casual, do-any-job-for-the-right-price type who could be involved in anything. Or they could have gone straight. Depending on whether Lefty Johnson is a different person from Two-Fingers Johnson, one or two people were last seen heading to Kent to pick apples. To find out where the rest of them went will take a week, maybe two."

"It's a lead though," Ruth said.

"Maybe. It won't tell us where they are now, and I think anyone involved in this crime is destined for nothing more than a shallow grave. Remember what happened to Hailey Lyons?"

Ruth couldn't forget, no matter how hard she tried.

"It's definitely Standage," Mitchell said before the door to the room had closed behind him. "Her house is dark, and no one's been there for at least the last two nights. Possibly longer, depending on which neighbour you ask."

"Any sign of a struggle?" Riley asked.

"No. But someone did go inside and look around. I'd say it was more a mission of curiosity than a thorough search."

"Could it be a marital dispute?" Riley asked.

"You mean that her husband could have taken their son away, and she hasn't reported it? I don't think so," Mitchell said. "Abduction is more likely. Specifically, I suspect she was blackmailed into giving them the designs, and perhaps access to the ink and paper, and then pressured into providing information about the case. Either because of Anderson's death, or because of whatever event triggered Anderson to steal that money in the first place, extra leverage was needed. Her child was kidnapped, the husband taken to look after the boy. Of course, this means that all three are likely to be killed as soon as she's no longer useful. That will be soon."

"Isn't that a leap, sir," Ruth said. "I mean…"

"Go on, say it," Mitchell said.

"Well, it seems like you're trying to get the facts to fit your theory," Ruth said. "She could have been having an affair and the husband could have had enough and gone to stay with family in Wales or somewhere. Or maybe she's the one orchestrating the whole thing."

"If it was the second, it's unlikely she would have come in to work," Mitchell said. "And it's even more unlikely she would have used serial numbers that had yet to be issued. As to your first point, Mr Standage is a surveyor for the Electric Company, and hasn't been seen at work. He would have told them if he was going away, or written to them after he'd left. We have someone who works at the Electric Company, and another who works at the Mint. That fills in some of the gaps that Turnbull couldn't. And that," he added as Ruth opened her mouth to utter another protest, "brings me to the last piece of news. Turnbull is dead."

"How?" Riley asked.

"Suicide. Poison. A capsule he had hidden in a button on his coat. That is the story being told in Police House. I don't buy it."

"But he was in custody," Ruth said.

"Exactly," Mitchell said. "Which means that if it wasn't suicide, they have someone on the inside."

"In the police?" Ruth couldn't believe it.

"Why not?" Mitchell replied. "If there can be an insider in the Mint, then why not the police?" He peered out the window. "The work day will finish soon. Standage will come out. We'll follow her. We'll question her, and then... I don't know. We've only got a handful of pieces, and that isn't enough to even tell what game is being played."

At half-past four, the door to the bank was closed. The last few customers trickled out until, at a few minutes after five, the employees began leaving, mingling with workers from the other offices nearby.

"No. Not yet. That's not her," Mitchell muttered. The flood slowed, until, by half past, the road was almost empty. "There," he said. "That's her."

But Ruth had already seen her. Standage stood by the door, looking up and down the street.

"Is she waiting for someone?" Ruth asked.

"I'm not— No, there she goes," Mitchell said. "She's heading south. Riley?"

The constable left.

"Now you," Mitchell said. "And remember what I told you."

Ruth nodded and hurried from the room. Mitchell's instructions had been brief. Riley, who Standage had never met, would follow the woman. Ruth, who Standage probably wouldn't recognise, would follow Riley from a distance of no closer than fifty yards. Mitchell would follow Ruth.

Beyond that, the sergeant had told her to try to look as if she was heading home after a long, tedious day. That, at least, wasn't hard.

Keeping the constable just in view, Ruth followed her through the centre of town, past market stalls and shops thrumming with after-work passing trade. At first, she thought they were heading towards the old priory, but the constable made an abrupt right turn into a compact terraced street. Another turn, another road, another dirt-trodden street. Large homes were replaced by smaller ones, and then by a row of boarding houses. The roads grew steadily worse as they left the old town of Christchurch behind and headed towards the ruined city of Bournemouth.

No one wanted to live near the glassy crater at the centre of the old city, and even four miles away, houses showed signs of blast damage. There were rough repairs to roofs, and some walls had been propped up, but no one had bothered removing the rubble from where buildings had collapsed. It was home to those people who'd never adjusted to life after The Blackout, yet who'd not given into death even twenty years on. Those lost souls kept their heads down as they tracked a path through the drifts of decaying leaves, their eyes fixed on some distant memory now forever gone.

Riley stopped. Ruth did the same until she saw the constable wave her on.

"She disappeared," Riley said. "Keep walking."

"Do you know where she went?" Ruth asked.

"Down one of the streets we just passed. I don't know which," Riley said.

They kept walking until they reached another junction and found Mitchell waiting there.

"You did a good job, cadet," Mitchell said.

"I did?"

"Yes, you were perfectly conspicuous. If there *had* been anyone keeping an eye on Mrs Standage they would certainly have seen you. There wasn't."

"I was bait?" she asked.

"Don't say it like that," Mitchell said. "You did the job perfectly. Now, we need to find her. It'll be a building nearby. Eyes open. You two take the west. I'll check the east."

A battered sign pinned to the side of an equally battered shop said that they were on Autumn Road. Something jolted in Ruth's memory. She looked around.

"No," Riley hissed. "Eyes down, shoulders slumped. Let your feet drag. Look up every fifth step, then down again, and use that time to think about what you saw."

Ruth thought the almost rhythmic bobbing of her head would have been more noticeable than had she gawked at every building. The more she saw of the district, the more she decided it didn't matter. They passed a shop she thought must have been closed since The Blackout just as a woman shuffled outside, a greasy package under her arm. Across the road was a far larger shop. The chipped paint and plastic sign proclaimed it to be 'Sandy Weathers. Electrical Repairs'. Underneath, though not quite as faded, was another sign in almost the same shade of red. 'And Her Sons'. There was no smoke coming from the chimney. That struck Ruth as odd since the windows were newly boarded up and the building was in better repair than the rest of the street. Then she realised.

"Keep walking," she said.

"What? You've seen it?" Riley asked.

"I think so," Ruth said, and led the constable into the first narrow alley they came to.

"Which one?" Riley asked.

"That shop with the black and red sign out front."

"You sure?" Riley looked up and down the alley, flattened herself against the wall, and then peered around the corner for a fraction of a second. "Why?"

"The sign," Ruth said. "Did you see the sign?"

"Sandy Weathers. Electrical Repairs," Riley said.

"And the other sign. 'And her sons'. Sandy *and her sons*. Andy Anderson. There's no way that can be a coincidence."

Riley took another look.

"Maybe. You stay here. Don't be seen. I'll get Mister Mitchell. No, not like that. Lean against the wall like you've nowhere in the world to go. Hands in your pockets. Slump your shoulders. Better. Stay out of sight."

Ruth did, for about a minute, but she couldn't resist peering around the corner. It looked more like a warehouse than a shop and seemed out of place. From what she could tell from a street where there was more rubble than roofs, most of the properties had been houses.

She pulled her head back from view and checked the time. It had been five minutes. Where were Mitchell and Riley? She peered round the corner again.

The door to the shop opened. She thought she heard something coming from inside. A man stepped out onto the street and closed the door behind him. Ruth wasn't sure, but that sound might have been a child's cry. She told herself not to jump to conclusions, yet she was certain that this was the building into which Standage must have gone.

The man was heading towards her. Ruth ducked out of view and weighed her options. Certainly there was nothing she could do about what was, or wasn't, going on in the shop. Riley would tell Mitchell, and that left Ruth with nothing to do but get backup. If the shop was connected to the crime, then so was the man and wherever he was going to. She would follow him, and then she would go to the commissioner and get the Marines he'd promised. She moved down the alley, into deeper shadows, and waited for the man to walk past. Any second now, she thought. Any second now. It was odd, though, she couldn't hear any footsteps.

"What's a girl like you doin' around 'ere?"

Ruth jumped back. The man stood in the alley's mouth, eight feet from her.

"Nothing," she mumbled, hanging her head. "It's a free country, init?"

"It's never been that. Let me 'ave a look at you." He stepped forward. She stepped back. He laughed. She took another step back.

"Don't make me chase you," he leered.

And she knew there was no point trying to run. He was too close. He would catch her. Where was Mitchell? Where was Riley? Then a voice reminded her that she was police.

"Big mistake," she said, tugging her revolver from under her coat. "I'm police and you're under arrest." The end of the barrel caught on cloth. She wrenched it free. But the man was already moving towards her. The gun was pointing down as his forearm smashed into her chest, and a vice-like grip clamped down on her wrist. As she fell, her finger curled on the trigger. The gun went off, but his grip didn't slacken. His weight on top, she slammed into the ground. Something sharp jarred against her shoulder and she wanted to scream, but his forearm was now pushing down on her neck.

"Bit young for police, aren't you?" he hissed, a mouthful of foetid air blowing into her face.

She tried pulling the trigger again, but her fingers wouldn't work. The pressure around her neck was growing. Her vision was narrowing. All she could see was his face, and she didn't want that to be the last thing she ever saw. With her free hand, she tried to claw at his eyes. He shifted his weight, stamping his knee down on her stomach.

With the sudden, excruciating pain came a memory of Friday afternoons at the academy. The mixture of boxing, wrestling, and riot control was always taught with one eye on the clock, and an assumption that the class was unnecessary. At the end of each session the instructor always finished with a reminder that when all else failed, they had their revolver. But her weapon was useless now.

This was it, she thought. This was death.

No. It couldn't be. Where was Mitchell? Where was Riley? Surely they'd save her. But no one was coming. She was on her own. Live or die. It was down to her.

"And if you've run out of bullets," their instructor had said, "club 'em with the barrel. Hit 'em with something that ain't your fist, unless you want an 'andful of broken bones."

Desperate, she scrabbled with her free hand, searching the ground for something, anything. Her fingers curled around stone. A brick. She swung it up in a ninety-degree arc, straight into the side of the man's face. There wasn't much strength to the blow, yet the man suddenly froze. His eyes widened. His jaw went slack, the hand gripping her wrist went limp, and he collapsed on top of her. The weight knocked the last of the air from her lungs. With her knees as much as her hands, she heaved his body clear, and crabbed away. Somehow the revolver was still in her hand. Gripping it two-handed, she pointed the gun at the man as she gasped for breath.

He was motionless. Unconscious, she thought, except she hadn't hit him that hard. Somehow, the brick was still stuck to the side of his head. Her vision cleared. Understanding dawned. It wasn't a brick. It was a lump of rubble, out of the end of which was a spike. No, half a spike. The other half of that jagged metal rod was now embedded in the man's brain.

She scrabbled away from the corpse until her back was against the wall, and kept moving until she was standing up, leaning against it for support.

He was dead. She'd killed him. Before that had a chance to sink in, a shot rang out. Then another. And she realised that there had been other shots as she'd fought with the man. The gunfire was coming from inside the shop.

She staggered out of the alley, and across the road. She had to investigate. She was police. She had to. Automatically, she reached for the door, pulling it open. She had to go inside. She had to. It was only after she'd stepped into the gloomy interior did she remember to raise her weapon.

To her left was a figure. She swung the barrel around, but again she wasn't fast enough. This man grasped her wrist, but unlike the dead man, his grip was gentle.

"What happened?" Mitchell asked, taking the gun from her hand.

"Someone came out. I killed him," she said. "I had to."

"This way," he said, leading her to a bench. Her foot slipped on something, but Mitchell had an arm at her elbow, catching her before she fell. She sat and looked at the floor. It was covered in dirt and dust, and blood. Two bodies lay near the entrance. Both had been shot. She stared at the bodies for a long minute and realised Mitchell had gone. She stood and walked over to the corpses. She peered at one body and then nudged the other with the toe of her boot until she could see what was left of the face. It didn't look like Emmitt or Clipton. For some reason that struck her as funny. She laughed.

"Come and sit down," Mitchell said.

"Where's Riley?" she asked, shrugging off his hand.

"Taking Standage and her family back to the police station. I thought they'd be safer out in public than in here."

"Standage was here?"

"And so were her husband and son. But I need you over here," Mitchell said.

"You do? Why?" she asked, this time letting him lead her over to a corner of the shop.

"They were expecting a collection this evening." That comment baffled her until she realised his hand was pointing towards the centre of the shop. It took a moment for her eyes to focus on the suitcases piled there.

"Were they going away?" she asked.

"It's the money," Mitchell said, "the cases that were taken from that abandoned house. It's going to be collected tonight. We've got thirty minutes before help arrives. Maybe longer. Keep your eyes on the front door. If they come, we'll have to fight."

She stared at the door. Then she realised her hands were empty. She reached for her holster, but touched unfamiliar cloth instead. Of course, she remembered, she wasn't in uniform, and then everything else came back to her all in a rush. The man, the arm on her neck, the hand on her wrist, the foul, stinking breath. She closed her eyes, but it wouldn't go away.

"It's all right," Mitchell said. "It's over."

Ruth shook her head, not in disagreement, but in an attempt to rid it of the image of the dead man, and the spike sticking out of the side of his head. She opened her eyes wide, gritted her teeth and focused on the door. The sergeant, she realised, was facing the other way. She turned to see what he was looking at.

"Keep your eyes on the front. I've got the back," he said.

"Right. Yes. Shouldn't I have a gun?"

He placed the revolver next to her. "Don't pick it up yet. Wait."

She looked at the gun, and then the door. Suddenly she felt cold.

"I had no choice," she whispered.

"You did what you had to do," Mitchell replied.

"I could have run, or called for help," she said. Mitchell said something, but she didn't hear what. She was lost in the past, replaying the scene trying to find someway that it could have ended differently.

"Mitchell!" a voice called from outside.

"Weaver?" Mitchell replied. "Is that you?"

"Yes. We're coming in."

Weaver wasn't alone. With the captain were a dozen Marines and a score of police.

"There's evidence here!" Mitchell snapped. "And you're trampling it into the dust. Don't you know how to secure a crime scene?"

Weaver threw him a glare. "Corporal," she said, addressing a Marine, "secure the area." She turned back to Mitchell. "Standage escaped. Riley is getting someone to bandage her head."

"What?" Mitchell exclaimed.

"Standage and her husband," Weaver repeated, "escaped as the constable was escorting them — on her own, I might add — through the city. They hit her over the head, left her unconscious, and got away."

"And the child?"

"Gone with them. Riley said that you thought the child was being held hostage to secure Standage's compliance. I think you are wrong. She is the one at the heart of this. We need to find her. I'll tear the city apart if I need to. I take it the body in the alleyway over the road is your work."

"It's mine," Ruth said.

"Yours?" Now it was Weaver's turn to sound shocked. "Are you all right?"

Ruth shrugged.

"I'll need a statement from both of you," Weaver said. "But I'll start with the cadet, then she can get home."

Ruth gave an account of what had happened. She wasn't sure what she should say, or when she should lie, so she kept to the truth. It didn't take long before she was finished.

"I'm going to have someone take you to the hospital," Weaver said.

"I'm fine," Ruth said.

"No, you're not," Weaver replied.

"I'll take her," Mitchell said.

"No, you won't. You have to explain what happened here, and why precisely you're here in the first place."

Ruth thought she was in the hospital for hours. After the doctor had given her a reluctant all clear, she looked at her watch and saw it was only six p.m.

"It's broken," a familiar voice said.

She looked up and saw Mitchell.

"What time is it?" she asked.

"Close to ten. I'm going to take you home."

She was too tired to do anything but follow him outside. There was a carriage waiting, pulled by two horses. The driver looked familiar, but it wasn't until they were at The Acre she realised it was Isaac's man, Gregory. She was too tired to ask about that, either.

"Where have you—" Maggie began, running out of the door. "Ruth, what happened? Henry?"

"It's a long story," Ruth said. "I'll tell you after I've changed."

She went inside, and upstairs. She sat down on the edge of her bed and then fell into it. Her last thought before she went into a deep sleep filled with nothing but dead faces asking unanswered questions, was that Maggie had called the sergeant by his first name.

Chapter 9
Strike A Match
20th September

"You shouldn't go in," Maggie said. "Stay at home."

"No," Ruth said. She'd considered it and thought of little else since she woke up. "If I stay here today then I won't go back at all. I don't know if… after last night, I…" She took a deep breath. "I don't know if this is something I want to do, just that I haven't had a chance to find out if I'm any good at it."

"You'll be entitled to a few days off, at least," Maggie said.

"Maybe, but not today. There will be questions to answer, and I'd rather get them over with. Anyway, if I stayed at home, you'd only do the same, and you've children waiting to be taught."

Ruth began the day by giving another, and far more formal, statement. The presence of the representative of the Home Secretary told her it was linked to the death of the man she'd killed. That interview was over quickly. The ordeal wasn't. On leaving, she was given instructions to go to the commissioner's office. He was waiting for her, and again, she had to go through the events of the night before.

"I wish you'd come to me," Commissioner Wallace said.

"There wasn't time," she said. "I mean… I'm sorry, sir, but there really wasn't. After I gave you that first message I was sitting by a window watching the Mint, and then we followed the woman, and it all… sort of… happened."

"Yes, I suppose so. We need a better communication system. We really do. Phone boxes in the street if nothing else. However, it's done now. Some of the criminals have escaped, but they will be caught. More importantly, there is no way that this operation can start up again."

"There isn't? What about Clipton?" she asked.

"He is irrelevant. It's the two Standages who were behind this."

"They were?"

"She had access to designs, ink, and paper," he said. "The husband knew how to lay electrical cable. Emmitt was the man who knew how to build the printers. Yes, he could build them again, but without the Standages, he will get no further. I am worried about their son, of course, but let us be grateful no other innocents have been caught up in this affair. As for you, you'll have to see the psychiatrist, and you'll be on light duties until you've been signed off. Unfortunately, Serious Crimes counts as light duties. Next time…" He shook his head. "Let's just hope there isn't a next time."

"How was the commissioner?" Mitchell asked.

"Not happy," Ruth said. "But he said it was over. We've stopped the counterfeiters."

"Well, yes. Perhaps," Mitchell said. "No, leave your coat on, we're going out."

"Where to?"

"You'll see."

Ruth followed Mitchell outside, and out of Police House. The streets seemed strange to her that morning. She felt somehow separated from the people as if their lives were unconnected to hers.

"Where are we going?" she asked.

"Nowhere in particular," Mitchell said. "Sometimes it's good to get out and see that the world still goes on."

It did. They took a shortcut down Religion Road, the narrow street where churches, chapels, and temples, the mosque, and the synagogue each occupied a different semi-detached house. They ambled through sprawling suburbs that ringed the trading and administrative heart of the city. Gardens were well tended. Communal pigs rolled around in their stys. An occasional engineer could be seen marking out where cables could be hung. Truant children laughed as they spied the police officers and ran away. Yes, life went on.

"What did they print in the newspaper?" Ruth asked.

"About last night? Nothing," Mitchell said.

"But three people died."

"And that will be reported. Eventually. I think they're waiting until after the trade deal to run the story."

"Are the editors happy with that?" Ruth asked. "I mean, isn't the newspaper meant to print the news?"

"Sure, but the advantage with only having one national paper is that whatever they print *is* the news and it's new whenever they print it. Delaying the story works out well for them. The ceremony and the radio broadcast, and people's reaction to it, will fill the editorials for the next few weeks. Maybe even longer. Then they can print this story, and it should keep them busy until the election."

"That's not how it should work," she said.

"That's life."

Ruth kicked at a pebble. She hated that answer. It was one that Maggie gave her too often. "And life goes on," she said.

"Precisely. It is what it is."

"But the case isn't over?" she asked.

"What do you think?"

"Emmitt and Clipton weren't in the warehouse. They weren't, were they?"

"No. Not when we got there," Mitchell said.

"And why *did* you go there? Inside, I mean. When Riley left me she said she was going to get you."

"We were heading back towards you when we heard a child's scream. We went inside. A few seconds later it was all over."

"Oh." It seemed entirely too brief an explanation. "Do you know the name of the man I killed?"

"No. Not yet. We'll find out, but it's Turnbull I'm more concerned about. Rather, I want to know who killed him, because I'm certain it wasn't suicide."

"Does the commissioner know that?" Ruth asked.

"I told him. I'm not sure if he believes me, or if it's that he doesn't want to believe me. He's very proud of what he's done with the police. I suppose it did need to be more organised," he added grudgingly. "You know he was a politician?"

"Yes. You said. So did he."

"He led an opposition faction in the last round of elections," Mitchell said. "Didn't win, of course, and in the end he lost his seat, but he did have a lot of supporters. The Prime Minister gave him the big chair in Police House in the hope of keeping the isolationists quiet. It worked. I… it's no secret I wasn't happy with that at the time, but the job seems to have mellowed him. He was a monarchist when he started. An imperialist as well, at least as far as an isolationist can also support empire building. But he's going to get the PM's seat when she steps down, and that's going to be soon."

"He told me," Ruth said.

They passed a field where turnips were being hoisted onto a cart. From the way the farmhands were cheering on the team working the row she guessed it was the last of that crop to be harvested.

"Was that why you left the police?" Ruth asked. "Because of his appointment?"

"What? No. No, it was… it was something else."

"What?"

He looked at her. "I suppose you deserve an honest answer to an honest question. It was to give Riley some space."

"Really?"

"Pretty much," Mitchell said. "I found her when she was ten, and she'd lived with me ever since. All of a sudden she was the age I'd been when The Blackout occurred, and she'd become a copper like I had. I missed out on having a life because we were too busy staying alive. I didn't want her to do the same, so I gave her the house, and I left. Sort of the reverse of how things were done in the old world."

"That's it?"

"More or less."

"It wasn't to bring justice to the parts of the world without it?"

He gave a short laugh. "No, though that's what I ended up doing. There weren't that many punishments in the early days. There was execution of course, but that was reserved for the worst cases. For the most part, people were exiled. That was as good as a death sentence, but some people survived it. After a decade or more of brooding on their fate, there were some pretty embittered psychopaths out there."

"Oh." She wasn't sure what to say. "How long did you do it for?"

"Just a few years. I would come back, periodically, and there were a few trips overseas."

"Really?" she asked with sudden curiosity. "Where?"

"It wasn't as glamorous as you might think, travel rarely is, and at the end of it, I'm back where I started. There's a lesson in there, though one I personally don't plan to learn from."

Ruth mulled that over. She was curious as to where he'd gone and what he'd seen, but there was something else far more pressing she wanted to ask. "Do you…"

"What?"

"Do you remember the first person you killed?"

"Rarely does a day go by when I don't," Mitchell said. "It was during The Blackout. I did it to save Isaac. Knowing what I do now, I still don't know if that was the correct decision."

"What do you mean?"

"No, that's a history lesson for another day, but what you did last night was very much the right thing, and you should never doubt it. It was self-defence, nothing more."

"And…" She hesitated again, but couldn't see the harm in asking, though she wasn't sure what help the answer would be. "How many people have you killed?"

"I don't know. You'd think I would. Certainly I remember a lot of them, but that's the problem. There have been so many, directly and indirectly, for whose deaths I am responsible."

"Indirectly? Do you mean immediately after The Blackout?" she asked.

"In a way. There was a time, you see, a moment, a second when I stood between the people and the mob. Do you know what the mob is?

144

No, when I was your age, I didn't understand it either. It was just a word they used in the news and history books. Like revolution and terror. I knew the meaning, but I didn't understand it because I hadn't experienced it. I learned quickly enough when I stood in front of a crowd of hundreds that was representative of thousands in the camp behind. When I looked at these people, some of whom I knew, scared, hungry, desperate, that's when I understood. The mob is what people become when decency is subsumed by our worst instincts. When the individual collectively loses its belief in anything bigger than the self. All it took was a spark, and we had murder, cannibalism, and the survival of the savage. I stopped it. Not me alone, but I was there. It was a brutal time of brutal law, and this democracy is the end result. The alternative…" He sighed. "It doesn't bear thinking about."

The road grew rougher. Mud had spread from the ditches and gates, covering the asphalt. It was only by the absence of ploughed furrows that Ruth could tell where the road had been and the fields now began. They reached a broken stile. Mitchell climbed over.

"I never knew England when it wasn't like this," he said, as he led her up a slight rise towards the corner of a field. "I think I would have liked to. I didn't see any of this until about a week after The Blackout, and then it was a nightmare landscape of smoke, fire, and screams. And we were the lucky ones."

"Who's 'we'?" Ruth asked.

"Isaac, me, thousands of others," Mitchell said. "The ones who took shelter in the London Underground. On our way from that city to the coast we gathered more. There were at least a hundred thousand of us by the time we saw the sea. Not everyone who emerged from a basement or bunker wanted to join us. Some thought we were crazy, and many more ran at the sight of our ragged column staggering south. Maybe we were crazy, placing our lives in the hope that the message Isaac had received was true, and there would be cargo ships waiting on the coast. But they were there. You've heard the stories, and I bet no two versions are the same, but that's how people remember it. There were the cargo ships and the cruise ships with their mostly American passengers, and then there was us, making our long walk. Then the stories jump to how we learned to dig and plant and plough and sow."

Mitchell stopped, halfway up the shallow slope, and turned to look back at the fug of smoke and smog hovering over the city.

"Billions died across the world. Millions died here. Not in The Blackout, but in the aftermath. It's a terrible thing, radiation sickness. If it's a low dose you might get better. But you can get a lethal dose, get sick, and seem to recover, only to fall ill again a few days later. That's what happened. When we arrived, footsore, thirsty, and far beyond weary, many people were dead and more were dying. Each passing day, the number of sick grew and all we could offer them was the comfort of companionship in their final hours. We almost gave up. Those days, those weeks, it seemed as if everyone would die. Then it was over. You know when 'over' was?" He started walking up the slope again. "It was when the number of dead was less than the number of graves we could dig each day. We used up the last of the fuel doing that. But we had food. We thought it was going to be okay. And then the other sicknesses came. Cholera. Typhoid. Flu. Then something else that no one could identify. People started dying again, and this time we didn't offer them comfort. We just hoped that we would be spared. All that death, it changed us. Some found religion. Others lost it. Some lost all sense of what it meant to be human, but a few of us decided we couldn't give up. We carved a society out of this small corner of England. Then we took back Scotland and Wales, and then we went to sea, searching for others who'd not been as fortunate as us. We hoped to find some bastion of civilisation that had held on to more than we had. People who could reach down and offer us a helping hand back up. We didn't find one. We were it. Call it Britain if you want, and if you think that matters, but most of us don't. If I had to call myself anything, it's lucky. Lucky to be on a stretch of coast rich in fish, with good soil, on an island linked by railways, and where preserving steam trains was a hobby. We had food thanks to… well, thanks to those cargo ships. Luck. Coincidence. Geography. Call it what you want, we have a duty to those not so fortunate, but we also have a duty to ourselves."

He stopped underneath a spreading apple tree.

"This isn't Utopia," he said. "We call them Marines and say we have no army. We say we're a democracy, but we've had the same leader for the past twenty years. We say we've got a free press, but we've only one newspaper. There will always be crime, misery, pain, and suffering. No, this isn't Utopia, but it's what we've got, and it's down to each and every one of us to try to make it the best it can be. We do that by each of us being the best person we can be." He picked up an apple. "Here."

She took it uncertainly, and her confusion must have shown.

"It is a nice day, Ruth," he said. "But there will be dark times to come, there always are. There will be days when it would be easier to turn our faces to the wall than face the enormity of what lies ahead. We don't, in the hope that others won't either. There's an old saying, something Isaac told me a long time ago; strike a match and sear the flame into your memory so that when you are surrounded by darkness, you can remember the light."

He reached into his pocket and pulled out a folded plastic carrier bag. "I'm often grateful for the waste of the old world," he said. "Here. For the apples. This will be the last of them until next year. Let's pick some and enjoy the fresh air, so when the wind howls and the snow falls, it's this moment you remember, not last night, nor whatever tomorrow might bring."

She took the bag and started collecting apples. It was strange to see someone like Mitchell doing something so human as gathering windfalls. For some odd reason she found it comforting.

Chapter 10
Homicide
21st September

The next morning, Maggie said nothing as Ruth got ready for work, though her disapproving expression spoke volumes. When she got to the cabin in the yard of Police House, Ruth found Riley there, alone, her head buried in a book.

"I'm sorry about your clothes," Ruth said. "My mother tried to wash them, but they were ruined."

"Don't worry about it," Riley replied.

"Where's the sergeant?"

"Mister Mitchell has been summoned," she said.

"By whom?" Ruth asked.

"The Home Secretary."

"To answer questions about the other night?" Ruth asked.

"Possibly. We'll find out soon." Riley returned her attention to her novel. It was a different one from before. The cover was illustrated with a soaring tower almost lost amidst a tempestuous sea. Ruth sat down at her desk and stared at the pile of reports from the fight at the docks. It seemed surreal to have to deal with something so mundane as a dockside brawl. She picked up the top sheet and began reading.

"Don't bother," Riley said.

Ruth looked over at her. The novel had been lowered.

"Why not?" she asked.

"Because it's a con," Riley said.

"Do you mean the paperwork?" Ruth asked. "Was it a joke, like the police sign?"

"I mean the fight," Riley said. "The oranges were stolen by the crew. The fight was staged to cover it up. Each person will blame someone different, knowing that unless there are at least two corroborating accounts, no one can be charged. That means the matter gets passed back to their ship's captain, who will be in on the theft. We know it, they know we know it, and there's nothing we can do about it."

"So why did you jump in the sea?" Ruth asked.

"Because I can't remember what a real orange tastes like," she said. She paused and seemed to be weighing up what, and how much, to say. "When Mister Mitchell… When we first met…" She stopped. "He rescued me. I was ten. There was a fight. A battle. Afterwards, there was a storm. Enough lightning and wind to destroy the world, or that's how I remember it. We hid in a house, a large one, in the middle of the New Forest. In the cellar there was a crate of drinks. The label said they were made with real oranges." She took another breath and then seemed to think better of saying any more. "I don't remember ever having eaten a real orange," she finished. "He said he took you apple picking?"

"The sergeant? Yes."

"He's a good man, but he's not very good with people," Riley said. "He wants to believe the best of them, but he's seen too much of the worst. He's conflicted, carrying a burden of guilt that weighs him down. He knows he's not as intelligent as he needs to be, so he tries twice as hard to compensate. Sometimes he gets it wrong. Did he say you did the right thing?"

"Yes."

"Good. It's true. It was self-defence. Don't ever hesitate to do the same thing again."

Ruth nodded. She looked at the report in her hand. "I think I'll finish these. I mean, it can't hurt, right?"

"Outside," Riley said, closing her book.

"I'm sorry?"

"You grew up alone, right? You were home schooled. Before last night were you ever in a fight?"

"At the academy," Ruth said. "In training."

"That doesn't count. They teach you how to hold a gun, and enough maths so you can count how many shots you've fired. It's a school, not a place that prepares you for this job." Riley walked over to the door. Ruth reluctantly followed.

Riley took off her jacket and hung it over the metal railings by the rusting ramp.

"Take off your jacket," the constable said.

"Did you learn to fight at the academy?" Ruth asked.

"No. There wasn't one when I started in the police. And your belt."

"Who taught you?" Ruth asked, hanging the belt with its revolver and truncheon next to the jacket.

"No more stalling. Come at me."

"What?"

"Attack me," Riley said.

Ruth inched forwards, her arms raised, her eyes on Riley's, watching for movement. She reached out. Riley sidestepped, lightly grabbing Ruth's wrist, and used the cadet's own movement to turn, spin, and drop her to the ground.

"All people are different," Riley said, "but everyone broadcasts their intentions. Eyes flicker, shoulders tense, fingers flex, a breath is held. Even if they don't, muscles have to move before a blow can be struck. Watch for it." She reached out a hand. Ruth took it and let the constable pull her back to her feet.

"Try again. No," Riley said, as she grabbed Ruth's wrist, and this time swept a leg out, scything Ruth to the ground. "Keep your elbows in." Still holding the cadet's wrist, Riley pulled Ruth back to her feet. "Again."

Ruth took a step back, trying to call to mind everything she'd learned in those Friday afternoon classes. It wasn't much. Elbows in, hands raised, shoulders hunched, eyes on the constable, she stepped forward. She feinted with her left and sent her right hand straight out, punching air as Riley glided out of the way. The constable's hands shot out in a two-handed flat-palmed push. Again, Ruth found herself on the ground.

"Don't forget your feet," Riley said as she helped Ruth back up. "Your goal isn't to fight. You want to take them down quickly and arrest them. Here." She extended her arm. "Grab my wrist. No, twist it. No, like this. Sweep your leg. Yes, but harder. Try again."

It took another two goes before Riley was on the ground.

"Again," the constable said.

By the time Mitchell returned, Ruth was breathless, but strangely exhilarated. Riley had barely broken a sweat.

"Fighting amongst ourselves?" he said. "That seems like a productive use of our time."

"You want a go?" Riley asked.

"No, please, carry on," he replied, walking into the cabin, and coming out again with a chair.

"How did it go?" Riley asked.

"Interestingly," Mitchell replied as he sat down. "And not at all how I thought."

"You're not fired?" Riley asked.

"It's the opposite. Well, not quite. I'm still a sergeant and you are still a constable. However, Serious Crimes is now an official unit that will specialise in homicide."

"Does that mean we're still investigating Mr Anderson's death?" Ruth asked.

"No," Mitchell said. "Weaver is still in charge of that. The Home Secretary made that clear. The commissioner did manage to get us a small concession. We are to be allowed access to Weaver's files so that we can consult on the case."

"What does that mean?" Riley asked.

"Politics," Mitchell said. "The commissioner doesn't like the Home Secretary, and that feeling is more than mutual. We've become a pawn in a game that is, I assume, some preamble to Wallace's return to the political arena. We did solve the counterfeiting quickly. Or it might be more accurate to say that we brought it to a quick end. As such, the Home Secretary wants us to solve some more murders. Specifically, the kind that can be printed in the newspaper to show she's the law-and-order candidate."

"Do we have a case?" Riley asked.

"Not yet. Two gets you ten that we have to wait until she finds an appropriate victim. That was a joke, cadet. Have you shown her how to disarm an opponent?"

Seemingly from nowhere, a knife appeared in Riley's hand.

"There are no rules. Remember that," Mitchell said. "Valour, gallantry, honour, those are words for the sport's ground. If you can, run. If you can't, take them down quick, and take them down hard."

"I already told her that," Riley said.

"Good," Mitchell said. "If someone comes at you with a knife, don't try to take the blade away from them, disarm them by breaking the arm. Show her how."

After another half hour, Ruth was bruised, sweating hard, and actually having fun.

"Our tax dollars at work," a man called out. His accent was a rich American, not too dissimilar to Mitchell's. "Not mine, of course," the man added.

Ruth looked around and was rewarded with a swat on the ear from the back of Riley's hand. She took a couple of steps back and waited until the constable turned to see who approached before she did the same. There was a man and a woman, both very well dressed, she in a black suit, he in light grey. Where the woman's clothes were almost a uniform, the man's were old-fashioned and elegant.

The sergeant stood up, not quite at attention. Riley followed, and Ruth, still breathing hard, tried to copy.

"No, please," the man said. "This is an entirely informal visit. You must by Henry Mitchell."

"And you are Ambassador Miguel Perez," Mitchell replied.

"You know who I am," the ambassador said, his grin growing even wider as he held out his hand to the sergeant.

"I do, sir. You're leading the delegation representing all the different factions calling themselves The United States of America. And you were in Maine when the first ship made contact with the Americas. I could never forget that." There was an edge to Mitchell's voice that belied the polite tone. "Cadet, you know how the cruise ships that came aground had mostly American tourists on board?" The question may have been addressed to Ruth, but the sergeant's eyes stayed locked on the ambassador's.

"Yes, sir," she said.

"That was the principle reason why, when we started sending ships out, we went to the trouble and risk of sending them across the Atlantic. People wanted to know what had happened to their loved ones. The ship, The Winter Sun, could have made landfall on any stretch of coast. It happened to be near Pinebreak Ferry, where His Excellency was in charge of a community of a few hundred souls. You know what he did?"

"Um… no, sir," Ruth said, quickly filling the ominous pause.

"He held half the crew hostage to guarantee that the ship would return," Mitchell said. "He took a gamble that when it did, it would return with food and medicine, not soldiers."

"And I was right," Perez said. "And look how it's worked out. We've got this radio broadcast in a couple of days, and a ceremony that will formalise the friendship between nations."

"Indeed, sir. How can I help you?"

"Actually," the ambassador said. "I'm here to thank you for that help you provided a few days ago. The matter by the shore?"

"Your assistant, yes, I remember," Mitchell said. "Has he talked?"

"Intermittently. I can't say we're getting that much use from him. A few names of people back in the U.S. but not much more."

"I see. Could I have a list of those names?" Mitchell asked.

"Of course," the ambassador said. "But I think the matter has been resolved. The addresses he stole were of oil fields that we're planning to re-open. Specifically, they gave the names of the legal owners who we know were stranded here during The Blackout. The details next to them were how we were going to prove these individuals, or their heirs, were who they claimed to be. As you probably gathered, my assistant, Fairmont, was selling the information. The gang buying it planned to use it to claim to be the legal owners themselves."

"After killing the real owners?" Mitchell asked.

"Fairmont says no," Perez said. "They'd told him that they would only assume the identities of people who were dead. I don't believe it, and I don't think he does either. We're changing procedures and sending in teams to collect DNA from those locations. The samples will have to be stored against the time we have the technology to run a comparison. I can't say whether you've saved us any money, but you did save us a great deal of embarrassment. I'm here to thank you for that."

Mitchell waved that away. "You're drilling for oil? You're bringing back the car to the U.S.?"

"We already have, in a small way. Refining is where we have a bottleneck, but as we drill more, we build more diesel power plants, and that enables us to refine more oil. Laying railway lines isn't an effective use of our workforce, nor is having them toil by hand in the fields, not when those fields used to stretch for miles. Give us a few years and we'll have tractors in them again. A few years after that, we'll have planes in the sky. All because that ship made landfall in Maine."

"Hmm," Mitchell grunted. "Is any of this gasoline coming to Britain?"

"It is, as part of the trade deal, though not for a few years."

"I can't imagine it will be much," Mitchell said.

"There will be enough. Not for cars, you don't need them on such a small island. It's the other uses, plastics and petrochemicals and all the rest, for which we'll be supplying it to your chemical works. And, of course, enough jet fuel for the planes to make the return trip."

"There will be planes? Landing here?" Ruth asked, unable to stop herself.

"There will," the ambassador said. "Is that a trace of America in your accent, were you born there?"

"No, sir," Ruth said.

"But you've at least one American parent?"

"Um... yes," she said.

"Then you're eligible to vote in the upcoming election." He pulled a folded sheaf of papers from his pocket and handed them to Ruth. "And you've not registered yet, either, sergeant. I did check. There are three copies there. I'll send Agent Clarke to collect them in a few days, but as I said, I came here to thank you. Clarke?"

The woman held out the small bag. The ambassador took it.

"This deal between Britain and America isn't really about trade, not in the sense everyone understands it," the ambassador said. "And it's certainly not about food. I know that the inconveniences of rationing

154

focuses minds on the canned fish, beef, powdered milk, and all the rest that's sent overseas, but we barely need it now. Even when the ships first crossed the ocean it wasn't food for which we were most grateful. It was the antibiotics. Within a few years we'll be shipping food to you. In return Britain will provide the pharmaceuticals, and precision tools, and then the circuitry. It's why your universities are expanding. They're preparing for the day when there's no need for tens of thousands of coalminers, and for when farms once again number their employees in tens not hundreds."

"The more things change, the more they stay the same, yes?" Mitchell said.

"It was ever thus," Perez agreed. "At some point, and I don't know when, we were at a crossroads. Perhaps it was back in Maine when I held that crew hostage, or perhaps it was when your Prime Minister decided to fill the ships with supplies rather than soldiers. Perhaps it was later, perhaps it was sooner, but at that crossroads we had a choice. We could regress to some twisted parody of the Victorian Wild West, with empires and despots. Or we could remember all that we'd collectively learned from history and try not to repeat those same mistakes. You see, as much as the food and medicines saved lives, it was the knowledge that we weren't alone that allowed us to reunify so quickly, and relatively peacefully. There were battles, certainly, but there have been no wars because reunification doesn't mean the strong taking over the weak. It's a return to law, order, and the comforts that many still remember. Knowledge, that's the most powerful force in this world. Knowledge that we weren't alone then and aren't alone now. That is the purpose of this ceremony, the broadcast, and the trade deal. That being said," he added, holding out the bag to the sergeant, "people do appreciate the tangible, and there are some things that you can't grow in this climate."

Mitchell took the bag. "Coffee beans?" he asked, looking inside.

"From Puerto Rico. A thank you for your work over the last few days. Not just that business with my assistant, but for exposing that counterfeiting ring."

"You know about that?" Ruth asked.

"Of course. You can't have a trade deal without money backing it. Your banknotes are used in the U.S. did you know that? People have faith in your currency and had you not caught the counterfeiters that faith would have been destroyed. Perhaps the trade deal would have gone with it. These are fragile times, but when has civilisation ever not been balanced on a knife's edge? Oil from America, coffee from the Caribbean, chemicals from Britain. The world turns, and in five years we'll be back in the air. In ten, we'll have satellites in orbit again."

"Those are lofty goals," Mitchell said.

"Is it worth having any other kind? But as I said, I wanted to say thank you. Enjoy the coffee. Think of it as a taste of what's to come."

"What was that about?" Ruth asked after the ambassador had left.

"That was what we call a stump speech," Mitchell said. "I think he was practicing. If he isn't planning to run for the presidency, I'll be surprised. Let me take those." He took the voter registration forms that the ambassador had handed to her. Ruth didn't try to stop him.

"I meant the stuff about you helping him," she said. "The assistant. The thank you."

"Oh, that, yes. There was an incident the day before you joined us, cadet," Mitchell said. "At about the same time as Riley was taking a swim in the sea, I was walking along the coast. It was more or less on the same route I take every night. I saw a group of three men acting suspiciously. I confronted them. One ran. I'd say he was around thirty, maybe a bit older. He had a white streak in his brown hair that didn't quite cover where half his ear was missing. I don't know what happened to him, but one of the others dived to the ground, and the third man shot at me. I returned fire, killing him. I caught and arrested the man who took cover. He is Lucas Fairmont, and he was the assistant to the ambassador. On his person was a list of names and addresses that corresponded, as you heard, to the rightful owners of the oil fields they are about to open up. Personally... well, the specifics of this trade deal are of no interest to me. I wanted to check the bullet we found in Mr Anderson against the guns I found on the man I killed."

156

"You think the two crimes are connected?" Ruth asked.

"I was worried that they were, but now I fear they are not," Mitchell said. "I had the bullet tested yesterday, and it doesn't match either weapon."

"And that's bad?" she asked.

"It means we'll see more crimes like these," Mitchell said. "After twenty years, people see power as once again worth killing for. There will be more murder, more innocent lives ruined. Progress!" He walked back into the cabin. "Forget satellites," he shouted from inside, "what about a decent criminal database? But if I get a fridge in my room before the decade is out, I'll be impressed." There was the sound of cupboard doors slamming one after the other. Then he came out again.

"You two continue training," he said. "I'll be back soon."

"Where are you going?" Riley asked.

"To find something I can grind these coffee beans with."

Chapter 11
The Ruins of Southampton
22nd September

"Don't close the door," Mitchell said as Ruth walked into the cabin. "We've got our first official case, a double murder in Southampton."

"Southampton? Does anyone live there?" Ruth asked.

"Two less people do now," Mitchell replied, almost with enthusiasm, as he pushed past her.

Riley, carrying the crime-kit, followed. "I've got it," she said as Ruth moved to take the kit from her. "Did you deliver the report to the Naval Office?"

"They were surprised to see me," Ruth said. She'd finished going through the accounts of the fight at the dock, had written an official response, and taken it to the Naval Office that morning. "But they took it."

"And will probably ignore it," Riley said.

"I'm not going to let them," Ruth said. "I added a request to interview each sailor."

"Really? Why?" Riley asked.

"As I see it, we're owed four crates of oranges," she said.

"Now she's sounding like a copper," Mitchell said. "But that's a battle you won't be able to fight until the ship comes in to dock. We've got a murder to solve. There's a train leaving for Kent in twenty minutes, and I'd like to catch it."

"Double homicide. Discovered by scavenger. Redbridge. Southampton," Ruth read as the train rattled east. She turned the note over. "That's not much to go on."

"You forgot that you have who the note came from," Mitchell said.

"It was sent at nine a.m. from the Ministry of Resettlement. Who are they?" Ruth asked.

"What do you know about scavenging?" Mitchell asked.

"You need a licence," Ruth said, remembering her and Riley's encounter with the cobbler a few days previously. "And ninety-percent of what you get is taxed unless you give it to the National Store."

"Broadly speaking, yes. Ninety-percent is taxed, and you can pay that tax in money or by selling the goods to the National Store, in which case the tax is waved. The amount the government pays for the goods is a paltry sum which is why the other ten-percent is so important. Usually that's made up of items found to order. Clothing in a particular size, books, specific items of crockery for those who can afford a matching set, and so on. Or it's luxury items like wine, spirits, real tea, spices, and other old-world goods that have survived the last twenty years. You can't sell those to a shop without the tax receipt, and they can't sell them on without a copy of the same receipt. Of course, they do, because there's no way of knowing whether the bottle of whisky on the receipt is the one on the shelf or the one that was sold the day before. The idea isn't to stop scavenging, or even to raise taxes, but to make looting less appealing than a life of farming or mining. There are exceptions and exemptions, of course, and those people who do make a living from scavenging depend on them. Books from Hay-on-Wye, for instance, or collecting research papers from Oxford. But you could look at this in another way. Scavengers spend their time clearing abandoned houses of anything valuable that the weather would otherwise ruin before people want to live there again. By putting it all into the National Store there's no need to divert resources into making new pots and pans for another generation. As to the sale of silk and wine and all the rest, I'm told that a luxury goods market is vital to the economy. Personally, I have my doubts."

"Southampton's different," Riley said.

"It is," Mitchell said. "It was hit by a far more powerful bomb than the one that devastated Bournemouth. It's a city of the dead that no one had time to bury."

"Then these scavengers must have a licence," Ruth said. "Because if they didn't, they wouldn't have reported the crime."

"I suspect they have something, but not a licence," Mitchell said.

159

Ruth waited for him to go on. He didn't. From his expression he was waiting for her to ask. Instead, she turned her attention to the window, watching the trees fly past as the train rumbled through the New Forest.

"We get out here," Mitchell said, as the train slowed, and then came to a halt. "This is Redbridge, the edge of Southampton, and the point where the train heads north, leaving the coast behind."

"It's a town?" Ruth asked, wondering why she'd never heard of it.

"It was an outpost and now it's a depot," Mitchell said. "A place for the train to take on water."

"Look up," Riley said.

Ruth did. There was a hot air balloon floating lazily above them.

"It keeps watch," Riley said.

"For bandits?" Ruth asked.

"Pirates," Mitchell said. "We've been strengthening the defences around Kent, so it won't be long before they try further up the coast. Come on."

The depot looked like an armed camp. It was a small old-world train station, ringed by a wall, behind which the top of an even higher fence was visible. That fence carried on for nearly a mile down the tracks, ending in... she squinted. "Are those shipping containers?"

"It was a port city, once," Mitchell said.

They went through the station and into a car park. A trio of Marines were playing dice against a wall, and a woman in railway green argued with a man over something to do with the price of duck. Mitchell led them towards a man standing on his own, near the guarded gate. At first glance he looked like one of those people who spent their lives wandering the country, homeless and alone. He was dressed in ragged leather and mismatched swatches of cloth, a trio of knives at his belt, and battered white trainers on his feet. But the face under the greasy hat was scrubbed if not exactly clean, so were his hands. Ruth guessed he was no older than thirty-five, too young to be one of those old-timers who'd never adjusted to the new world. Though he was shifting from foot to foot in nervous agitation, he didn't seem afraid.

"You're waiting for us?" Mitchell asked, approaching the man.

"Are you police?" the man asked.

"Don't the uniforms give us away?" Mitchell replied

"Did you come about the murder?" the man asked.

"Will you take us there?" Mitchell replied.

The man weighed that up for a moment before nodding.

Ruth threw a quizzical look at Riley. The constable shook her head.

The gate was opened, and they went outside. There was a cart, pulled by a team of hardy ponies, being tended to by a boy of around ten.

"Is this your son?" Mitchell asked.

"Aren't all children of the tribe my sons and daughters?" the man replied.

Everything was a question, that was clear, and this person was… weird, Ruth decided.

It was a short journey, made in silence, though that was filled by the smell. The cart was filthy, held together by grease as much as by wire and bolt. The padding on the seats was of uncured leather, and Ruth didn't want to even think what they were stuffed with. The ponies, however, were sleek and well groomed.

After five minutes, they came to a halt outside an abandoned school at the top of a curving avenue. As Ruth jumped down from the cart, she saw the canopy of the balloon hovering overhead, barely a mile away. They could have walked, she thought, but guessed the cart ride was somehow symbolic because a large group waited for them outside the school. About fifty adults, she thought. Inside the building she could make out the faces of children, unwashed and unkempt. The cart's driver went over to the group, as the boy unhitched the ponies.

"What's going on?" Ruth asked.

"More or less what I expected," Mitchell said, which was no more illuminating than the back and forth questioning had been.

Mitchell approached a woman at the centre of the group. She wasn't the oldest there, though she was at least fifty, but she was obviously in charge.

161

"My name is Mitchell. I am police. I am here about the two bodies," he said.

The woman looked from him, to Riley, to Ruth, and then back at Mitchell.

"Are we not here to start a new life?" the woman asked, and with the question the group behind her unstiffened, though the suspicion didn't leave their eyes.

"I remember you," Mitchell said.

"Do you?" the woman replied.

"Are you here on resettlement?" Mitchell asked.

"Don't we all seek shelter at journey's end?" the woman asked.

"And life is a journey with only one end. I remember you saying that," Mitchell said. "Who found the bodies?"

Half the group, mostly the younger ones, glanced towards the man who'd driven the cart.

"Who else, but me?" the woman asked.

"Perhaps we could talk?" Mitchell suggested.

The two walked away from the group, and it seemed the conversation moved more freely now that there was no one to overhear.

"Thank you," Mitchell finally said, and loudly enough for the entire group to hear. "I wish you all well, here in your new home."

"Sir?" Ruth prompted, as she and Riley followed the sergeant down the avenue.

"You've not heard of resettlement, have you?" he asked.

"They're bandits," Riley said. "Or they were."

"Really?" Ruth asked.

"From the north," Mitchell said. "It's cheaper to offer them land and hope they'll assimilate than to send the Marines in to kill them. They've been given these houses, that school, and what's left of an old rugby club to turn into fields. But primarily they're here to sort through the old container port that's on the other side of the railway station."

"Do they always speak in questions?"

"Yeah, that's a new thing," Mitchell said. "It's understandable, I suppose. Civilisation abandoned them, so they had to come up with their own customs. A game taught to children becomes the habit of adults swiftly enough."

"And the bodies?" Riley asked.

"There are two of them, in a house down here," Mitchell said. "This group arrived yesterday evening. The bodies were found when they began surveying their new home this morning. It was a few hours before dawn, and she couldn't give me a more precise time than that. This house here, I think." He stopped in front of a three-storey terrace. "The front door's missing. Do you see the glass? The windows were blown in. Riley, you take downstairs. Cadet, you're with me. They said the bodies were upstairs." He stepped inside. "I think we can say…" He paused, peered at the sodden, rotten mess of a carpet lining the stairs. "Careful on this. Yes, I think we can say these bodies arrived here before last night. They would have noticed people walking around their territory."

The stairs creaked as Ruth put her weight on one. She shifted her foot to the edge.

"And they call themselves a tribe?" she asked.

"They felt abandoned," Mitchell said. "To survive, we all did things that we wish we could forget. Some did things they can't live with. Those people were alone a lot longer than most and had to find a way of coping with the guilt. Creating their own mythology was—" He stopped speaking as he reached the open doorway to an upstairs room at the front of the house. "Riley!" he yelled.

Ruth tried to see past Mitchell, but he held out a hand to stop her. The constable came running up the stairs, pushed past Ruth, and came to a stop in the doorway. She said nothing, just shook her head. Finally, Mitchell allowed Ruth to step forward and see for herself.

The room was small, crowded with furniture, and filled with the smell of damp edged with the increasingly familiar coppery tones of blood. On a sofa facing the window was the body of a man she didn't recognise, a revolver still held in his right hand. In an armchair against the far wall was the body of one she did.

"That's Marcus Clipton," she said.

"It is," Mitchell said. He carefully knelt down and peered at the floor. Then he turned his head to look towards the two bodies. "Nothing but scuffmarks. No discernable footprints. Riley?"

The constable stepped lightly over to the bodies. "Recent," she said. "A day. Maybe two. No longer. Clipton's been shot from close range. Single gunshot wound to the chest." She looked closer. "Through and through. The bullet's lodged somewhere in the chair. The other man was stabbed. The knife is still present. From the angle, it was an underarm blow, entering just below the rib cage. There's a revolver still in that man's right hand."

Mitchell looked at the two bodies, tilting his head left and right.

"Sir, do you think—" Ruth began.

"No more questions, cadet. Not now," the sergeant interrupted. "Get out some evidence bags."

He stepped into the centre of the room, turning a full, slow circle, his eyes on the floor. He turned around again, this time looking at the ceiling. Then he knelt down. Ruth followed his gaze, but couldn't tell what he was looking for.

"It appears obvious what's happened," Mitchell said. "Clipton came here to kill this man. The man was expecting it. He was stabbed, but shot Clipton before he died, and they both collapsed into the chairs as they breathed their last. One more loose end tied up. Wonderful. That just leaves the identity of this man." He turned another slow circle. "Yes. Annoying, too," he added, a little more loudly than Ruth thought was necessary, "since we're not allowed to investigate Clipton's murder. We'll bag the evidence though, don't want to leave it where one of those scavengers might purloin it."

He walked back to Ruth, took an evidence bag, and pulled a small jar and a brush from the crime-kit.

"Sir, do you—" Ruth began.

"Cadet, I am sick and tired of your constant questioning. Silence, please, while I work."

164

She frowned, but said nothing as the sergeant went back to the body. He knelt on the floor and peered at the unknown man's shoes. A clasp knife appeared in his hand. He scraped something off the sole and into a bag that was then thrust up at Ruth.

"Another," he said, and moved over to Clipton, before repeating the procedure. "Don't mix them up," he added.

He returned to the man, took the lid off the jar, dipped the brush in, and then dusted the handle of the knife. Kneeling, he peered at the blade, his head inches from the wound. Gingerly, he picked the revolver up by the barrel, and dusted the handle. He turned it towards the light, tilting it this way and that until, finally, he nodded. He opened the chamber.

"Fully loaded. One round fired." He emptied the cartridges into one evidence bag and placed the now unloaded revolver into another. Then he peered at the man's hands. "Interesting," he said, standing up. "I'll take Clipton. Riley, search this man."

Starting at the man's ankles, Riley began a thorough search that turned up nothing until she reached his jacket pockets. "I've found a ration book. His name is Rahman Gupta. He lives at 12E Fennel Street."

"Sounds like a boarding house," Mitchell said. "Anything else?"

The ration book went into a paper evidence bag.

"A pocket watch in his right-hand pocket," Riley said. "A very old one. Gold case. No inscription. No wedding ring. There are keys. A pen. A linen handkerchief. Some money."

"Any twenty-pound notes?" Mitchell asked.

"Three one-pound notes. Five penny-stamps."

"Hmm. Pity," Mitchell said. "Clipton must have emptied his pockets before he came out to do this job. It suggests he thought he might die here. That tells us… yes, he almost certainly came here alone. Let me see that pen."

Riley held it out.

"A fountain pen," Mitchell said. "Interesting. And there's ink in it. Good. I suppose the next thing to do is find out how Mr Gupta is connected to the counterfeiting. Well, we might as well start with his home. There's no point hanging around here."

Ruth stood back as Mitchell marched out of the room. She looked at Riley, and opened her mouth, but the constable shook her head. Ruth gathered the evidence bags and followed the sergeant outside.

"We'll send for the coroner," Mitchell said, his voice back to its normal tone once more.

"Do you want me to stay here to watch the bodies?" Ruth asked.

"There's no point. Gupta and Clipton aren't going anywhere, and those scavengers will make sure no one else comes in. They've very strict rules governing the dead. I'll go and tell them. Or ask them, at least. You two start heading back to the station. I'll catch up."

"What's going on," Ruth asked as, using the hot air balloon as a guide, they headed back to the train station.

"You might as well wait for Mister Mitchell to tell you," Riley said. "But think back on what you saw. Did anything strike you as odd?"

"Other than the sergeant?"

"Think about it."

She did, though she hadn't reached any firm conclusions before the sergeant caught up with them outside an old garage.

"Stop here," Mitchell said. "Have you ever heard of bugs?" he asked Ruth.

"As in insects?" she asked.

"As in electronic listening devices," Mitchell said. "I don't know if there were any in that room, but there might have been."

"Why?" she asked, confused.

"That scene was staged. Badly staged. It's almost as if whoever did it had never been to a crime scene before. First of all, Mr Gupta had no ammunition in his pocket, nor a holster for the revolver. Second, the gun was in his right hand. That pocket watch was in his right-hand pocket. Taken with the ink stains on his left hand, I'm certain he was left-handed. Third, there was no blood on the floor, just a lot of scuffmarks through the dust. Fourth, there were no discernable prints on the knife or the revolver. Fifth, remember how the bodies were positioned? We are supposed to believe that Gupta was stabbed while sitting down. With that wound it's highly unlikely. On being stabbed he then shot Clipton. Taking the entry wound, exit wound, the hole in the back of the chair, and the stippling around the wound, he was sitting down when he was shot. And it was from point blank range, not by a man seated on that sofa. To summarise, in order for this crime to have played out the way we are supposed to think, Clipton stabbed Gupta. Gupta then pulled a revolver out of his pocket. He pushed Clipton into the chair and shot him. Then, as he staggered back to the sofa, he paused to clean up any blood he dripped onto the floor. He switched the gun from his left hand to his right, and then he died. Or, more plausibly, they were both killed by someone else."

Ruth ran through that explanation. "And you think they were recording us with electronics? Why?"

"Turnbull was killed in custody. This is our first official case, and the victim happens to be Clipton. His body is found relatively close to the city, yet at the same time outside of anyone else's jurisdiction. The body is in one of the few properties where it was certain to be discovered. Not just that, but the killer knew exactly when the scavengers would arrive, and that they wouldn't disturb the crime scene."

"Who did it?" Ruth asked.

"I don't know, and we're not going to find out here. Riley, I want you to speak to the Marines in the depot, and then talk to the train station staff. I doubt Gupta or Clipton came through here, but someone had to scout out the location. Perhaps they were lazy enough to use a train. Then go and see the commissioner. Tell him we've found Clipton, but leave it at that for now."

"And you?" Riley asked.

"We're going to do what they expect us to do. We'll go to the boarding house and find out who Mr Gupta was."

"And then?" Riley asked.

"We need help, and if we can't trust our colleagues, we'll have to rely on those we know to distrust. Go to Isaac. We'll meet you there."

Chapter 12
Grief

"You can tell a lot about the people who live in a house by their front garden," Mitchell said. They were on a pleasant, tree-lined but leaf-clear street to the west of the main commuter station. "And the key feature about these houses is that there's no hedge, wall, or fence dividing them."

"Do you think they're all boarding houses, owned by the same person?" Ruth asked.

"The six terraces either side of the road are. I'm not sure about the detached houses at the end. Or perhaps it's two people who each own one side of the road. But it doesn't look like a collective." He pointed towards a woman, kneeling in the garden outside the door to number eight.

"Excuse me, ma'am," he said. "Are these boarding houses?"

"They are," she said.

"Including number twelve?"

"That's right," she said, standing up. "Why?"

"Do you live here?" Mitchell asked.

"I'm the owner. What's this about?"

"Do you know a Mr Rahman Gupta?"

"Yes? Why? What's happened?" Her tone switched from wary to frantic.

"I'm very sorry to inform you that he's dead," Mitchell said.

The woman's face collapsed, and for a moment Ruth thought the woman would follow.

"How did it... how?" she whispered.

"Perhaps we could go inside," Mitchell said.

The woman nodded and led them towards the nearest door. She paused halfway along the front hall and glanced down at the muddy path she'd tracked along the scrubbed floor. She shook her head and led them into the kitchen.

"Please, sit down," she said. "I can make you some tea?"

"There's no need. What's your name, ma'am?" Mitchell asked.

"Garland. Ingrid Garland," she said.

"And you own these houses?"

"The entire row. My mother owned the house before. We took in refugees, you know? And that became…" She sighed. "How did he die?"

"We'll have to wait for the coroner's report before we can say," Mitchell said.

"But was it… was it an accident?"

"It's too early to say," Mitchell said. "When did you see him last?"

"Two days ago. He didn't come home that evening, or last night. But he often sleeps at work."

"And where's that?"

"The chemical works. He's quite important there," she added.

"How long has he been a tenant?"

"Oh, for nearly fifteen years," Garland said.

"That's a long time," Mitchell said. "He never wanted a place of his own?"

"He had one. A farm. Him and his brother and sister. It's about thirty miles away. It's why he kept a room here. He'd work at the factory some days, but often finished after the last train. Sometimes he'd sleep at work, and sometimes he'd come here, and other times he'd take a few days off and go back to the farm."

"The chemical works didn't mind?"

"Mind? About five years ago, he told them that he sometimes woke in the middle of the night with an idea but forgot it by the time he'd found the box of matches. They had electricity installed before the week was out. He's that important to them, but he's diligent, too. He works twenty-hour shifts, and I think he'd work longer if he could. Worked." She sniffed. "He took me there, to his farm. Such nice people, just like him."

"Did he have many visitors?" Mitchell asked.

"Here? No. There was just—" She stopped.

"Just who?" Mitchell pressed.

"I was going to say there was just him and me."

"You were close?"

She shrugged.

"No one came looking for him over the last week? No late night callers or anything out of the ordinary?" Mitchell asked.

"No, why?" she asked.

"It's a routine question," Mitchell said. He took out the keyring. "Can you identify the keys?"

"That one's for his room, and that's for the front door."

"Thank you. We should take a look at his room."

It was immaculately tidy, about twelve feet long by twenty feet wide, but seemed larger due to the sparse furnishings.

"A bed, a desk, a wardrobe, a shelf. I'd say this room was rarely slept in, even when he was here," Mitchell said. "But it's been dusted to within an inch of its life." He ran a finger along the edge of the single shelf. "There's not a speck of it. The wardrobe has… three pairs of trousers and five shirts. A raincoat. Underwear. Socks. Hat. Scarf. Two pairs of gloves. That's it. Other than the scarf and hat, which are a bright reddish pink, it's all subdued colours and old fabrics."

"Not hardwearing clothes," Ruth said. "That confirms what Ms Garland told us."

"How did you come to that conclusion?" Mitchell asked as he bent to peer under the bed.

"There's a large garden outside that's halfway between an allotment and a field. Except for a few chairs underneath the trees, it's all been ploughed, dug, or planted. I'd say that everyone who lived here must spend some time working outside."

"Except for Mr Gupta," Mitchell said. "And there are no chemical stains on his clothes. No jackets either, so he didn't have to dress up for work. Maybe he changed there."

"Or he wasn't employed at the chemical works, and there is no farm for him to disappear off to," Ruth said.

Mitchell pulled a book off the small shelf above the desk, flicked through it, and handed it to Ruth. "Here," he said. "It looks like a journal. Look for anything incriminating. A sketch of a banknote or something."

Ruth turned a page, and then another. "You think there will be one?"

"Not really, but we have to look."

Ruth flicked through the book. It was three-quarters full, the handwriting was small, the letters carefully formed, but all were of the same hand.

"It's not really a journal," she said. "There are no dates. It's his thoughts and ideas, and a list of problems and how to solve them."

"Like what?"

"Anything," Ruth said. "Everything. This page is about increasing the yield of wheat. The next page is… I think it's about how to build a better light bulb." She turned another page. "And this is just a lot of formulas. No, wait. He's scrawled something about diesel in the margin."

"Let me see." Mitchell took the book, glanced at the page, and handed it back. "That's a calculation on the time and cost of producing bio-diesel, and the net increase in food production it would bring on a hundred-acre farm."

"How do you know that?" Ruth asked.

"Because I've seen that before, or something similar. During the first winter after The Blackout, everyone wanted to know if we could get the tractors running again. But we needed every calorie we had to stay alive. If the climate was different, or if we'd been more geographically spread out, or if we'd not had the steam trains, or if the roads weren't packed with all those stalled cars… It happened the way it did." He turned a page, and then another. "No pictures. A few doodles. But nothing obviously incriminating."

"Why are you looking for pictures?"

"Because we'd certainly notice if an entry about counterfeiting had been written in a different hand," Mitchell said. "However, we might assume a drawing of a twenty-pound note was done by Mr Gupta. Remember that the killer assumed we'd fall for the staged crime scene. But there's nothing here." He picked up three letters from the bookshelf. "All of these are written by a woman named Clementine. Return address is Away Farm. Probably a sister, or a sister-in-law, perhaps? Not a wife or a girlfriend, but someone to whom he was close. It's all about farming. Very bucolic, and all dated within the last two weeks. Check the tacks on the carpet."

"What for?" she asked.

"Are they new, or newly scratched? Does it look like the carpet has been removed?"

Ruth knelt down near the door, combing through the thick pile.

"It seems Ms Garland's account of her lodger tallies with what we've found here," Mitchell said. "Did you find anything?"

"No. Do you really think it likely someone would remove the carpet to hide some clue?"

"Probably not. They'd leave it somewhere obvious. But there is a reason Mr Gupta was killed. We didn't find it on his person. We haven't found it here. We'll try the chemical works next, and then the farm. That reason is key, I'm sure of it."

He pocketed the journal, and they left the boarding house.

The chemical works was a short walk from the boarding house and was one of the few larger factories situated in the town itself. The giant red and blue 'Satz!' signs either side of the wrought iron gates were a familiar sight from every tin of ersatz tea Ruth had ever opened.

"We're here to see the director," Mitchell said to the guard standing in a small sentry box by the gate.

"And do you have an appointment, officer?" the guard asked, with a theatrical glance at the book in front of her.

"It's official police business," Mitchell said.

"Oh, really?" the woman replied.

"All right, look," Mitchell said, stepping closer. "We can continue this back and forth for a bit, but at the end of it, you'll either open that gate or I'll arrest you for obstruction. Why don't you save us some time, and yourself some trouble, and tell your boss we're here regarding Mr Gupta."

The guard gave Mitchell a resentful glare, and threw another at Ruth for good measure, before leaving her box and heading into the building. She wasn't gone long.

"Someone will be out shortly," she said before pointedly turning her back on them.

Mitchell nodded his head towards the gate, and they walked away from the sentry box. Ruth looked up at the chimneys towering over the beige painted building.

"What was this before it was a factory?" she asked.

"A soccer pitch," Mitchell said. "You see over…" He turned around, squinting at the redbrick buildings opposite. "Well, I don't remember which ones, but the chemical labs started off in those houses. It was after the meningitis outbreak. That was the final straw. We had cholera and typhoid, flu and pneumonia, and then there were the everyday infections that everyone seemed to get. People were dying all the time, but when the children started to die, thousands at a time, that's when something had to be done. We went to the old pharmaceutical labs to find the formulas. Not all of us made it back."

"You mean you?" Ruth asked. "You went?"

"Me? Yes, among others. Don't look so surprised. Because of my proximity to Isaac, and because he'd had that message about the cargo ships, I found myself in the room where the decisions were made. I wasn't sitting at the table with the admiral and the PM, but I was there, and so I fell into policing. There wasn't much investigating to do. There were crimes, of course, but they were the kind where it was obvious who'd done it, or where you knew from the outset you'd never prove who had. With more time on my hands than those working a plough, I was volunteered whenever someone was needed to go to the wrong side of the Thames. Anyway, they built the labs in those houses and recreated the vaccines, but there's only so much you can do in a converted terrace, so we built the chemical works. At first for the vaccines and antibiotics, but we soon had a stockpile, so they started on aspirin and the like. Then it was paint, gunpowder, fertilizer, bleach, toothpaste and, well, it's a marvel how much of what we call civilisation is dependent on chemistry. It certainly made the difference between survival and living."

"Would you need a chemistry lab to make ink for printing banknotes?" Ruth asked.

"Yes, and that's exactly where my thoughts were going, but hang on. Someone's coming."

A squat, bow-legged man waddled towards them from the main building.

"I'm Mr Worley," he said, as the guard opened the gate. "Have you found Rahman?"

"Was he missing?" Mitchell asked.

"Why else would you be here?" Worley replied.

"Can we go inside?" Mitchell asked.

"What's happened?" Mr Worley asked.

"I'm afraid Mr Gupta is dead," Mitchell said.

Worley's face went slack, almost as if every muscle relaxed at the same instant. "Dead?" he asked.

"Yes, sir," Mitchell said.

"You're sure?"

"We are."

"I mean, are you sure it's him?" Worley asked.

"Yes, sir, we are. Can we go inside and talk?"

"I... Yes. Yes. You... yes," he murmured. "How?" he asked as he led them towards the building. "How did it happen?"

"We're still investigating," Mitchell said, "but it appears to be murder."

"Murder?" the man almost squawked the word in surprise, as he stopped and stared at them.

"What was your relationship with the man?" Ruth asked.

"What? Oh, I was his supervisor," Worley said. "I'm deputy director, in charge of research."

"What kind of research?" Mitchell asked.

"Every kind," Worley said.

"Perhaps we can see his lab?" Mitchell asked.

"Yes. I will have to inform the board, I suppose."

"Mr Gupta was that important?" Ruth asked.

"Dr Gupta," Worley corrected her. "And he was very important."

"Indispensable?" Mitchell asked.

"I hope not. This is his lab."

Ruth had only the haziest of notions as to what a laboratory should look like but glassware and jars of chemicals featured prominently. This room had nothing but blackboards, whiteboards, and long sheets of paper pinned to the walls. There were three desks in the middle of the almost empty space. One piled with loose sheets of paper, the other two creaking under the weight of scores of well-thumbed textbooks.

"What exactly did Dr Gupta do here?" Mitchell asked.

"He preserved the future," Worley said. "Every breakthrough that was about to happen before The Blackout, every theory, thought, and idle speculation, it all comes here. Dr Gupta was one of the scientists sorting through it, cataloguing it, ensuring that as we rebuild we don't waste time reinventing that which was already discovered."

"That doesn't sound like chemistry," Ruth said.

"It's not. People think of this as the place that makes their tea, paint, and soap, but it's far more than that. We are the repository of knowledge, the guarantors that as we recover, we don't repeat the mistakes of the past."

"But specifically, what was he working on?" Mitchell asked.

"Something to do with friction. I don't know precisely what, except that the research notes he was working on originally came from Cambridge. I'm not a scientist, you see."

"But you were his supervisor?" Ruth asked.

"Precisely. I made sure he had anything he wanted. Water, tea, pens, paper, what have you. If I could understand the work he was doing then I would have a room like this of my own."

"And when did you last see him?" Mitchell asked.

"Let's see. Well, yesterday, at about three. Perhaps a little earlier."

Ruth frowned. "Three in the afternoon?" she asked.

"No, in the morning," Worley said. "I'm here when he's here. I lock up after him, and I try to make sure I unlock before him, though he sometimes would start work during the middle of the night."

"Did you see him leave?" Ruth asked.

"No," Worley said. "As I said, I locked up. When I left, he'd gone. To his bed, I presume."

"Did he often stay late?" Mitchell asked.

"Sometimes he would stay all night, sometimes he'd leave after a few hours. There was a lot of thinking in this job, you see, and he didn't need to be here to do it. He had a farm, you know? He'd often go back there and take his work with him."

"And that was allowed?" Ruth asked.

"Well, it's hardly a state secret. That's the point, don't you see? A summary of each discovery is filed at the university. We want to share this information with the world, not hide it away where it might be lost again."

"How much was he paid?" Ruth asked.

"A thousand pounds a year," Mr Worley said. "As well as whatever supplies he wanted for his farm. That was mostly fertilizer and tools."

"Really?" Mitchell said. "And was he well liked?"

"I liked him. He was a nice man. Diligent. Kind. Polite when he remembered to be."

"And what did everyone else think of him?"

"There isn't anyone else. As I say, anyone who can understand the work he did would be employed at it themselves. I have a secretary, and there are assistants who organise the filing, but I don't think any of them really knew Dr Gupta. I wouldn't say he had friends here, but he certainly had no enemies."

Mitchell picked up a piece of paper from the desk, and then another. He put them down. "What about ink and toner, is that made here?"

"Ink? What type of ink?" Worley asked.

"For banknotes. Do you supply the Mint?"

"We do. That's on site, somewhere. I'm not sure where."

"I see. Did Dr Gupta have a locker? Or a locked drawer?"

"No."

"Anything that would require a key?"

"I keep the lab locked when he's out, but who would want to steal anything?"

"And if he needed the lab unlocked when you weren't here?" Ruth asked.

"A guard would do that, or a secretary or an assistant. As I say, there aren't any secrets in here."

"I see. That's very helpful. Thank you for your time, Mr Worley," Mitchell said.

"Oh. Yes. Will you keep us informed?"

"Of course."

"I don't like this," Mitchell said as the train rattled north, taking them towards the farm from which Dr Gupta's letters had been sent.

"Do you think Dr Gupta was involved in the counterfeiting?"

"We're meant to think he was involved, I'm sure of that. That alone makes me suspect he was innocent. We'll inform his relatives because it's what we should do, and it was what we are expected to do, but it's a distraction. I doubt we'll find anything at this farm other than grief. His death has been dangled in front of us, and that makes me wonder who's holding the string."

"You mean the killer?"

"Not precisely. Dr Gupta's murder could have been committed by any hired thug. Similarly Turnbull could have been killed by almost anyone in uniform. But there is someone behind all of this, the person who sent us to that house. That's who I want to find. Dr Gupta seems to be innocent, and unless we bring an end to this conspiracy, more innocents will die. I won't stand for that. No, I won't."

And the detective was silent for the rest of the journey.

Away Farm was the largest that Ruth had ever seen and came complete with its own station. On the far side of the platform was a siding at which a string of cargo wagons was being loaded. She watched as a cart was drawn up next to a large metal hopper. The horses were unhitched and led away as a pair of labourers began emptying the cart into the rectangular metal bin. A few feet further along another cart was nearly empty.

"Full!" a farmhand shouted. A rope was tugged, a pulley squeaked, chains rattled and the full hopper swung up and over the top of the nearest cargo wagon. There was a shouted back and forth of "Left a bit.

Right a bit. Lower. Steady her. There." The hopper was opened, and the potatoes tumbled down into the train car.

"Let's see if we can catch a ride," Mitchell said, pointing to where the team of horses was being led to an already emptied cart.

"We're looking for Away Farm," Mitchell said.

"You've found it," the driver replied. "It's not good news is it? Police never come with good news. I can drive you to the house. Get on."

"You work there?" Ruth asked as the cart set off down a patched road.

"We all do. Everything around here is part of the farm," he said, waving a hand to indicate the fields either side of the road where dozens of people laboured.

Mitchell gave an encouraging nod of his head that Ruth took to mean she should keep the man talking.

"How many people work here?" she asked.

"Technically, the station is run by the railway," he said. "And there's a few hundred casual labourers depending on the season. But we've got forty-three families living here, along with ninety-seven people on the government scheme. You know the one? You work as a hand for five years and then get the option of a place of your own. No one leaves here though. We just take on more land. Keep expanding, that's the plan. Always has been."

"Well, how big is the farm?" Ruth asked.

"Depends on how you measure it. There's the fishing and the hunting, and there's the dairy herd, though that's more for ourselves than export. We've got some woodland that we're starting to bring under the axe, but I suppose a townie like you is only interested in what you can eat. It's over a thousand acres of arable and crops. Wheat and potatoes mostly, but we've also got some greens, and a bit of grazing. We feed ourselves, and about five thousand others."

"That's five people per acre?" Mitchell asked. "That's far higher than the national average."

"All told, it's closer to six," the driver said, "and we're aiming for seven by next year's harvest. Mechanical Mechanisation, that's what Dr Gupta calls it. You see those markers?" He gestured towards a double row of poles, two feet apart that ran parallel to the road on the other side of a drainage ditch. "We're putting in a miniature railway as soon as this harvest is done. We'll get the food from the barns to the station without the need for so many horses. Less feed, you see. And that's only the start. Dr Gupta thinks we can manage close to twenty people per acre. That's his target."

"And who is Dr Gupta?" Mitchell asked.

"He's the brains behind the place. You won't find him here today. He works in the city half the time, on account of we can't keep up with him."

There was no envy or jealousy in the man's voice, just pride. From what he'd said, it was justified. The national target was that a hundred acres of potatoes should feed four hundred people for a year. A hundred acres of wheat should feed a hundred. It was around these figures that the quotas were set. Chemical fertilizers helped. Animals could be grazed on land unsuitable for crops, and it was rare for a fishing boat to return without its nets laden. But the export of so much food aid, and the farming targets and rationing scheme that enabled it, were increasingly contentious. There was a saying: one for the farmer, one for the miner, one for the American, and one for everyone else.

"Why are you here?" the man asked.

"We've come to see the owner of the farm," Mitchell replied.

"Well, you'll want Clementine or Richard, then. Richard will be in the stables. Clementine, you'll find in the big house." He nodded towards a gate that led up a drive towards a rambling mansion. "But I've got to go back to the barn. Got to get those wagons filled, and then we make a start on the broccoli."

They jumped down from the cart and were halfway up the drive when there was a shout. The word 'police' echoed ahead of them until a woman came out of the mansion's main door.

She saw them, stopped, and stared as they approached. Her lips moved silently as her shoulders alternately slumped and stiffened.

"Tell me," she said, when they were still twenty feet away. Her expression was one of knowing dread, tinged with that impossible hope that for once two police officers had come with anything other than the worst possible news. "Just tell me."

"It's Rahman Gupta," Mitchell said. "I'm afraid that he's dead."

The woman took the news like a physical blow, staggering back, and reaching for the ornate pillar by the side of the door for support. Her head shook, and she let out a pitiful wail that carried across the landscape.

"And you're his brother?" Mitchell asked the man who'd ran out from the barn at the sound of the woman's cry. The four of them sat at a worn-smooth pine table in the kitchen of the big house.

"Richard Point. His adoptive brother. Unofficially. We sort of adopted each other back during the first year. That winter. You remember it? Me, Rahman, Clemmy, and… and Jamie. She died. And now Rahman? This world of ours, it grinds away, doesn't it?"

"Rahman said he had a plan," Clementine whispered. "He always had a plan. He didn't plan for this."

"How did it happen?" Richard asked.

"We're still investigating," Mitchell said. "Tell me about him."

"Rahman? Like Clemmy said, he had a plan," Richard said. "That was during the winter. That first winter." He looked over at Ruth. "You don't know how lucky you are. Your generation complains about our food going overseas, but if you'd lived through the hunger you wouldn't begrudge it. Your parents might tell you stories, but you weren't there. You didn't see the horror, smell the fear, taste the despair. Believe me, it was palpable. We had to queue for food, and it wasn't much, and each day it got worse. You had to eat it before your bowl could be stolen from your hands." He squinted at Mitchell as if trying to work out if he recognised him. Then he shook his head. "Rahman's plan was simple. There was food in the camp, but not much else. There was no hope. No future. But there would be food out in the fields, growing wild. We left. We walked. We kept walking. He kept us walking until we reached here and only stopped because none of us could go any further. We lived on roots and berries and what animals we could trap. Compared to what we'd had in the camp, it was a feast. Then Rahman made us go back. He had a new plan, you see.

180

That's how it was with him. One plan after another, and he'd always plan a dozen steps ahead."

"He always had a plan," Clementine sniffed.

"We returned to the camp," Richard continued, "and we got more people. Kids, just like us. The ones who'd die if they stayed. That's how it all started, and it's how it all grew. Rahman came up with a plan, and we followed it. He read anything and everything. He took old ideas and modern tools and came up with a way to make it all work. Then we needed fertilizer. That was, when? The third year? The fourth? By then, we were shipping food back to the city. He went with it, and went to the lab where they made the antibiotics. He told them how to make the fertilizer. So they did, and they offered him a job."

"He refused it," Clementine said. "He wouldn't work for them."

"But he was working for them now?" Mitchell asked.

"Not really," Richard said. "Technically he was a professor at the university conducting research who just happened to have a lab in the factory. That's the arrangement they settled on. First he was an undergrad, then he was studying for a PhD, and then he was a professor. It was a conceit, really, and it amounted to the same thing, but he refused to work for anyone. It was… it's complicated. Life wasn't easy during those early years. You kicked a lot of people out of Twynham. Exile you called it. Where do you think they went? And here was us, a bunch of teenagers with a lot of food."

"I'm sorry about that," Mitchell said.

"It wasn't your fault, was it?" Richard said. "And we got help in the end. It all got sorted out. But now this." He shook his head.

"Do you know what he was working on?" Mitchell asked.

"Increasing yields," Clementine said. "That was what he was always working on. He got three tractors working this summer. On biodiesel. He doesn't like coal. Too dangerous for the miners, and the health… risks… didn't…" She stumbled to a halt.

"He said if we really wanted to feed the world we'd need hydro and aquaponics," Richard said. "Of course, we'd need a lot more electricity."

Mitchell glanced up at the bulb hanging from the ceiling. "I would have thought this was too far away from the power station to be on the grid."

"We've turbines, and a water mill," Richard said. "And we'd plans for a biogas plant. Or Rahman did."

"And we still will," Clementine said firmly. "His work won't stop."

"But was there anything else, anything he was doing at the chemical works he might have talked about?"

"Why do you ask?" Richard said.

Mitchell looked from one farmer to the other. "Rahman was murdered," he said.

Clementine took a sharp breath.

"Why?" Richard asked.

"I don't know. Did he have any enemies? Anyone you've sacked or—"

"No. Absolutely not," Richard said. "Some people do leave here. Not many. Most like the place too much to leave. They can see what we're trying to do and want to be a part of it. There are a few who just don't fit, but they probably wouldn't have ever met Rahman."

Mitchell nodded. "One last thing. Do you know what these keys open?"

"That's the gun safe," Richard said, pointing to one. "And that's the ignition for a tractor. I don't know about the other three."

Mitchell peeled off the key to the safe and the other to the tractor and laid them on the table. "We'll let you know when you can collect his other possessions," he said.

"Do you think you'll catch whoever did this?" Richard asked. "Honestly?"

"I will try," Mitchell said. "I can't promise you more than that."

Mitchell quietly fumed until they were at the end of the mansion's long drive.

"We have done all that is expected of us. We have informed the family. We have been to Dr Gupta's place of employment. We have established that there is a link between him and the counterfeiting by way of the ink. It's a tenuous one, but what can we expect from someone who thought I wouldn't notice that crime scene was staged? We have done what is expected of us, now it is time to do the unexpected."

"You said, earlier, that we are going to see Isaac," Ruth said. "How can he help? From what you said, he's just another criminal."

"Quite. He told me he would have news on Anderson today. But as to the rest you will have to wait until we get there."

Chapter 13
Footage

When they boarded the train, Ruth thought they would head back into town and to the old church where she'd first met Isaac. They didn't. After about twenty minutes, Mitchell grabbed her arm just as there was a clunking thump of one carriage hitting another.

"We're getting off here," he said as he pulled open the door to the slowing train. "Wait."

Saplings sprouting out of untamed undergrowth rushed by at what seemed an impossible speed.

"Wait, until after the bridge," Mitchell said. The train slowed, but not enough for Ruth's comfort. There was a whistle. "Now!"

She jumped, rolled as she landed, and slipped on a rotting stump, grazing her palm on a jagged road sign half buried in a patch of nettles. Silently cursing the sergeant, the train, and, belatedly, the killer responsible for them being out in the middle of nowhere, she stood. As the train disappeared into the distance, the sound of its engine and rattling wheels was replaced by the living symphony of the forest surrounding her.

"Did we have to jump?" she asked.

"The alternative is telling anyone who might be following us precisely where we're going."

"And where's that? For that matter, where are we?"

"Let's see," Mitchell said, brushing at his knees. "The farm is about fifteen miles to the north, maybe a mile or two to the west. That crashed plane where we found Anderson's body is about twelve miles to the east. Twynham, or the centre of it, is another fifteen miles down those tracks. Maybe a little further, so we want to go about a mile west." He looked up, down, and then along the impenetrable thicket blocking their way. "This isn't quite where I told the driver we'd get off." He looked north, and then south.

"You told the driver?"

"He wouldn't have slowed the train if I hadn't. But this is definitely not where I wanted to be."

"You're lost?" Ruth asked.

"Of course not," Mitchell said. Ruth wasn't sure she believed him. "This way," he said and started walking along the tracks. After a hundred yards, he pointed to an animal track that cut through the undergrowth. Ruth tried to guess which creature had made it because it was something far larger than a fox.

"Are there wild animals out here?" she asked.

"Of course," he said.

"I mean dangerous ones."

"Possibly. But they're mostly nocturnal."

The brief flash of relief vanished when she saw the sergeant's shadow and realised how low the sun was on the horizon. But her trepidation was almost as quickly replaced with a sudden awareness of how hungry she was. They'd grabbed a baked potato from a stall at the station on their way out to the farm, but it had been a long time since breakfast.

They reached the end of the track and joined an old road, crammed with abandoned cars. They were a familiar sight, but she'd never before seen so many in one place. She leaned forward, wiped her sleeve over a mud-encrusted windscreen, and jumped back. There were bodies inside, two in the front, two smaller ones in the back. Their mouths lolled open and receding skin exposed yellowing teeth set in mummified heads.

She spun around as a hand touched her arm. It was Mitchell.

"Come on," he said.

"Who are they? Where were they going?" she asked.

"They were trying to get away."

"Away from what?" she asked. "Why did they stay in the car?"

As he led her away, she saw inside other cars where the windows had been broken, allowing insects to turn corpses to skeletons.

"I don't know," Mitchell said. "It wasn't radiation. At least I don't think it was. These weren't driverless cars. It looks more like a convoy. There were some missiles that were tipped with chemical weapons. As I understand it, the AIs used those when they wanted to kill the people but leave the electronics intact. It might have been that. Or maybe it was mass suicide."

"I thought the AIs didn't care about people," Ruth said.

"They didn't, in the same way that people don't care about ants until they find them running across the kitchen table. They were busy at their own war, but that didn't mean people didn't try to stop them. There were kill switches in power plants that could be turned off, server farms that could be blown up, and fibre optic cables that could be cut. When people tried, they started killing us."

"Don't you worry about them coming back?" she asked.

"No," he said.

"But they're bringing back radio, aren't they? For this transatlantic broadcast."

Mitchell sighed as he pointed at a side road leading to the south. "This way. Look, don't think of them as technology. Think of them as people. Dead people. You can't bring them back. New ones might be created, but maybe this time we've learned our lesson. Enough people worry about the mistakes of the past that they won't be repeated. You just have to hope that the new mistakes we make aren't quite so catastrophic. Here it is."

The track ended at a junkyard where cars were piled one on top of another. Behind it was the ruin of a four-storey concrete block of an odd design Ruth had never seen before. She kicked away the weeds growing up around a scorched sign and saw it identified the place as a leisure centre and swimming pool.

It wasn't a junkyard, she thought as she followed Mitchell towards the block. It was a graveyard for the vehicles. Had someone towed them here? Or driven them? There were none of the usual signs that the building was inhabited. No smoke from a cooking fire, no patch of earth filled with lovingly tended vegetables, no squawk of chickens or snuffle of a pig. It was a place completely devoid of life. Then she saw Gregory step out of the shadows, a sawn-off shotgun nestled in his massive paw. He waved in what could have been a warning or a greeting before gesturing towards the shattered glass door behind him.

"I guess we go inside," Mitchell said.

The old lobby had a viewing window from which the pool, empty of water but half full of rubble from the broken roof, was visible. Standing on the lowermost diving board was Isaac. He raised an arm in a lazy salute.

Ruth followed Mitchell down a long flight of stairs, through a dank, dark changing room, and out into the pool. She saw Riley first, sitting on a bench next to a young boy of around six. A man sat next to the child, and next to him was...

"That's Mrs Standage. They caught her!" Ruth exclaimed.

"Caught? She isn't a prisoner," Isaac called back, his voice echoing around the empty chamber. "Didn't you tell her, Henry?"

Ruth realised that Standage wasn't in handcuffs, and Riley seemed indifferent to her presence.

Ruth turned to Mitchell. "What didn't you tell me?" she asked.

"I couldn't risk her facing the same fate as Turnbull," Mitchell said. "We staged the escape."

"I took her to Isaac before I went for backup," Riley said. "I pulled the stitches out from where I'd cut my head when I fell off that horse. The blood did most of the work."

"Why didn't you tell me?" Ruth asked.

"You didn't need to know," Mitchell said. "But things have changed."

"Did you go to Dr Gupta's farm?" Isaac asked.

"We did," Mitchell said.

"He was a good man," Isaac said. "One of the best. I tried to recruit him. He wasn't interested."

"Good for him," Mitchell said.

"Seeing as he's now dead, I wouldn't say that," Isaac replied. "But he was the most thoroughly honest of men. A truly decent man who cared about others over himself. The world needs people like him, and far fewer of the kind who killed him."

Ruth glanced over at Riley. The constable looked bored, and that was the only reassurance she had in the cavernous chamber.

"Do you know why Dr Gupta was killed?" Ruth asked.

"Yes," Isaac said. "I believe it was so that you would waste your time asking that question."

"That's no answer at all," Ruth said. "Why did they do it? Why did they copy the banknotes but not spend them? Why?"

Isaac smiled, or at least his mouth opened exposing perfectly white teeth, but there was no humour in the expression.

"Power," Mitchell said. "It's what it all comes down to. It's what it always comes down to."

"Power?" Isaac echoed, as he took a step along the diving board. "That is like saying the motive of a robbery is to get rich. Some people prize pain and misery above all else." He took another step and was at the edge of the diving board. "Fortunately, there are more people who value love, friendship, and…" He waved a hand at Mitchell. "Even justice. But in this case the answer is control." He bounced back on his heels. "Control of Britain?" He bent his knees and jumped, twisting in the air so he landed with only his toes on the board, his heels over the rubble-filled pool. "Or control of the world? That is the real question."

"Cut the theatrics," Mitchell said. "Tell us what you know."

"Mrs Standage?" Isaac said. "You're up."

The woman stood, nervously. "Um… my son?"

"Of course. Mr Standage, please take your boy outside. Watch the sunset. We'll be leaving soon."

The man looked at his wife before gathering their son and heading out the door.

"Mrs Standage?" Mitchell prompted.

"It was as I was telling your colleague," she said. "I had no choice. They threatened my son. They came to my house in the middle of the night and said they'd kill him. At first they only wanted to know when the new notes were going to come into circulation."

"Who was this?" Mitchell asked.

"There were three of them. The two that you killed in that shop when you rescued us, and the other… I don't know his name. He was older, with a scarred face."

"Emmitt. When was it?" Mitchell asked.

"March."

"And these new banknotes they were interested in weren't the twenty-pound notes they forged?" Mitchell asked.

"No, it's the ones they were planning to bring in next year," Standage said.

"Go on, what happened after you told them?" Mitchell asked.

"Well, before I could do that, I had to find out the answer. Not many people in the Mint knew the date the new notes were being introduced. It wasn't something that was openly discussed though everyone knew they were coming. Mr Grammick had even asked my opinions on the design. There's no monarch on the back, you see. He didn't like that, but he was overruled by someone in government."

"You gave them the information? How?" Mitchell cut in. "Was it in person? A letter?"

"They said they'd find me, and they did. I was picking Luke up from school. One of them, Carl he said his name was, started walking beside me. I told him that the new notes would enter circulation at the end of January with the announcement made at Christmas. He said thank you and disappeared. I thought it was over, but a week later they broke into the house again, this time while we were having dinner. They didn't want me. They took my husband away. I thought they'd kill him, but he came back three days later. They wanted an electric cable laid between a factory and a house. He works for the Electric Company, you see."

"It's the same house we found the printer in," Riley said.

"He didn't know which factory, or where the house was," Mrs Standage said.

"And after that?" Mitchell asked.

"It was about another week, and they wanted a copy of the design for the note. I would have told someone. I would. Except this time, they took David and Luke away. They said they'd be released when I brought them the copy."

"And that's what you did?"

"Yes. I'm sorry. But I gave them the wrong serial numbers. That way I'd be able to see if the notes were used."

"These designs were on a computer?" Mitchell asked.

"An un-networked machine, yes."

"How many other people had access?"

"Mr Grammick, a few technicians. I didn't. Not really. I had to break in when Mr Grammick was at a meeting."

"After you stole the design and gave it to them, was your husband released?"

"The very next day."

"Tell them why you didn't report it," Riley said.

"They had police on their payroll. They said they controlled the entire police force."

"And you believed them?" Mitchell asked.

"Oh, I don't know. I did at the time. David didn't know where this house was and I couldn't offer much description of the people. We talked about it, about what information we could tell anyone and then, well, we didn't forget about it, but they didn't come back."

"Until they did," Mitchell said.

"Yes. One day I got home, and found it empty except for that man, Carl."

"What did they want this time?" Mitchell asked.

"I... I don't know. Maybe they wanted David so they could set up a new place to print the money from. They would ask me about the investigation, but I think it was out of curiosity more than anything else. I had to go to that old shop after work, you see. David and Luke weren't there, not until the night you came... and..." She finally broke down, and sobbed.

"It's interesting, isn't it?" Isaac said. "There are a few details that Mrs Standage has skipped over, but I think she's covered the salient points. My dear," he added, turning to the woman, "why don't you go and join your son and husband. As soon as the sun sets, we'll take you to a place as safe as anywhere can be on this planet."

Ruth waited for Mitchell to object. He didn't.

"That's more or less what I got from her that night we rescued her," Mitchell said after Mrs Standage had left. "So why did you keep her around?"

"I thought you might have some more questions for her," Isaac said. Then he turned to Ruth. "You asked what this was about. Do you know the Prime Minister is stepping down? There are many people waiting to take her place. Why bother with a revolution when you simply need to win a parliamentary rebellion? That is what this is about. Who benefits from a colossal fortune in counterfeit money that is discovered before it can enter circulation? Only someone who wishes to disrupt the status quo. The trade deal, the election, the direction that society is moving; it doesn't matter which because the cause is the same. At the root of this is the desire to be the one who controls the fate of the people."

"A politician?" Ruth asked. "You're saying an MP is behind this?"

"What else makes sense? Here is the ability to become the richest person in the country, yet the money was left unspent."

"Get to the point," Mitchell said. "Do you have anything useful for me?"

"How about the identity of a suspect?" Isaac replied. He walked over to the bench, picked up a metal case, and opened it.

"That's a computer!" Ruth said.

"Indeed," Isaac said. "Pixels are so much more reliable than ink, and far more dramatic, of course."

He tapped at the keyboard until a window appeared. Ruth squinted at the image. There were cars, a lamppost, a building with a wire fence, and a person coming out of a gate.

"Where is it?" Mitchell asked.

"It's a recording taken from a CCTV camera in the staff car park of a prison on the Isle of Wight," Isaac said. "But the more pertinent question is when, and the answer is six days before The Blackout."

"How did you get it?" Ruth asked.

"The feed was simultaneously sent to the surveillance room in the prison and to a secure archive which I gained control of some years ago," Isaac said. "Leave the rest of your questions until later," he added, and pressed another key. The image began to move. Ruth watched a woman walk from the gate to a car. The short clip stopped as she reached it.

"I can't make out her face," Mitchell said.

"There's no need. For some reason, none of the AIs thought to fire a missile into the data centre for the DVLA. The register of car owners is just one of many databases I rescued from damp and decay. You see, I started with the address of Mr Anderson, which led me to the prison. The prison led me to a house on the same street on which Mr Anderson lived. That gave me the car, and that returned me to the prison, and to this footage."

"The name," Mitchell prompted.

"Let us start with Mr Anderson. His real name is Charles Carmichael, and he is named after his father, who, at the time of The Blackout, was imprisoned on the Isle of Wight." He pointed at the screen. "At which prison, that woman ran a rehabilitation programme attended by Mr Carmichael Senior. About two months after she started working there, she moved into a house on Spring Close, six doors up from the Carmichael family. An odd thing to do, don't you think?"

"I'd say it's highly suspicious. What's her name?" Mitchell asked.

"Patience. Watch." He tapped at the keyboard. The image changed. Another clip began to play. This one showed the woman, and a man still wearing prisoner garb, run from the building as smoke billowed from a burning car at the edge of the frame. The clip stopped, with the two figures halfway across the car park.

"This was taken eight hours after The Blackout," Isaac said. "It ends at the moment that power was cut to the island."

"I know that woman," Mitchell said. "Play it again."

"If you want," Isaac said. "Or I could tell you that it was Weaver."

"Weaver?" Ruth asked. "You mean Captain Weaver?"

"The very same," Isaac said. "And the man in that footage is Mr Charles Carmichael Senior."

"It's a coincidence," Riley said.

"You've seen it?" Mitchell asked.

"And it doesn't prove anything," the constable said.

"She knew what Clipton and Emmitt looked like," Ruth said. "And well enough to give a description for them to print drawings in the newspaper. How else do you explain it?"

"You don't," Mitchell said. "She knew what they looked like because she knew Anderson. Presumably she knows the others as well. She's the insider in the police. She must have staged Clipton and Gupta's murders, and she'd have had access to Turnbull. I thought she was quick getting to the house where the printer was, well, this explains how. She knew exactly where to go. It was clever of her to bring Marines rather than police to the crime scene, what better way to ensure that the evidence was trampled into the dirt?"

"It doesn't explain why she did it," Riley said.

"I suspect that she is working for someone else," Isaac said.

"Who?" Ruth asked.

"Oh, I've no idea," Isaac said. "Probably someone in the opposition, since exposure of the counterfeiting would bring down the government. Beyond that, any name I gave would be a guess."

"And there's no point speculating," Mitchell said. "Let's go and ask her."

"Let me do that," Isaac said. "Gregory doesn't say much, but he's rather good at getting answers."

"This is a police matter," Mitchell said.

"Oh, don't start that self-righteous babbling," Isaac snapped. "Where is your warrant? Where is your writ? Where is your right? You may carry a badge, but there's no more authority in that than there is in my gun, and at least I don't pretend otherwise."

"There's a line, Isaac, one that I won't cross. It's why I have the badge, and why you have this." He waved his hand to take in the desolate decaying building.

"I see," Isaac said, and all pretence at good humour was gone from his voice. "And will you be taking her with you?"

It took Ruth a moment to realise that Isaac meant her.

"She's safer by my side. But if you want to help, go back to Southampton. Search that house in which we found Clipton's body. See if there're any bugs or other surveillance equipment."

"That sounds like make-work, Henry."

Mitchell shrugged and walked back towards the stairs.

Chapter 14
The Informant

There were a dozen freshly oiled bicycles in a rack behind the leisure centre. They took three and travelled back to the city as dusk settled around them.

"Sir, where are we going?" Ruth asked.

"Weaver's house," Mitchell said.

"And then what will we do?"

"We'll get her to confess," he said.

Ruth knew it wouldn't be as simple as that. "How?" she asked. "I mean, are you going to torture her?"

Mitchell slowed, but didn't stop. His answer was long in coming and short on detail. "No."

"Then what *are* you going to do?" Ruth asked.

There was another agonisingly long pause. "Fine," he said, though she wasn't sure to what he was agreeing. "We'll search her house. There will be some clue. I'm not sure what, but we'll find something that will lead us to whoever is behind all this."

"And if we don't?"

"We'll worry about that then. What other choice do we have?" Mitchell asked. "Who can we trust? Whatever they are expecting, right now it isn't this. Perhaps if we act quickly, with surprise on our side, we may catch them unawares."

"That's a lot to hope for," Riley said.

It was after eight p.m. when Mitchell brought them to a halt at the head of a quiet street with a working lamppost at the northern end. The commuters and after-work-shoppers had long since gone home. Children were on their way to bed, and the roads were deserted. Flickering lights and the occasional snatch of happy laughter escaped from around curtained windows in a street that was a place of homes, not boarding houses.

"It's halfway down," Mitchell said, waving vaguely at the eastern side of the street. "The allotments run behind the gardens."

Ruth told herself that it was too late to protest. The video was incontrovertible proof that Weaver knew Anderson. But what exactly did it mean?

They crept along the edge of the allotment. Ruth alternated her gaze between the narrow path with a drainage ditch either side, and the guttering light of a night-time gardener in the far corner of the field.

Mitchell slowed. Ruth did the same. When he stopped, she saw that Riley was no longer with them. Mitchell pointed a little ahead and over a wire fence to a woman weeding by the light of a candle-lit lamp. Dressed in faded red overalls, and wearing a blue and white bobbled hat against the evening's slight chill, Ruth didn't immediately recognise Captain Weaver.

Mitchell raised a cautioning hand and then pointed at the ground. His mouth moved in a silent command, but it was too dark for Ruth to make out the words. She nodded anyway. Mitchell almost seemed to vanish as he moved stealthily towards the garden.

Ruth stayed in place for a few seconds, turning her head this way and that, occasionally catching a glimpse of a shadow moving through the undergrowth. Then she inched closer to Weaver. Step by cautious step, with her eyes fixed on the captain. She couldn't place what, but something was very wrong. She drew her revolver and took another step. And another. She was ten feet, the low wire fence, and a thin row of newly cut raspberry canes away from Weaver when something clinked against stone somewhere near the house. Weaver glanced over her shoulder and then returned her attention to the soil. Ruth didn't dare move any further.

There was another sound, of two hard surfaces scraping against one another. Weaver spun and rolled as Mitchell stepped out of the shadows. He had his pistol raised, but the captain had a gun, too, and it was pointing at the sergeant's chest.

"You!" she hissed.

"Put it down," Mitchell replied.

"You first," Weaver said.

Ruth stepped over the wire fence, her revolver gripped in both hands, her doubt and uncertainty over their actions growing with each step.

"You've got five seconds," Weaver said.

"I'll give you three," Mitchell replied.

"Then you're—"

But Weaver stopped talking as Ruth pressed the barrel of her gun against the small of the captain's back.

"Please lower your gun," Ruth said.

Mitchell handcuffed Weaver to a chair in the kitchen and then sent Ruth to the front door. When she opened it, she found Riley waiting on the porch.

"There's no one outside," the constable said, closing the door behind her. "No one's watching."

"Check upstairs," Mitchell said.

The house was empty except for the still-silent Weaver.

"From your lack of questions, you know what this is about," Mitchell said, after Ruth and Riley had joined him in the kitchen.

"I'm sorry to see that you've involved the cadet in this," Weaver replied. "And I'm disappointed that you've chosen to stick by him, Riley, but I suppose that was the inevitable end to this miserable affair. I thought he was dead. I *wished* he was dead. But it's too much to expect people like Isaac will simply crawl off and die. I have to admit that I hoped you would do the right thing when you learned he was behind it. Twenty years too late, certainly, but I did hope."

"What are you talking about?" Ruth asked.

Weaver looked at her, and then at Mitchell. "Ah, so he hasn't told you? I don't know what he *has* told you, but—"

"Stop," Mitchell interrupted. "Just stop. All right. Why do you think we're here?"

"You've discovered that man you call Isaac is behind the murders. The counterfeiting was part of a plot so that he could use that ragtag cult of his to seize power. On learning this, you finally gave in and sided with him, as I knew you would."

"An interesting defence," Mitchell said. "But no. Tell us about Charles Carmichael."

"You know his name? I'll tell you about him if you tell me why he was killed."

"I don't mean the son. I mean the father," Mitchell said.

"His father? What does his father have to do with this?" Weaver replied.

"Maybe we should start again," Riley said. "We are here because we have evidence that indicates you were the one supplying information to the conspiracy behind the counterfeiters."

"What?" Weaver sounded surprised. "Me?"

They'd got it wrong, Ruth thought. As she looked around the small kitchen with its neat little stove, the woven red placemat on a table set for one, she realised they'd got it *very* wrong. The lid of the pot on the stove began to rattle. Ruth picked up a cloth and lifted the pot from the heat. She picked up the box of matches and lit the candle on the table. Then she realised the other three were watching her.

"There's no point arguing in the dark," she said. "Captain, perhaps you should go first. You say Isaac is behind this?"

"I take it you've met him?" she replied.

"I have, but I think it would be quicker, and I would personally prefer it, if for once someone would give an answer that wasn't a question."

"I suspected it from the beginning," Weaver said. "This crime was committed by someone with access to computers, and by people for whom murder is simply a chore. What I lacked was any proof of his involvement. Until now."

Ruth picked up the candle and walked into the living room.

"What are you looking for?" Mitchell asked.

"I don't know," she said truthfully. The living room was as neat, clean, and homely as the kitchen. There were no old photographs. Those were something people either had a lot of or none at all, depending on whether they wanted to remember the world before. What Weaver had was books.

They filled the shelves lining each wall. Even the two armchairs were positioned for reading; one by the window, the other by the fire, with a candlestick placed where a mirror would best reflect the light. It didn't seem like the home of someone conspiring to bring down civilisation, nor was Weaver acting like one. As Ruth walked back into the kitchen she asked herself whether she trusted Mitchell. Maybe. Up to a point. Did she trust Isaac? Not really. As for Weaver, she wasn't sure. She glanced at Riley. Yes, the constable was someone that Ruth trusted, though she couldn't say why.

"Well?" Mitchell prompted. Ruth realised they were all waiting for her.

"What we think," Ruth said, "is that you killed Turnbull, and that you were working with whoever is behind this conspiracy to ensure that the investigation didn't discover them. We have footage of you from during The Blackout, helping Charles Carmichael escape from prison. You lived next door to the family. You knew the dead man."

Weaver blinked. Then she laughed. "Seriously, that's your evidence? That's why you think I'm somehow involved in all of this?"

"You have another explanation?" Mitchell asked.

"Carmichael was my informant," Weaver said.

"Which one, father or son?" Mitchell asked.

"Both," she said. "Before The Blackout, I worked for MI5. You know what that was?"

Ruth shook her head.

"The Intelligence Services. Charles Carmichael Senior was a member of a gang that controlled the flow of cocaine and heroin into southern Britain. We'd arrested most of them, and locked them up, but their gang continued running things from inside the prison. Carmichael was offered immunity and a new life for him and his family if he would turn on the gang and provide us with information. I was just an analyst, but I had the qualifications to work on a rehabilitation project inside the prison, so I became his handler. I moved close to the family to become part of the gang's periphery. Then The Blackout occurred. I was in the prison when the rioting started. Carmichael saved my life. We got out of the prison, off the island, and back to the mainland, and then we got out of the south.

Cue forward a couple of decades and Charles Junior came looking for me. I didn't know he'd come south, but he'd fallen in with some bad people. He wanted out and offered to trade the information for a new life. He told me about the counterfeiting. He gave me descriptions of Emmitt, Clipton, and the others. What he didn't tell me was their location. That was his bargaining chip. He disappeared for a while. When he reappeared he said that he'd give me all the proof I needed if I could get him a new life. The next I heard of him was when you found his body. I suspect the banknotes on his person were stolen as proof of what he was saying. It was unnecessary. He could have just told me the address."

"Can you prove any of that?" Riley asked.

"Of course," Weaver said. "In the living room, there is a shelf with nothing but Charles Dickens. Take the books off and take the back of the shelf out. There's a safe there. The combination is 7. 19. 39. 12. 1."

Riley went into the living room. There was the sound of books being dumped onto the floor, a crack of wood being broken, and then a metallic clicking of a dial being turned.

"It's a handwritten transcript," Riley said, coming back into the kitchen. "An account of a meeting between Weaver and Carmichael, signed at the bottom by both of them. It seems he was giving her information."

"It could be fake," Mitchell said.

"Oh, for the love of... of course it could be fake," Weaver said. "But short of summoning Charles's ghost here to this very room, how else will I prove it? There's a grey folder with his new identity in it. He was going to work at the radio relay station in Newfoundland. Why else would I have that?"

"As part of your escape plan for when the crime was complete," Mitchell said.

"You honestly think that if I wanted to escape, I'd go to what's effectively a government facility in Canada?" Weaver snapped.

"There's an I.D.," Riley said, placing a laminated card on the table. Though the unsmiling face was younger, it unmistakably belonged to Captain Weaver.

"That's from when I was in MI5. It's how I got the job in the SIS," Weaver said.

"I believe her," Riley said. She pulled out a key and uncuffed Weaver before Mitchell could object. "And it's not Isaac," she told the captain.

"He *is* capable of counterfeiting," Weaver said, rubbing her hands. "And of bringing down everything we've built."

"Yes," Riley said. "But if he was behind it, there wouldn't have been any clues left behind. Mister Mitchell, Captain Weaver, we were all wrong. Perhaps we should start again."

Ruth now saw what the commissioner had meant. Weaver was a captain in the SIS, the branch that dealt with these types of crimes, and she'd worked in a similar field before The Blackout. The captain had been investigating the counterfeiting right from the start, and doing it well. By comparison, Mitchell had blundered around, stumbling across clues and forcing them into a shape that proved to be wrong. But not completely wrong, she thought.

"What about Turnbull?" she asked. "Who killed him?"

"I have my suspicions," Weaver said.

"Which are?" Mitchell prompted.

Weaver shrugged.

"No," Riley said. "Someone in the police is working with the counterfeiters. It isn't us. It isn't you. That means we have no choice but to trust each other." She looked again between Mitchell and Weaver. "At least for tonight. Tomorrow, you two can go back to hating one another, but here and now, the investigation has to come first."

"Turnbull was killed by a cyanic compound," Weaver said, her tone grudgingly reluctant. "A button had been pulled off his jacket and broken open. Inside was a cavity that corresponded to the shape of a pill. On his neck, however, was a small injection mark. When Charles first came to me, he told me that Clipton had bragged that there were members of the police involved. Prior to his death I'd found fifty officers whose expenditures didn't match their incomes. Of the original fifty, thirty-five had access to the man before he died."

"Thirty five suspects? Like who?" Mitchell asked.

"The officers who worked the cells," Weaver said. "Or in prisoner transfer and processing, and five who went to interview other suspects. In addition there's the legal representative from the Home Office, and the trustee who sweeps up. And it's definitely not her."

"You're sure?"

"She's in for assaulting her boyfriend," Weaver said. "It was absolutely self-defence. We'd drop the charges, but she's too scared to leave. No, it's one of our colleagues, I'm certain of it, I just don't know which one."

"And no senior officer had access?" Mitchell asked.

"No."

"We're looking for someone who knew that Serious Crimes was being assigned to investigate murders before I did," Mitchell said. "Rumours spread fast, but you can't plan a murder like Dr Gupta's in a matter of hours. Whoever it is, has to be someone right at the top."

"They wanted the bodies to be found," Ruth said. "They wanted the money to be found."

"What's that?" Weaver asked.

"They wanted them to be found," Ruth said. "The crime scene was staged, you see, and the location was chosen so the killer could guarantee the bodies would be found and reported." She remembered what Isaac had said. "And all so that we would spend our time trying to find a link between Dr Gupta and the counterfeiting, right? Except there isn't one, is there?"

"And?" Mitchell prompted.

"The whole point of the counterfeiting was to bring down the government, right? And didn't you say," she added, speaking to Mitchell, "that Dr Gupta's death was staged by someone who'd never seen a real murder?" She turned to Weaver. "And didn't you say that there was someone from the Home Office in the cells?"

"Turnbull's court appointed legal representative," Weaver said. "He came in, saw the man, and got a summary of the deal Mitchell offered him."

"And wasn't it the Home Secretary who asked for Serious Crimes to be turned into a homicide unit?" Ruth asked. "She's a politician, right?"

"But she's in the cabinet," Mitchell said. "If the government loses the election, she'll end up in opposition."

"When the PM stands down, the Deputy will take over," Weaver said. "He'll win the election because of the Prime Minister's popularity. No one in the party would support a change of leadership unless the election was lost. Without the party losing, she can't even mount a challenge. But if they do lose, the Home Secretary would be a contender."

"Then she'd have to wait five years before taking office," Mitchell said.

"If she can arrange all this, no doubt organising a vote of no confidence won't be difficult," Weaver said.

"We're missing something," Riley said.

"Yes, proof," Weaver said.

"So how do we find it?" Ruth asked. "Do we go and search her house?"

"You really haven't trained her very well," Weaver said, addressing Mitchell. "No, you don't hold a gun to someone's head and ask them to confess, particularly not a cabinet minister. You have to get the Prime Minister's permission first, and then you need to ensure that the people doing the searching are those that you can trust. In this case, the same Marines that I've been using ever since I suspected the police department had been infiltrated. What you don't do, *cadet*, is rush in with your gun drawn. Mitchell, you and the cadet go and inform the commissioner. I will tell the PM. Riley will get the Marines."

"No, Riley will go with you," Mitchell said.

"Fine. It will take twice as long, but I'm not going to argue," Weaver said.

Chapter 15
Unmasked

Mitchell hammered a fist on the commissioner's door. The wavering candlelight, distorted by the door's ornate stained glass, moved slowly closer. The door opened.

"Mitchell? Deering? What's going on?" the commissioner demanded.

"It's a conspiracy, sir, one that strikes at the heart of government," Mitchell said.

"That's a tad over dramatic for this time of the evening," the commissioner said. He leaned forward and peered at Mitchell. "You're serious?"

"Yes, sir."

"Well, you better come in," he said. "You as well, cadet. Is it just the two of you?"

"Yes, sir," Ruth said.

"My wife's away, and taken the staff with her, but there's a fire in the study. We might as well be comfortable while you tell me whatever this is about." He led them through the dark house, towards a doorway lit by a flickering orange glow. "I will say, cadet," he added, "that when I asked you to keep me informed I wasn't expecting this."

Ruth said nothing as the man ushered them into his study.

"Let's have some light," Commissioner Wallace said, and pressed a button on a desk lamp. The shade began to glow, ever so softly. "An energy efficient bulb," he said. "It's nearly the last of the old world stock we found in a warehouse near Woking. It takes a while to warm up, but they don't burn out as quickly as the ones they're making these days. Now, please, sit down, and tell me what's going on."

The commissioner took a seat behind the desk. Mitchell, clearly agitated at the delay, sat in a chair opposite. Ruth sat on the chair next to him.

"It was never intended that the money should be released onto the market," Mitchell said. "It was meant to be discovered in order to trigger a mass recall of banknotes. When the public were informed as to the reason why, they would lose faith in the economy, and so in the government. Taken with the Prime Minister's resignation, this would cause the government to lose the election. This would enable the mastermind behind the crime to take over the leadership of the party, prior to wining in five years."

"Well, that's an interesting theory. I take it you are here because you actually have a suspect? A politician?"

"Yes, sir. The Home Secretary."

"Her? Really?" Wallace said, leaning forward. "What evidence do you have to support this theory?"

"One of her representatives went to see Turnbull in his cell before he was murdered."

"Yes, a lawyer, I believe. What else?"

"She was the one who wanted Serious Crimes to deal specifically with murder, and our first case was the discovery of Clipton's body. That can't be a coincidence."

"Probably not, but I need something more tangible than that."

"The murder of Clipton and Dr Gupta was staged," Mitchell said.

"You're certain?"

"It was done very badly," Mitchell said.

"How so?" Wallace asked.

"The gun and knife had been wiped down. There was no blood trail on the floor. Gupta was left-handed, but the gun was in his right hand. Most importantly, the angle of the gunshot and knife wound were wrong for the way the bodies were positioned."

"Ah, I see." Wallace leaned back in his chair. "And *why* was the crime scene staged?"

"Probably so that I would waste time trying to find a link between Dr Gupta and the counterfeiting," Mitchell said.

"Waste time? Why would they want you to do that?" Wallace asked.

"I… I don't know. Turnbull did say something to me about how they were nearing the end."

"The end of what?" Wallace asked.

"The printing, presumably. They must have had enough banknotes," Mitchell said.

"And what were they planning to do next?" Wallace asked. "You say the Home Secretary is behind this. Was she going to scatter the forged notes about the streets? What I'm asking is how, precisely, were they planning to destroy the economy?"

"I don't know," Mitchell admitted.

"Ah. Then no, I'm sorry, but at present I don't see any connection to the Home Secretary," the commissioner said.

"No other politician had access to Turnbull," Mitchell said.

"Nor did she, not really. She may not even have known the lawyer in question. There are dozens of them, and legal representatives are allocated according to a rota. No, I really don't see the link."

"All right, what about Serious Crimes being turned into a proper unit? Not only that, but we were assigned to deal with murders. Then, before the ink was dry on those orders, Clipton's body turns up in a house outside anyone else's jurisdiction. The killer had knowledge of the scavenger tribes and their customs, and knew the bodies would be reported and left undisturbed."

"Yes, but how does that specifically implicate the Home Secretary? Are you saying that there's no one else it could have been?"

"I know it doesn't sound like much—"

"Honestly, Mitchell, it doesn't sound like anything," Wallace said. "I've read the coroner's report on Turnbull. I agree that it looks like murder. With what you've just told me about Clipton's murder, I agree it sounds as if it was staged. Everything else isn't even circumstantial; it's barely even speculation. Dr Gupta was killed for a reason. I would suggest we find out what that is, and focus on finding who killed him. He was an important man. His loss is almost as damaging to the nation as the counterfeiting could have been. As to Turnbull, I will personally take over the investigation into his death. Between the two of us, we'll find something, and then, and only then, will I consider taking this to the Prime Minister. As it stands, however, I really can't."

"Captain Weaver's already gone to the PM," Mitchell said.

"She has? You've… spoken to her?"

"This evening, yes."

"I see." Wallace drummed his fingers on the desk. "And Weaver concurs, does she? She agrees with you?"

"She does."

"Ah, that's a shame."

"Sir?"

"Give me a moment to think this all through," he said, his eyes fixed on Mitchell. "Yes. I see," he muttered. "There are many other conclusions that could be drawn from your evidence. Though I will admit yours is a plausible one, but there is another that is more likely."

"What's that?" Mitchell asked.

"Your theory is based on the assumption that the public will be made aware that a vast fortune was forged. That would require the newspaper to actually print the story. It won't. There will never be a trace of this in the press if for no other reason than the collapse of our society would be terrible for their circulation. The editor enjoys the kickbacks from the advertisers, no matter that they are paltry amounts compared to the bribes in the old world. No, they won't print a word, and so the public will never know about this."

"But you have a better theory?" Mitchell asked.

"I do," Wallace said. "One you seem to have overlooked. It is all about this trade deal. The ambassador and the PM may talk about idealism and the future, petrol and coffee, food and antibiotics, but the key word is trade. That is dependent on a functioning economy. You see, while this matter will never be made public there really is no way of keeping it from the Americans. When they learn that our currency can be devalued by someone wiring together a few old copiers, the deal will collapse. But you *are* right that it is a politician who will benefit. I have something that might tie all of this together." He leaned down and pulled open a drawer. "Yes. Here it is. I think this is the answer."

He straightened. Mitchell started moving before Ruth saw the gun in the commissioner's hand. As Wallace raised the pistol, the sergeant stepped away from the chair. There was a single, percussive shot, and Mitchell collapsed to the floor.

"Pity," Wallace said, moving the gun to point at Ruth. "There are some questions I would have liked him to answer. Principally among them is why he wanted you assigned to his unit. Do you know? Do you? No, I can see from your face you don't. I thought it might be explained by some family resemblance, but there isn't one. Perhaps you take after your mother, but it hardly matters now."

Mitchell gave a grunt. Wallace shifted the barrel to point down at the man. Ruth stood. The barrel moved again.

"No. Don't," Wallace said.

There was a groan from Mitchell. Then a twitch that curled him almost into a ball. Then he was still.

"A shame," Wallace said, "but it would have happened sooner or later. I told you, cadet, he really wasn't suited to this type of police work."

"You... Why...?" she stuttered.

"I doubt you would understand. Why does a farmer wake up in the morning? There are far easier ways of earning a crust. Each of us has a role to play, some plough, some make, others lead. That didn't change in the last ten thousand years, so it should be no surprise it hasn't changed in the last twenty. Without leadership, fear grows. It festers. Order collapses. It was ever thus. It is unfortunate that you've told Weaver, and that she has gone to the Prime Minister. A lot more people will die tonight because of it. Now, let us start with whom else you have told. Constable Riley? Of course she knows."

Ruth looked down at Mitchell's corpse. Except he wasn't dead, not yet. Blood was spreading across his side, but his arm was slowly moving towards his foot.

"You shot him!" she yelled, trying to keep Wallace's attention.

"Yes. Quite. But save yourself the trouble of asking any more cogent questions than that. It's only in bad fiction that heroes get an explanation at the end. This is not fiction, and you are not the hero."

"But... but you're the commissioner!"

"So? Emmitt would have shot you back at that house if I hadn't wanted the money found. Yes, of course I wanted the money found, and found by Mitchell. That was the point of Serious Crimes and everything else. I knew I could rely on him to blunder around and get in the way of any real investigation. Of course, that man, Anderson, had to steal those notes, and Clipton bungled his execution so you arrived at the scene a few days earlier than I had planned for. But you found it without much prompting. We adapt. We always adapt. Emmitt was correct about Standage, at least he was correct about Mitchell following her. Do you know what happened to the woman and her family?"

Ruth wasn't going to answer that, but she had to keep him talking. "You wanted the money found?" she asked instead.

"Stop repeating me. Yes, and it all worked as planned. Now, other than Riley and Weaver, who else have you told?"

Ruth shook her head and as she did, she saw Mitchell's hand curl. Was he trying to signal something? She turned back to Wallace and looked the man squarely in the eyes. Her revolver was in the holster, the button down, and she couldn't now remember if it was loaded. It didn't matter. She'd never draw it in time.

"Has this really all been about power?" she asked.

"If that is an explanation you understand, then fine, why not. Please, this is your last chance. Start with the names of everyone you've told. If you don't, more will die just so that I can be certain that no one was left out."

She shook her head.

"The world must seem like such a simple place to someone of your age, divided into good and evil, with no room for anything else. It isn't like that. It never has been." He raised the gun.

There was a shot. And another. The commissioner collapsed wordlessly to the floor.

"But maybe it should be like that," Mitchell croaked, as the gun he'd drawn from his ankle holster dropped to the floor. "Do you think you can give me a hand?"

"You're alive!"

"State the obvious," he muttered as Ruth bent down. His shirt was soaked in blood. She tore it open. There was something rigid underneath. The bulletproof vest.

"I don't think it stopped the bullet," she said.

He winced as he prodded at his side. "No. It's stopped too many bullets, and this was the one that finally got through, but I think it slowed it down."

"I'll get help," she said as she helped him into the chair "It's not far to the hospital."

"Wait," he said.

"I won't."

"The bullet's lodged just the under the skin," he said. "I can feel it. It's fine."

From the amount of blood, she doubted that.

"Check the desk, see what he was working on," he said.

She picked up the top sheet. "It's a speech," she said, "for the signing ceremony. I didn't know he was meant to speak. No, wait. It's a script with timings for the broadcast. It's what the Prime Minister is going to say, then the ambassador, then the presenter before they switch to the reply from America."

"Anything else?"

"There's a map of the spot where they're doing the broadcast," she said. "And I think these are the details of the trade deal."

"Let me see."

She handed them to him. "Sir. He said... he said he wanted to know why you wanted me in your unit."

"Yes," Mitchell replied. "Yes, I heard."

"He said something about a family resemblance."

"We're not related," Mitchell said.

"But—"

"There's a time and place for questions like that," Mitchell said. "It isn't now. Check his desk. The drawers."

"I really should get you—"

"Please," he said. So she did.

"What am I looking for," she asked, as she opened one drawer, and then another.

"The next part of his plan, the final part that ties all of these smaller pieces together. Failing that I'd settle for a list of whoever he had working for him in the police department."

She took out papers, letters, and blank sheets. It was possible that there was some clue hidden within them, but not that was obvious at a casual glance.

"Maybe he's got a safe like Weaver has," she said as she turned to the last drawer, the one in which the commissioner had kept his gun.

"Yeah, maybe. I should have realised," he said. "A staged crime scene that looked like it had been done by a copper who'd never seen a real one. A politician with access to police records. It's obvious now, but then it always is after you've been given the solution."

There were more papers, but any of them could be innocent or incriminating and she doubted she would ever know which. She lifted them out and placed them on the desk. There was something else, lodged at the back of the drawer. It looked like an old coin. She bent down and picked it up just as Mitchell groaned, more loudly than before.

"That's it," she said. "I'm going to get help."

This time, Mitchell didn't object.

Chapter 16
The Broadcast
23rd September

Ruth stared at the coin that she'd taken from the drawer of the commissioner's desk. On one side was something that almost looked like a backwards 'L'. Around it, with each word separated by five stars, were the words 'THE TRUTH LIES IN THE PAST. It was an odd thing to put on a coin. Odder still that it was in English. On all the old coins she'd seen, the inscription was always in Latin. Perhaps it wasn't a coin, but some heirloom or keepsake from Wallace's childhood. It didn't matter. She'd give it to Weaver later, but for now, she put it back in her pocket and picked up her fork.

Yesterday, she'd run to the hospital, and raced back with the ambulance. They'd loaded an increasingly pale Mitchell inside just before Riley arrived, looking to see what was taking them so long. If things had moved quickly before, they'd sprinted after that. She'd explained what had happened to Riley, and then to Weaver, and then to an admiral and a man in a suit who worked for the Prime Minister. Fortunately, she didn't have to speak to the woman herself though Weaver had. Around two a.m. the captain of the SS Britannia, who was supervising the sailors searching Wallace's house, told her she was in the way. She'd gone home.

Maggie was still up, and when Ruth had told her what had happened, her mother had left the house with barely a word. Ruth didn't understand why, but had been too exhausted to care. Despite that, she'd not slept well, and woken long before dawn to an empty house.

She'd stared at the cold stove for a long minute before donning her uniform and heading into town. Dawn was barely breaking by the time she'd arrived at Police House. The cabin in the yard was as dark and empty as her home had been. The rest of the building was buzzing with rumours though even the most implausible weren't as outlandish as the truth. She'd dodged questions from Simon Longfield and a dozen others who'd learned that she was somehow involved. More by accident than design, she found herself at Wallace's office. It wasn't empty. Weaver was there along with half a dozen men and women in Naval uniform, all methodically tearing the room apart.

"I didn't know where else I should go," Ruth had said. "So I came to work."

"Good for you," Weaver had replied. "But you can't be in here. This is a crime scene."

"What are you looking for?" Ruth had asked.

"I know Wallace didn't kill Turnbull himself, but a man as arrogant as that is bound to have left a clue that will lead us to the murderer. It's why the Navy is here. We don't know who we can trust."

That had cut through Ruth's confused fog like a knife through the heart.

"You can trust me," she said. "And I can help."

"I can, but you can't. It's a matter of procedure. Appeals procedure," Weaver qualified. "I don't want the killer getting off on some technicality."

"Oh. Yes. Of course. I'll... um... do you know where Riley is?"

"She's guarding the stage by the antenna. From what you said about your confrontation last night, and from what I found in Wallace's home, I think he might have been planning to disrupt the ceremony. But you can't help with that either. Take some time off, cadet. You got caught up in something big, something you weren't prepared for. By rights you should have had time off after Emmitt shot that woman in front of you. Certainly you shouldn't have been allowed back to work after you killed that man in the alley. Had Wallace not wanted to keep you around to inform on Mitchell, you would have been forced to take some leave. Go home. Go fishing. Go anywhere that isn't here. There will be plenty of work to do in the days to come."

Ruth had left the office with Weaver's words ringing in her ears. The captain was right, of course. Ruth had merely been caught up in something, and had done nothing to actively help in the investigation. She'd killed a man, yes, but that only meant one more suspect they couldn't interrogate. She'd been the one to suggest it was the Home Secretary who was behind the conspiracy. That had led to her and Mitchell going to the commissioner's house, but it didn't qualify as 'help'. She'd asked a lot of questions, and got very few answers back, and now it seemed unlikely she would get any more. The only tangible good she'd done was to keep Wallace distracted long enough for Mitchell to shoot him. It wasn't much, and she couldn't help think that her presence had distracted the sergeant from realising the truth earlier. In fact, she was certain of it, because, on leaving Police House, she'd gone to the hospital. There she'd been confronted with the most confusing sight of the past few days. Maggie had been sitting by Mitchell's bedside.

"How is he?" Ruth had asked.

"He'll live," Maggie said. "And be released as soon as he wakes. It was a shallow wound, but he lost a lot of blood. Give it a few days, and he'll be fine."

"Good." Ruth had looked at the sleeping sergeant, then at her adoptive mother. "Maggie, why are you here?"

Maggie hadn't answered immediately. "He saved my life," she'd finally said. "It was a long time ago, but I've never forgotten."

"Was it during The Blackout?" Ruth had asked.

Maggie had sighed. "Yes, and after."

"Why didn't you tell me?" Ruth had asked. "I mean, you acted like you'd never heard of him."

"I asked him to keep an eye on you when you applied for the police," Maggie had said. "I didn't want you to know. I'm not sure that was the right decision."

She'd wanted to ask for the details of how the sergeant had saved Maggie's life, and a million more things besides. It wasn't the right time. Maggie looked older and frailer than Ruth had ever seen her. Instead, Ruth had laid a hand on Maggie's shoulder, and watched the sleeping sergeant, until restlessness overtook her, and she'd left.

Life in the city carried on oblivious to the events of the night before. It was absurd and infuriating. Ruth had paced through the streets until her feet had taken her to the outdoor stage from where the signing ceremony was going to be broadcast.

The antenna towered above the cliffs. It was impossible to tell where it began and the scaffolding ended except by watching the engineers scrabbling up and down, hammering out and screwing in their last minute adjustments. Ruth couldn't get near it. The common in front of the stage was empty, the nearby streets roped off and guarded by Marines.

"You shouldn't be here," Riley had said when one of the Marines had finally relented and gone to find the constable.

"I had nowhere else to go," Ruth had replied. "I thought I could help."

"The Navy is running things," Riley had replied with a shake of her head. "I'm here as a token. A representative of the civil power so it doesn't seem like a military coup. I couldn't let you through the barrier even if I wanted. You've got a day off. Enjoy it."

"Oh. Yes." Ruth looked behind Riley to the stage in front of the apartment building. In front of the stage were rows of empty chairs that ran across the common all the way to the next empty apartment block. Agent Clarke, the woman who'd been with the ambassador on his visit to Serious Crimes what seemed like a decade ago, was pacing up and down the vacant rows.

"Can I get a seat for later?" Ruth had asked. "I'd like to see the ceremony."

Riley shook her head. "They're not going to use the seats. The only audience will be listening on the radio."

"But there are all those chairs," Ruth had said.

"Weaver thinks that the commissioner planned to disrupt the ceremony. It's possible someone might still try. No one is being allowed to get close. They would have moved the equipment inside, but it's too late for that. The engineers had a fit when I suggested it." She'd grinned.

Ruth tried to smile back.

"Come back this evening," Riley had said. "I'll see what I can do."

Ruth had taken to the streets again. Increasingly hungry, she found herself wandering through the town until she reached the Golden Hind – the pub opposite the shoe shop owned by Xavier Collins. The windows of the shop had been cleaned, and there was no sign of those lurid trainers. There was a new sign, too, promising shoes repaired while a customer waited in the pub.

Ruth scraped at the horseradish and mustard sauce that was the pub's speciality in search of the potato underneath. Theoretically, it was a nice day. The streets were clean and busy. The sun was bright, though it had failed to burn off the morning's chill. Everyone who walked past seemed content, but Ruth felt a great sense of disquiet. In her mind she replayed the conspiracy as it had happened, and then as Wallace had planned it. There was a piece missing, but she couldn't place what it was.

At half past three, she gave up, and began a meandering walk back towards the outdoor stage, intending to watch the broadcast and then go home via the hospital. She reached it fifteen minutes before the broadcast was due to begin, and the Marines wouldn't let her near. She craned over their uniformed shoulders, trying to spot Riley, or even Agent Clarke, but the only person she could see was a young man with a notebook, looking lost amidst the empty seats. She backed away. There wasn't even a crowd. Everyone else, she guessed, on seeing they couldn't get close had gone to some pub or home where they could listen on the radio. She could do the same, of course, but what would be the point? The speeches weren't important. It was the fact that there *was* a broadcast that mattered. That they'd trained engineers, and had electricity to spare, and that there was somewhere else on the planet that would broadcast a reply, that was the real achievement. From what she'd seen of the script on the commissioner's desk, the words were forgettable, full of vague sound bites that promised a lot without... without...

There was a man, on his own, loitering by the side of the building ahead, and there was something odd about him. Was it the white streak in his brown hair that ran from his crown to where the top of his ear was missing? Or was it something else? Something about the way he was looking up and down the street almost too casually. The building in question was on the other side of the common from the apartment block on which the antenna had been built. It was covered in almost as much scaffolding as the radio mast. With the introduction of electricity to the area, she supposed it was being renovated. The man didn't look like a labourer told to stop hammering until the broadcast was over. He didn't look like anything except that he didn't belong.

Ruth kept walking, not quite towards him, but as if she was angling for the old hotel at the bottom of the hill. A small crowd was queuing outside, wanting to get inside to listen to the broadcast. The man turned his head. Left, right, left again, this time looking at her. He looked away, almost too quickly, and then back at her. Ruth pretended to ignore the man as she got closer. There was something about him. Was it the hair? It must be. Had she seen him before? She didn't think so. The man turned and began walking down the road.

It was nothing, Ruth thought. She was getting paranoid, that was all. Then, when he reached the end of the building, the man abruptly ducked around its corner. That was suspicious. Too suspicious. Ruth quickened her pace. As she reached the end of the block, her hand dropped to her belt, flipping the button on her holster, drawing the revolver. She turned the corner and saw... nothing. The man had gone.

There was a clear view of the road on the far side of the building, the cliffs beyond, and the path that led down them to the beach. He wasn't there, and there was no way he could have disappeared. That left the door to the building. It looked sealed. She stepped closer and tried it. Despite looking secure, the door swung silently outward.

Her heart began to beat faster. She tried to calm it. What was the danger? Where was the threat? The building was at least four hundred yards from the stage. An image of Emmitt came back to her, standing in that field, the sleek old-world rifle in his hands. But that shot had been made at a distance of fifty yards, sixty at most. No, she told herself her fears were the product of nothing but sleepless paranoia.

Except four hundred yards wasn't far, not for a shooter who'd had training. She stepped into the doorway, her revolver tracking from left to right. It was a stairwell, with a door leading into the ground floor, and stairs leading up. Be rational, she told herself. Yes, of course it was possible that someone might have a gun that could accurately hit the stage from here, but was it likely?

There was no crowd, she realised. No spectators to spoil the shot. The PM would be standing on the stage near the microphone as the ambassador gave his speech, and then he would wait for her to do the same. Those speeches had been timed and scripted. The commissioner had had a copy of that script on his desk, with the timings written in the margin. They might be off by a few seconds, but not much longer.

She tried the door that led into the building. It was sealed. She crossed to the stairwell and began to climb.

And Wallace had had a map of the stage. With that and the script, someone would know exactly where the microphone was, and when the Prime Minister would be standing by it. They could have practiced somewhere out in the wasteland until they knew they could make the kill.

Elbows bent, revolver pointing upward, Ruth began to climb the stairs.

But it wasn't Emmitt that she'd seen, just a man with a white scar in his brown hair, missing half an ear. She took a breath, and spun around the landing, pointing the gun up. There was no one there.

Where had she seen the man before? She hadn't, she was sure of it. Yet there was the vague sense of recognition whenever she thought of his face.

She reached the first landing and another door. She tried it. It was sealed. She breathed out, and realised that she was alone in the building, except, perhaps for that man. She knew she should go and get help. The words of Captain Weaver, and Ruth's own self doubt, kept her putting one quiet foot in front of another as she climbed the stairs.

The second landing ended in another locked door. She thought she could hear voices coming from above her. One sounded American. Familiar. There was a crackling hiss behind the voice. It was the ambassador, speaking on the radio. Then she knew how she'd recognised the half-eared man. He matched Mitchell's description of the man who'd run when he'd arrested the ambassador's assistant.

Ruth was at the third landing. The radio broadcast was coming from one floor above. It was too late to turn back.

The gun's grip was slick in her hands. The stairs loomed above her. The door to the next landing was wedged open, and she could hear the voice on the radio more clearly.

"This is a time to formalise the centuries old friendship between…" the ambassador was saying. Ruth tuned it out.

The wedged-open door led to a corridor off which there were four closed doors either side. The corridor ended fifty yards away in another open door. She inched forwards, quietly raising one foot then the other. You are police, she repeated in her head. Not for comfort, or reassurance, but to drown out the other voice that kept asking what she'd do when she reached the open door. She reached it all too quickly.

There was one man in the room, a rifle in his hand, the barrel, and his eyes, pointed at the stage visible over his shoulder. It wasn't the half-eared man she'd seen outside. It was Emmitt, and he hadn't seen her.

Over the radio, an announcer said, "Ladies and gentlemen of two continents. I present Mrs Emma Wolton, Prime Minister of…"

The barrel of her revolver wavered as Ruth took aim. "Don't…" The word came out as a whisper. "Don't move!" she said, this time in a loud bark. Emmitt turned his head slightly, but barely glanced at her before turning back to the window.

"I'll shoot," she said, and he just ignored her. For a moment she couldn't believe it.

"I will," she said.

"If you remembered to load your gun," he replied softly, shifting his stance, taking aim. "I'll take my chances."

Over the radio, the Prime Minister said, "Thank you all. I cannot tell you how glad I am to be here today…"

Time slowed as anger flared, at herself for being someone just caught up in events, at Maggie for her secrets, at Mitchell and Isaac for their guarded conversations, and at the commissioner for deceiving her and everyone else. Then it boiled over into fury at the sheer arrogance of Emmitt. Her finger curled on the trigger. A final flash of doubt crept over her as to whether she *had* loaded the gun before the revolver bucked and the gun roared.

The shot sounded strange, almost as if it had echoed. No, it wasn't an echo. Emmitt had fired too. There was shouting coming from the radio now. Emmitt turned. His face was expressionless as he raised his left hand to his right arm.

"You broke my arm," he said, in that same soft voice. He strode towards her, crossing the room before she had a chance to react. A rough slap knocked the gun from her grip. The backhand knocked her against the wall. His fist curled, and she dived to the ground before he had a chance to throw the punch. She rolled to her feet, looking for her gun, but it was on the other side of the room.

A knife appeared in Emmitt's hand and sliced through the air between them. Ruth ducked again, dived, rolled, and grabbed the pistol, bringing it around and up just as he threw the blade towards her. She kicked herself out of the way as the knife plunged into the floorboards where her arm had been. When she brought the gun up, Emmitt was already out of the door, running down the corridor. She took aim, but there in the doorway at the end of the long hallway was the man with the missing ear. In his hand was a gun. He fired. Ruth ducked as the bullet tore splinters from the doorframe. She pushed herself to her feet, and then to the doorway, spinning around, gun levelled, but the hallway was empty.

Over the radio she heard the Prime Minister saying, "I'm fine, really I am. Sorry, everyone, a light fixture exploded. As I was…"

Ruth didn't think. She didn't hesitate. She just ran. Along the corridor to the stairs, bounding down them, three steps at a time, all doubt was gone. They would run, but she would chase, and she wouldn't let anything stop her from catching them. She reached the building's entrance and dived outside, rolling across the grass, expecting one or both of the men to be waiting either side of the door. They weren't. They were running down the hill towards the path that led to the beach.

She ran across the wild-grown grass, and jumped over the low wall and down onto the road. Her feet hit the ground with a resounding slap of leather on concrete. The half-eared man heard it, turned, and fired. The bullet hit stone somewhere to her right. Ruth didn't stop. Emmitt did. He yelled something Ruth didn't hear, waited for the other man to catch up, and then took the gun from him. His right arm hanging loosely by his side, Emmitt raised the pistol in his left, and fired. The bullet came nowhere close. Ruth grinned and sped up.

The two men started running again, along the path that curved down the cliffs. They were a hundred yards away. Ninety. A hundred. Ruth could feel a dull ache rising up her legs. She wasn't gaining, but she couldn't give up. Not now.

They reached an old one-bar gate that blocked the end of the winding road. Emmitt had to slow to duck under it. He paused at the other side to fire. Again he missed. It was too great a range, Ruth thought, and he was right-handed, not ambidextrous. The two men set off again, dodging around the wooden beach huts to the sand-strewn path that ran alongside the beach. Ruth didn't slow as she neared the gate. She put a hand out, ready to jump over it. At the last second, realism caught up with her feeling of invincibility, and she dived underneath, grazing her hand as she sprawled back to her feet.

When she rounded the beach huts, she saw there was less than seventy yards between her and them. Slowly but surely, she was gaining on them. Emmitt glanced around. The other man did the same. Emmitt barked something. The man put on a burst of speed, but he couldn't sustain it. He was tiring, Ruth thought. Emmitt wasn't. Even with the wound in his arm, his stride had an easy gait, suggesting he could keep going for hours. It didn't matter. She only needed to arrest one of them.

Sixty yards. Emmitt looked back. Ruth raised her gun. Emmitt finally sped up, leaving the other man behind. He tried to keep up, but couldn't. There were fifty yards between her and the half-eared man. Thirty. Kicking up sand, dodging twisted metal from the decaying hulks lining the beach, the distance shrank. Twenty, and the man stumbled. Ruth raised her gun again. No. No, she couldn't. The man was unarmed. She switched her aim towards Emmitt, but he was at least a hundred yards ahead.

The half-eared man stumbled again. With victory within her grasp, Ruth found a last burst of speed. Sprinting the final few yards, she dived forward in a one-armed tackle that knocked the man down.

"You're under arrest," she barked, pressing her knee into his back, bringing her gun up, looking for Emmitt. He'd stopped, still a hundred yards away. He raised his pistol, fired, and missed. Ruth returned fire, and missed. Emmitt gave an almost sardonic shrug and shot at her again. The bullet struck sand on the beach to her right.

The other man struggled.

"Stay down," Ruth said. "He's not aiming at me. He wants to kill you. Stay down and you might live." She wasn't sure how true that was.

Emmitt fired again, and again the shot went wide. Then he waited as if giving her a turn.

She aimed, carefully, and then stopped. How many bullets did he have left? One or two? It didn't matter because she realised that it wasn't his gun and he didn't have any spare ammunition. He was waiting for her to waste her bullets at an ineffective range, and then he'd get closer as she was reloading. She held her fire, and smiled.

The standoff continued until Emmitt finally took a step towards her. Then she pulled the trigger. It was a miss, but a close one. He stopped, and raised the pistol to his forehead in a mocking salute. Then he turned around and ran away along the path.

"Remember," she hissed at the man as she pulled out her handcuffs, "he was trying to kill you." She cuffed the man quickly. When she looked up, Emmitt was gone.

She pulled the man to his feet, and saw his face was covered in blood. He'd broken his nose in the fall, and gashed his forehead, almost exactly underneath the scar that turned that streak of hair white. From the way he staggered as she pushed him towards the cliffs, she suspected he had a concussion. When he fell to his knees and threw up, she thought that confirmed it. Because of that, by the time she saw the Marines running down the beach towards them, they were barely a hundred feet from where she'd arrested him.

At the head of the Marines, almost as if they were racing one another to stay out in front, were Agent Clark and Riley.

"Emmitt," Ruth said. "He went that way. He's injured. I shot him in the arm. The right arm. I think it's broken. He's armed, but I think he's only got one bullet left. And he's not a very good shot with his left hand." She bit her lip to stop herself from babbling any further.

"Emmitt? He's the one with the scarred face?" the American agent asked.

"That's him," Riley said.

Without another word, Clarke started running in the direction Emmitt had gone.

"Go with her," Riley ordered the Marines, and they did.

"Let's get him back," Riley said, hauling the suspect back to his feet. "You did good."

"What about the broadcast?" Ruth asked.

"The Prime Minister was shot, but it was only a glancing blow. She gave a slightly shorter version of her speech, and then they cut to the pre-recorded broadcast. No one will ever know."

"But she was shot?" Ruth asked.

"She'll be fine."

"Emmitt escaped," Ruth said. "Again."

"You managed to wing him," Riley said. "And you caught a suspect. That's not bad for a cadet. Weaver will be pleased."

"And Mitchell," Ruth asked, though she wasn't sure why.

"He'll be pleased you're still alive."

Epilogue
TRUTH

Ruth sat at the small desk in her bedroom staring at the odd coin she'd found in the commissioner's drawer. Coincidences did happen, of course they did, but not like this.

THE TRUTH LIES IN THE PAST. She read the inscription again, and then reached up to the bear that sat, almost forgotten, between a collection of dog-eared detective novels. She'd been clutching the bear when Maggie had found her wandering alone in the immigration camp. Other than the rags she'd been wearing, it had been her only possession.

Around the bear's neck was a singed ribbon. Carefully, she untied it and laid it flat on the desk. On it, one word was visible. 'Ruth'. That was how she had gotten her name. Except it wasn't 'Ruth' but 'RUTH'. There was a ragged hole in front of the 'R' and the ribbon ended after the 'H'. She held it up to the light. Could the letters 'THE T' have once preceded the 'R'? Possibly.

She picked up the coin again. When Maggie had found her, the only word of English that Ruth had known was 'five'. Separating each word of the coin's inscription were five stars. Coincidences did happen, but surely not ones this large. Surely not.

She brushed a little dust off the bear and then placed it back on the shelf. After a moment's thought, the coin and ribbon went next to it.

There was a connection, she decided. That meant there was a link between the coin and her. Not with her directly, but perhaps with her real parents. Of course, that meant there was some link between them and the commissioner. She mulled that over. It was unlikely to have anything to do with the counterfeiting. That, she decided, was the coincidence in all of this. But what should she do?

"Be a detective," she said. "Find the proof."

Which was easy to say. She would begin with the commissioner. Not with what he'd done recently, but who he'd been in the past. Then she would find out where the camp was from which Maggie had rescued her. She would go there and then… then she would see.

She took the uniform down from the hanger. It was already looking ragged. Some stains just wouldn't come out. She'd have to put in for a new one. As she dressed, she wondered whether she should make that request of Mitchell or Weaver. She left the house, but she didn't head directly to work. Instead, she went to the home of Mr Foster, their landlord.

She knocked on the door. When there was no answer, she tried hammering.

"Coming! I'm coming!" she heard from inside, followed a moment later by feet stamping down the stairs.

Foster opened the door bleary-eyed and sour-breathed. "What the hell is it? What are— Why are you dressed as a copper?"

"I'll keep this brief," Ruth said. "I get paid in three months' time. We'll pay what we owe then. You can evict us if you want. But if you do, or if you ever threaten us again, I'll have my colleagues tear your house apart looking for contraband. Every day, Foster. We'll rip out the floorboards and dig up your pitiful excuse for a garden. That's a promise. Understand?"

"You can't—" he began.

"Try me," she said, her eyes fixed unblinking on his.

He stared back. Seconds crept towards minutes. Finally, he blinked.

"Fine," he said, and slammed the door.

Feeling as if she'd won a victory greater than when she'd arrested the man on the beach, Ruth started cycling to work. The case was far from over. Emmitt might have escaped, but they had a suspect in custody, and there were many questions she wanted to ask him. In her short time with Serious Crimes, she'd learned that there were always questions. Perhaps if she asked enough, she would start finding answers.

The end.

Printed in Great Britain
by Amazon